The Rug Broker

FRAN MARIAN

RED HILLS PRESS
TUCSON, ARIZONA

This is a work of fiction. All the characters and events portrayed in this novel are either fictitious or are used fictitiously.

The Rug Broker

Published by Red Hills Press
Tucson, AZ 85748

Illustration by Peggy Jackson

http://www.therugbroker.blogspot.com

ISBN: 0-9787848-0-4

Printed in the United States of America

First Edition September 2006

For Bryna –
Her spirit lives on in my heart.

Acknowledgments

I am indebted to Captain Mike Rhyner of the Tucson Fire Department, Station 9, who told me how a cave rescue is carried out, and to Walter Gaby, owner of Outrageous Rugs, who taught me how the Oriental rug brokering business works. Thanks, too, to Meg Files, novelist, poet and teacher at Pima Community College; Alan M. Petrillo, novelist, journalist, editor; Carlene Jones novelist and editor; and to my cousin Vivian Weber who traveled to Turkey with me to visit that country's extraordinary weavers. And, never last in any sense of the word, to my husband John and other family members for their love and encouragement, which opened the door to the muse in the first place.

1

It struck me as ironic that I felt more confidence driving in a foreign country than I did mothering my five-year-old son who was asleep in the back seat of the rental car. Istanbul's familiar landmarks were everywhere: a lace curtain fluttering in a third-story window; the corner grocer with fresh breads stacked in the window; and the newly-painted, banana-yellow Kelebek Hotel directly ahead. But I'd never felt confident with my son, and now that my husband was gone, the idea of raising him alone terrified me.

The late afternoon shadows were lengthening as I made a final turn on the narrow cobblestone road, pulled up to the hotel entrance and waved to the door captain. He was the same crisply uniformed man who'd offered his welcoming smile on each of my prior visits. He opened my door, then reached in the back to retrieve our bags. I saw him withdraw with a jerk.

"You have a traveling companion, Mrs. Reardon?"

"Yes, my son. Can you carry him for me, Adal? And tell the desk clerk I will register later, after we are settled. I don't want to wake him."

He nodded, positioned his body, and lifted Skipper like he was a Ming vase. I whispered my thanks. Skipper was sleeping soundly and I was looking forward to the same for myself after traveling more than twenty-four hours – Philadelphia to New York, New York to Frankfort and on to Istanbul. As we passed the lobby's ornate ironwork staircase and received another wave, this time from the desk clerk, my eyes fell once again on the Persian Mashad. A thousand people might take this rug for granted, but not me. After five years of brokering, I could still be struck with wonder at the pink, purple and red colors that could be coaxed from the cochineal beetle.

For several seconds I lost myself in the rug's beauty. The subtle shades and stylized flowers with their curvilinear stems drew me into a world of wonder I never questioned, perhaps afraid that if I understood the magic, it would vanish. At times I felt the rugs were the only things holding me together, having the power to mend me with their threads. It was a momentary respite but enough to remind me of the buying trip I'd planned for the next few days, and my hopes that bringing my son along would help me to build a new relationship with him. Just thinking about it boosted my spirits.

Our rooms, a small sitting room and large bedroom on the first floor, were decorated in the style of a nineteenth-century Ottoman house, which it had been until it was turned into a hotel in 1989. By the time our luggage was opened and the staff retreated, Skipper was snoring softly in a single bed next to a window, lace curtain billowing in evening's light breeze, and a pale blue duvet pulled up to his shoulders. Against the opposing wall was a queen-sized bed for me, but my exhaustion had lifted, maybe with thoughts of the rugs. I walked to a corner window and enjoyed the minarets in silhouette against a darkening sky. Such scenes always reminded me of my childhood home where my parents had covered the walls with photographs and art from Lebanon. Suddenly, the memory of my brothers' angry voices intruded on my pleasure.

"You're crazy to think of going to Turkey now. You just lost your husband; Skipper just lost his father. Take some time to heal, for God's sake.

We'll take care of you, Nora. We love you."

Val and Philip would never understand me. They couldn't help me to heal any more than they could counsel me about my son. Their ideas were mired in a Father-Knows-Best sitcom fantasy, one that may have worked for our parents but didn't work for me.

I pinched off their voices, undressed, and filled the bathroom's lion-footed tub. A few minutes later, relaxed with warm water to my neck, a sound like faraway thunder was followed by a mild shimmy. An earthquake?

I listened for other sounds, conscious that my heartbeat had accelerated. But it was quiet. Then suddenly there were footsteps and loud voices outside our door. I grabbed my robe and slipped on my shoes. When I stepped into the hall I collided with Adal.

"Please, go outside. I will carry your son."

By then Skipper was awake and refused to be carried. We quickly joined others who had poured from the hotel and surrounding homes.

"It's just a little earthquake," I said to Skipper.

"Cool," he said, looking around at the people who were wearing a mix of pajamas and street clothes. "What happens now?"

I looked at Adal for an answer.

"We must wait for the inspector to tell us it is safe to go back. Excuse me, I must help," he said, seeing a confused-looking older couple at the hotel entrance.

A short time later a caravan of vehicles with sirens and flashing lights pulled up at the entrance. They stormed into the building and we watched as lights went on in every window. Then, finally, the inspectors gathered at the hotel entrance and, after much discussion among themselves and with others by cell phones, we were allowed to return to our rooms. Skipper was asleep in minutes. It had been an adventure for him, one I feared he'd share with his uncles at the first opportunity. I could already hear Val's response:

Why would you work in a place where the earth can swallow you whenever it wants? With his words in my head, sleep didn't come as easily for me.

Morning sun cast a bright band across the hotel room from the window to the wall. My first thoughts were of the tremor, which in the morning light seemed like more of a dream than reality. I turned my attention to the pale green striped wallpaper I'd missed the evening before. What else had I overlooked? Hand-woven cotton with an inlay of cream-colored crocheted strips covered the room's windows as well as a small round table at the foot of my bed. Another narrow table rested against the wall, supporting a lamp with a bright green ceramic base, a small coffeemaker, and a red glass ashtray. The night before I'd dropped in several Turkish coins to declare its new use. A wicker chair and settee with colorful kilim cushions were the only other furnishings.

Back in the bathroom the mirror told me I'd missed more than the room's details – my hair was a disaster. This time I turned on the shower, pulled my nightgown over my head, and stood before a floor-length mirror in the bathroom. My hair hung on my shoulders in lifeless brown clumps. My body, too, appeared to have lost its tone. Perhaps sagging spirits translated to skin and muscle. All the more reason to get back to the things I loved and create a new bond with my son. I'll soon turn things around, I said to my reflection. A sour look responded and I turned away.

Outside the shower door an hourglass-shaped black rug stretched out on the tile floor. Brown bats formed a line through the center. It was Chinese-made, I was sure, and then I remembered that bats are a symbol of good luck in that country. I hoped the Chinese were right.

With a towel wound tightly around my breasts, I propped myself up on the settee and watched Skipper until he stretched, opened his eyes and sat up.

"Welcome to Turkey, Skip."

Without answering, he flipped the duvet aside and ran to the window. "Last night when we were in the street I saw a mosque at the top of the hill. Can we go? I want to see inside."

Thousands of miles hadn't changed my son. No small talk, his mind had already fixed on an agenda for his first visit to a foreign country. Even the evening's excitement was a thing of the past.

"I'll fill the tub so you can take a bath. Then we'll go get something to eat."

"Girls take baths. Boys take showers."

"Fine. Don't forget to wash your hair."

The phone rang. It was Muharrem, my Turkish agent, right on time. He was unaware of the minor earthquake we'd experienced.

"This is very often for us. It is nothing. How is your son? Your flights are good?" There was an edge of excitement I hadn't heard before in his soft, deep voice. I soon learned why.

"If it is possible, Mrs. Reardon, can we adjust our schedule? A broker in Torbal is most anxious to sell his inventory. He has a buyer who cancelled. Also he is the Mayor of Torbal, a very important man. I have already told him you are interested. Is it possible? I believe you would be most happy with his rugs and his prices."

The reason for his fervor was suddenly clear. This, most likely, was a contact Muharrem hadn't been able to make in the past. Now he had the opportunity and he didn't want to miss it. Since I learned long ago to respect his instincts, I didn't either.

No foreigner conducts business in Turkey without an agent, and I discovered early on how lucky I was to hire him. Muharrem El Habashy had turned out to be my best asset. Not only did he provide me with information about a broker's reliability and the authenticity of his wares, but also he managed to discover intimate facts about the broker himself. It was this kind of information that propelled me to success.

"Well…" I could feel my own excitement building, but there

were new considerations. Torbal was about fifty miles west. I would be gone for three or four hours. Could I leave Skipper?

"I'll need someone to stay with Skipper, but I'm sure the hotel can help. Pick me up in an hour. I'll be ready."

I turned to see Skipper standing in the doorway, wrapped in a towel. He looked angry.

"You okay?"

He turned and walked back into the bathroom.

Torbal looked like all the other small Turkish towns I'd seen on previous trips – small stone buildings, rebar jutting from unfinished roofs, randomly placed narrow roads, goats and sheep in abundance. We drove by several *bakkal*, the traditional Turkish grocery stores. Women and children milled around until we approached, then they smiled and stood still, watching us pass. Men, dressed in suit jackets, dark pants and woolen caps, clustered on chairs outside a coffee house. Like the women and children, their eyes followed us.

Fifteen minutes later we arrived at a long, windowless building on the edge of town. An elegant copper and silver shield hung on the carved door.

"It is the Mayor's family crest," Muharrem said, hands wringing, adjusting his black suit jacket. He was a formidable-looking man in his 30s, dark hair and heavy eyebrows, at least six feet tall and solidly built. Deeply pocked olive skin made him look tough, but he was gentle and polite and I felt safe when we were together. I relaxed and got ready to share a new experience with him.

Before getting out of the car, I quickly tied on a headscarf. Although unnecessary in the cities, I'd been told small villages like Torbal often observed strict religious conventions and women never appeared in public bareheaded. The women I'd seen earlier were wearing scarves and even though Turkish law didn't require them for foreigners, I wasn't taking any chances.

The showroom, a sharp contrast to the dingy village we'd driven through, was fitted with mirrors and gilded art on the walls. A door opened on our left and Muharrem stepped forward to introduce me to Mayor Nerman Ysilada. He surveyed my entire face slowly and deliberately. I stiffened, avoided looking into his eyes, and hoped he was satisfied with his first impression. In one way or another, the men I dealt with managed to let me know they preferred working with their own gender. It was a challenge I gladly accepted. I'd wanted to be an Oriental rug broker since high school and an insignificant matter like gender wasn't going to deter me. Sometimes, when I looked into the eyes of Turkey's young women, I told myself I was plowing the way for them.

Mayor Ysilada led us into a side room, asked us to sit, and poured tea from a large brass samovar. He moved with the grace of practice, but offered no chatter. Often I learned about personality traits from the small talk preceding negotiation, but since it appeared I'd get nothing from him, I shifted my thoughts to his outer appearance. The hair peeking beneath his embroidered skull cap was thick and silver, and his cream-colored shirt and flowing cotton pants were crafted from fine, hand-woven cloth - pleasant to the eye but lacking clues as to how I should deal with him.

The Mayor had three sons whom Muharrem had discovered were soccer fans. My *bakşiş*, the gift expected by Turkish custom, was three soccer balls. The boys were summoned, arriving in t-shirts and blue jeans, looking like teenagers everywhere in the world. Obviously they'd been instructed in good manners and the Mayor smiled broadly when his sons received the balls, bowed, thanked us, and promptly left the room. I wondered how many times they'd been through the ritual. In any event, Ysilada seemed more relaxed and my hopes for a more friendly negotiation spiked. Or so I thought.

Ysilada dropped his smile and we sipped our tea in silence until I asked the Mayor about the ages of his sons.

"They are all in school."

Certain my Turkish had been correct, I glanced at Muharrem, but he was staring into his cup. No former experience had prepared me for the awkward atmosphere. In most cases my encounters suffered from too much effort to be friendly. Even when a negotiation failed there would be long, complicated explanations for why a deal could not be reached. And always I was encouraged to visit again because they had enjoyed my company, or because they wanted to introduce me to others, or take me to points of interest nearby – anything to maintain friendship and goodwill. Ysilada, on the other hand, offered more tea and when we assured him several times that we had had enough, he led us into the storeroom.

"Your rugs are most attractive. How much would you ask for this?" I said, moving my hand over an Iranian Bidjar runner, fifteen feet long with a dark blue polychrome border, an ivory field with continuous medallion and flower details.

"You have excellent taste, Madam Reardon. This rug is $3,000 American dollars."

"Ah, forgive me, Mayor Ysilada, but I am able to spend only $1,000."

He stepped back as if I'd slapped him. "You insult me. You insult my family with such an offer."

A wave of heat rose from my neck. "No, Mayor Ysilada, I assure you. I have the deepest respect for you, your family and your village. But I have traveled far, bringing my family with me. Also, to obtain the best shipping fees, I must fill the largest possible cargo container. You see, Mayor Ysilida, I hope to purchase many of your rugs at the very best prices." It was a critical speech and I hoped my Turkish was equal to the task.

He didn't respond, rather he turned his back on me and walked over to Muharrem, took his arm, and disappeared with him into another room. My hopes fell. Something was wrong, my tactics perhaps. Most of my dealings had been with rural weavers. Were negotiations with a man of status like Ysilada, a mayor, conducted differently? I should have known, should have researched the situation with someone. Now it was too late.

I watched the door for Muharrem to come and escort me back to our car. Would Ysilada return to say goodbye at least? Nothing more would be said about the rugs, I feared, and I would never know what I could have done better.

But when the door reopened, the Mayor approached me with a smile. I smiled in return and casually lifted my hand to my hairline where I felt the weight of a line of sweat about to slide. Muharrem entered behind him, giving me no clue as to what had transpired between them.

"I see," he said. "In that case this rug may go with you to America for $2,000."

It took several seconds for me to pick up the conversation that had ended so abruptly moments ago. I glanced again at Muharrem and saw the corners of his mouth curve upward. I tossed back my head.

"My limit is $1,500," I said, turning away slightly toward the door, enjoying the game.

Ysilada scowled and turned his back. He took several steps away from me and I thought the negotiation might be over for certain. I glanced again at Muharrem, but he had moved away as he normally did while I was negotiating. I wondered if "normal" could ever be applied to negotiating in the Middle East.

"It will be as you wish. I want only to please you. Come, look at my kilims," the Mayor said, pointing the way to another room.

By the time Muharrem and I left, my dress was clinging to my back, but I had a full cargo container at a very acceptable price. I arranged for Muharrem to check with Ysilada in two hours to be certain a money transfer I'd arranged earlier had reached the bank in Torbal.

It was mid afternoon when Muharrem dropped me off at the hotel. As I stepped into the hotel lobby, I could hear Skipper screaming. I rushed to our suite and saw the manager's daughter, who'd agreed to stay with Skipper, cringing behind a chair. Skipper was kicking and punching her. I pulled him away and he turned his anger on me, biting and scratching like a wild animal. It took all my strength to pick him up, put him in the bedroom and slam the door.

I pulled a handful of Turkish lira from my purse and gave it to the terrified girl who stood with one hand on the doorknob and the other outstretched to me. I understood her terror. I'd felt it myself whenever something I said or did enraged my son. I leaned against the wall thinking that perhaps the girl had done something to him, but I knew better. I moved toward the bedroom but then decided to deal with him later. *Deal* – that was Jared's word. *You never deal with him; you just distract him with a new toy*. It was true. I didn't know how to handle Skipper's anger. But it was also true that Skipper never threw temper tantrums when he was with his father, so how would he know what it was like?

From the moment I brought Skipper home from the hospital Jared insisted on taking care of him so I could get on with my career. As a senior partner in his law firm, he could arrange his own appointments, and we hired a housekeeper to fill in the gaps when I traveled. Jared was thrilled with my ambition and eager to make business suggestions that might help me. It was a happy time that didn't last.

Skipper had stopped screaming but I no sooner sat down than the phone rang. It was Muharrem. The money had not transferred. The bank had no idea where the money was, he said, and Ysilada was furious. "He says he will not trade with deception. What goes wrong?"

I glanced at my watch. It was eight in the morning in Philadelphia, an hour before the bank opened. "Stay by the phone, Muharrem. I'll call you as soon as I can."

I made coffee to pass the time and while it perked I walked to the bedroom door, opening it slowly until I could see inside. Skipper was asleep on the floor, his mouth relaxed and slightly open. The lips that had bared teeth like a growling dog just minutes before were pink and sweet. I left the door ajar and sat by the phone.

An hour later the bank had corrected its error and I called Muharrem and Ysilada.

"I'd bring the funds myself, Mayor Ysilada, but my son needs me here. I'll call again tomorrow to verify that everything is in order."

"Your son, he is ill? Perhaps there is something I can do. Or my wife? She is a nurse."

"No, no, thank you," I said. This was Turkish tradition: Ysilada was responding as all Turks do with family and friends, and now that we had a business agreement, I, too, was a friend.

His words should have been comforting, so why was my face wet with tears? I reached for a tissue and saw blood. My nails had dug into my palm.

2

Skipper was absorbed in the world at thirty-six thousand feet above the earth, and for that I was grateful. While the plane's engines labored to return us to Philadelphia, he lobbed question after question: "Can birds fly this high? Why are the clouds white?" My answers were no more than grunts, but he didn't seem to notice.

I had no answers – not for him, and certainly not for how to balance my work and my family responsibilities. As soon as I thought everything was working well, something happened to tear it apart. I didn't need more roadblocks in the way of rebuilding my life, but they fell into my path anyway. Muharrem had called just as we were leaving the hotel.

"There has been an accident," he said. "Your shipment, your rugs, they are gone."

"What? What do you mean, gone?" I dropped my purse on the floor and sat my suitcase on its wheels.

"I am not sure. There are yet no details. Only Mayor Ysilada, just now, he called me to say his truck ran off the road and burned. The driver is alive. He jumped from the truck before the flames. This is terrible for you, I know. Can I do something?"

I shook my head, not wanting to believe him. Last night, Skipper aside, I had at least one reason to be pleased. My inventory of rugs had increased with the finest quality in my years as a broker and though the process was premature, I'd already made a list of clients I knew would be eager to buy. But now this...

"I really don't know. We're on our way to the airport. I'll call you as soon as I can."

It was still hard to believe our conversation. I stared at the airplane seat in front of me, a blue and tan pattern as repetitious as the words in my head. When I tired of the seat I stared at my hands and rubbed my fingers like they were rosary beads. But no good solution shot forth from the seat or my fingers. Clearly, I'd have to cut my clients' rug orders to a bare minimum and hope my warehouse inventory would suffice. My clients' options would be limited, not a condition they'd faced before and one that hurt my pride. And my finances were severely damaged. It wasn't clear to me how my insurance would work in this instance. The rugs were mine, but they were in Mayor Ysilada's truck. Whose insurance was involved and at what point? I didn't know. What I had for the next twenty hours was the counterpoint of roaring engines and questions in my head - not all of them having to do with rugs.

In retrospect, were my brothers right about Skipper? *Mama and Papa would turn over in their graves if they knew you were taking Skipper away so soon after loosing his father. He needs time to heal. My God, Nora, what are you thinking?* I glanced over at Skipper. He was slumped against the window, sleeping peacefully. I knew he enjoyed being in Turkey. What's more, Jared often spoke of exposing Skipper to other parts of the world. *I don't want my son to think the American way of life is the only way.* I agreed with him - then.

Philadelphia International Airport was boiling with activity when Skipper and I joined the river of travelers winding their way to the baggage claim. As we stood by the carousel, studying the parade of black cases, a gravely voice broke through the background bustle. "Welcome home, baby sister."

I spun around to see Philip's smiling face. He scooped Skipper up in one arm and hugged me with the other.

From his raised vantage point, Skipper shouted, "There's my suitcase, Mommy, and yours too."

We yanked them from the carousel and followed Philip to the parking garage. From behind, Philip was a copy of our Lebanese father - broad shouldered, olive skin and black hair and eyes. Val and I were lighter – green eyes and chestnut hair. But unlike Val, Philip gave me the chance to think for myself. No wonder it was Philip I chose on those rare occasions when I wanted to discuss a problem.

Both of my brothers were electrical engineers. I felt they put extra effort into building their business so they could support the four of us. It was a philosophy we all understood, one that Mama and Papa hammered home every time we left the house together. *Val, Philip! Take care of your sister.* The fact that I was now an adult, fully able to care for myself, hadn't changed a thing. The family mantra lingered sans audio.

As we drove along the narrow Philadelphia streets, Skipper supplied us with a continuous commentary, and, gratefully, not a word about the tremor in Turkey. "They drive too fast and they smoke. They make kebabs, but yours are better, Uncle Philip."

Philip tried to comment but Skipper had more to share. "They have mosques instead of churches and they pray together with their faces on the ground and they take off their shoes. I didn't see any girls praying. Mommy said she didn't know where the girls prayed."

Finally we approached our row of brownstone homes and I spotted Val waiting at the door. He rushed to us, extended a hand to Skipper for a mock handshake and then broke into his throaty laugh when Skipper looked surprised. He lifted Skip into his arms and smothered him with kisses. This was the welcome Skipper was used to.

"Your mustache tickles, Uncle Val."

"Why do you think I keep this mustache? Do you think it's to make me handsome?"

I was next. His exuberance was infectious, warmly familiar.

Val and Philip always had keys to our home. It was obvious they'd arrived earlier in the day to get things ready for our homecoming. A huge vase of yellow roses, my favorite, was on the Chippendale table just inside the door, and wonderful, rich aromas wafted from the kitchen.

In less than half an hour, Val was ladling lentil soup into large round bowls and piling warm crusty bread into a basket. His long hair was plaited and bound bluntly at the nap of his neck. He loved being in the kitchen, maneuvering his wiry physique around my counters. He knew where everything was and, from the metal mountain piled in the sink, it appeared he'd used it all. In the meantime, Philip lugged suitcases up two flights of stairs to Skipper's room and then up another flight to mine.

After dinner, when Skipper was asleep, we sat together in the den enjoying the fire Philip had laid. I dreaded the topic I knew would eventually come.

"Sometimes trauma alters our judgment. I'm sorry you had to learn the hard way, but you're home now and, you'll see, it's for the best. Skipper doesn't always tell us how he feels. It's up to us to know." It was the speech I expected from Val.

Sometimes my brothers acted like they knew all there was to know about children. But, in fact, Philip had never married, and Val's wife of only five years died before they could have a family. Skipper was the only child they'd ever cared for.

"He's fine – you can see that, can't you?" I took a deep breath. "He had a temper tantrum, not cardiac arrest."

"See? You don't get it." Val said. "You should've had more sense than to leave him with a stranger after such a traumatic experience. Sometimes you amaze me." Philip placed his hand on Val's shoulder and Val looked at him and rolled his eyes.

I slouched deeper into the sofa pillows.

"Let's go, Val. We've covered enough territory for one night. There'll be others."

At the door, Val said he and Philip had been looking for a house. They were tired of apartment living. "We want enough room for an office and a big garden. We've been keeping our eyes open and I think we've found something. After you get caught up, you'll come and see."

And I'd bet my best carpet there were several rooms for Skipper and me.

Skipper and I settled into a routine. I enrolled him in the first grade at Wister Academy. Every morning we walked to school together and I spent the rest of the day on the phone with clients until it was time to pick him up. He began connecting with old friends in the neighborhood and some days he'd meet them in the park to play. He seemed really happy, a fact I was eager to share with my brothers who called almost every evening. But keeping them abreast of Skipper's doings was one thing, sharing my own thoughts was quite another.

With each passing day, I felt more restless. The present routine might be good for Skipper but it was becoming increasingly boring for me. I found myself searching for new ideas in the journals and newsletters I received from Oriental rug societies. From the beginning, Turkey had been the focus of my buying trips, but Turkey was only one player in the rug business. India, Pakistan, Tibet, Africa, the Balkans and China were others. I already knew these countries produced rugs of quality and beauty. Now I was reading about the new designs and techniques that were emerging. Why not expand my horizon?

One afternoon my eye caught a small notice in the "Oriental Network," a British journal: *An eighteenth century wool rug,* *woven in India for the late Mogul court, sold recently for $805,500.* My skin tingled. The antique market involved so much more than just buying a beautiful rug. Those who bought them were collectors for the most part, and collectors made challenging customers. They also were rich customers. Perhaps this was where my future lay. Antiques would take lots more money, but I'd make more too. Surely there were antique dealers in Turkey. And there was Muharrem. My adrenaline pumping, I placed a call to him.

"What you are asking is absolutely no problem for me," Muharrem said. "As you know, I have a network that reaches into every corner of my country."

It was the kind of confident response I expected from him. If my new endeavors promised more income, he would push windmills against the wind. He said he'd find a contact for me and would be in touch in a few days. In the meantime, I put my new idea on the back burner and called Val to begin planning a party for Skipper's approaching sixth birthday.

"What do you think of a sailing party for Skip on your boat?"

"It's a great idea. You know, there are some small coves less than a mile from the marina. We could sail there, build a fire on the beach to roast hot dogs and play some games."

"Perfect. I'll talk to Skipper about the friends he'd like to invite and we'll probably have some parents too. How many can you handle?"

"Ten to fifteen would be fine."

That evening I told Skipper what we were planning. But instead of the happy response I expected, he ran away from me and I heard his bedroom door slam. I waited a few minutes before I went to his room.

"Skipper?" I said, outside his door. "I thought you'd jump at the chance to go sailing like you used to with Daddy and your uncles."

"No." His voice sounded muffled. I opened the door and saw him on the floor wrapped in his bedspread.

"I don't understand. You love sailing."

"I hate it. I hate Uncle Val's boat." He wrapped the bedspread tighter around himself. Nothing he said made sense. I scanned his room hoping the right words would come to me and rested my eyes on Skip's favorite picture. It was one Val took when we were all sailing on the Chesapeake Bay. Skipper was eighteen months old, naked except for a captain's hat and tiny deck shoes. Jared was at the helm holding him on his lap when suddenly Skipper grasped the wheel and turned the boat sharply to the left. Val snapped the picture and gave it to us the following Christmas. Below the photo he'd written: "Skipper at the Helm." The nickname stuck. We never called him Tommy or Thomas again.

I grabbed the photo, gathered him up inside the spread and sat him on my lap. Two puckered spots showed where he was clutching the fabric.

"Don't tell me you can't remember how much fun you had when we went sailing together. Look at this picture of when you were a little boy."

He began to cry.

"Daddy would want you to remember the fun we had. He'd want to see you sailing and having fun on the boat." My throat tightened.

"Daddy's dead. He isn't here anymore."

"Oh, you're wrong, so wrong. We can't see Daddy anymore, that's true, but Daddy's in our hearts." I found his hand and placed it on my chest. When he quieted down, I folded back the bedspread from his face, hugged him and kissed his head. "Daddy's inside you too, and you know what?"

"What?"

"Daddy wants us to be happy even though he knows we miss him." My throat was so constricted the words were more air than sound. "Uncle Val and Uncle Philip miss sailing with you. Won't you think about it?"

He didn't answer, but he wasn't crying anymore. I swallowed and pulled him close. It wasn't just his words that touched me; it was the uncharacteristic emotion, part of him I rarely saw. We lay together until his breathing became slow and steady and I was sure he was asleep. I slipped out and closed the door.

Several days later Muharrem called. "I have found the perfect person to work with you: Carlos Ghazerian. He lives in Ankara, but travels throughout Asia and specializes in rugs with history. He is most willing to work as a wholesaler and wants to know when you can come to Ankara."

"Good work. Who pays Mr. Ghazerian?"

"He is a broker for many dealers. The dealers pay him a commission when he finds buyers for their rugs."

"So his profit would not be part of my cost, correct?"

"Correct. This is the answer you wanted, yes?"

"I still have many questions about him."

"Yes, I will send you more information. Already he has asked me many questions about you. You can trust me to tell him of your skill and your-"

"Thank you. Let me call you in a week or so with my plans." After our conversation, I hung on to the receiver with the distinct feeling I was inching my way to the crest of a roller coaster and was about to lose myself in the acceleration.

In less than a week a package arrived from Muharrem. Mr. Ghazerian had studied law and economics at Harvard, and also received a master's degree in international law in Washington. His father, recently deceased, had been curator of Istanbul's Museum of Art, which maintained many of the Asian world's finest rug treasures. Furthermore, the Ghazerian family estate included a large and valuable collection of rugs.

I was ready to pack my bags and board the next available plane, but that would be skipping over the hard part – how to convince my brothers. They'd not only object to another trip to Turkey, they'd hate the idea of expanding my business. I dreaded the inevitable confrontation, but the specter of humdrum days seemed worse. A straightforward, logical explanation, accompanied by a delicious dinner would have to do. I began planning the meal, one that included all our favorite family recipes.

The kitchen in our Colonial brownstone home had been remodeled several times before Jared and I moved in. It had all the modern conveniences with one exception: a raised wood-burning fireplace with a swinging bar that held a cast iron kettle - our capitulation to historic accuracy. It was fully operational but we never used it. For Jared and me, the most important feature in the kitchen was a small table and four chairs. There was a large dining room, but it saw use at holiday time only. Jared said he liked being close to the food and got no argument from me. I came from a family that loved everything about mealtimes. This was the table I set for dinner with my brothers.

Val arrived first and immediately joined me in the kitchen to lift each pot lid. He wasn't disappointed. I'd made his favorite beef burgundy.

"And for dessert I've got lemon mousse and Mama's poppy seed strudel." I reached into a drawer and handed him a spoon so he could sample the stew.

"You must have been cooking all day." He lifted the spoon to his mouth. "Ah, terrific. Are you softening us up for something?"

"Well, I do have news, but it can wait until after dinner."

We were mellow with wine and good food when the doorbell rang. Skipper sprinted to answer.

"It's Marty," he shouted back to us. "We're going to the park to play ball with his dad and then I'm staying overnight."

I shrugged in answer to my brothers' raised eyebrows. "Our boy is growing up," I said.

Back at the table, Skipper introduced Marty and his dad, neighbor Jack Denby, and then he scooped up his backpack and gave us each a hug and kiss.

"Great job with the introductions," I whispered in his ear. He smiled and dashed for the door to join his friends.

Jared had been relentless about good manners. At the time I hadn't liked the harping, but I could see that Skipper liked impressing grownups so I never said anything.

"He's becoming a small hurricane," I said, "but I love seeing him excited, don't you?"

"Jared did a good job raising Skipper," Val said.

Heat rose from my neck and I got up to fill the wineglasses again. We walked together to the den, carrying our glasses. Philip went out to the deck to grab an armful of logs and we watched as he laid a fire. Soon the wood was crackling soothingly and the smell of vaporizing pecan drifted through the room.

"I've decided to expand my import business to include antique rugs. Muharrem has made a contact in Ankara for me, and I'm planning a business trip there soon," I said without taking a breath.

Val's face clouded. "Nora, what's the matter with you?" He got up from his chair and stood over me.

"Let me finish, will you?"

"No. I won't let you finish. We should never have let you get started with this business in the first place," he said.

"We? Who put you, or anyone else, in charge of my life?"

We were on our feet, facing each other. I swallowed, wanting to run, but felt my anger root me like an oak tree in a windstorm.

"Mama and Papa would never have approved of what you're doing," Val said.

Something exploded inside me. "Mama and Papa? Have you forgotten what happened to Papa, how the university just decided they didn't need him anymore? It killed him. And it killed Mama too. So don't tell me they wouldn't approve of what I do. They'd be the first to cheer me on. They'd understand the need to protect myself and Skipper."

I was screaming, but couldn't stop. Val began to blink spasmodically.

"It was because of what happened to them that I swore I'd have my own business. No one was going to fire me from a job and leave me with nothing."

"Mama and Papa knew we'd always take care of you," Philip said, placing an arm around Val's shoulders.

"Well, that's not what I want. Do you ever stop to ask me what I want?" I pushed forward and glared at both of them.

"Stop thinking about what you want for a minute and think about Skipper and what he needs," Val said. His eyes were fluttering.

"You're not being fair," I said. "Everything I do is for Skipper. I never want him to be helpless or without his own resources. I want to show him how to be successful and independent. He's learning these things from me, and I won't let anyone get in my way. Jared is gone. Skipper has only one parent: me. I'll teach him and, damn you both, I'll do it my way."

"Jared wouldn't like what you're doing, Nora," Philip said.

I knew that gentle voice, but it wasn't going to make me back down this time.

"You're wrong, Philip. Jared and I discussed my business even before we got married. He helped me in every way. He loved my determination." I kept my voice under control but could feel the anger building.

"Nora, Nora," Val said. "Jared may have encouraged you before Skipper came along, but-"

I began to shake and walked to the fireplace to speak to the fire. "There's something you don't know. After my last trip, right before his accident, Jared was going to leave me."

They started to protest, but I didn't let them. "It's true. First he said he was proud of me, and then changed his mind and told me he wanted a divorce. He was going to take Skipper away from me." I barely got out the last few words.

"I don't believe that. If he did, it must have been in desperation, a desperate move to keep you home," Philip said.

It was no use. They didn't understand anything and never would. I turned around. If I felt like crying a moment ago, the urge was gone.

"I'm leaving for Istanbul next week. I'll stay for about two weeks, maybe a bit longer if that's what it takes. You can take care of Skipper or I'll find someone else."

Disbelief spread across their faces. At that moment, I hated them. I'd listened to enough of what they felt, what they thought I should be. I left the room and ran up the stairs to my bedroom. They'd figure it out, or they wouldn't.

I heard the door close below and threw myself on the bed. If they didn't like who I was that was just too bad. Bile burned in my throat and my stomach churned. Had anyone ever understood me? I thought Jared did, but I guess he really didn't.

"Jared, you deserter," I screamed into the bedclothes. Did he look when he crossed the street to his office, or was he thinking of some case he was working on? Why didn't that stupid woman keep her eye on the street? She said she bent to pick up her child's toy. She said it only took a second, only a second to change everything.

3

From the fourth floor of my hotel, I had a panoramic view of Ankara's business district. Cars, buses and people moved along the streets and sidewalks and several steel and glass skyscrapers lined up like glitzy dominoes. Most people were dressed in Western attire, but I saw a few traditional Turkish costumes here and there. Across from the hotel there was a small park, dense with trees and small tables along the outer edges. Groups of two and four men were playing board games.

I caught Muharrem's eye as he emerged from his car and signaled that I'd join him. My stomach fluttered with excitement as I snatched my purse and took a last look at myself in a mirror. I'd arrived the day before by air shuttle, wanting to be fresh and well rested for the meeting with Ghazerian. I needed the time away from the family, and it felt good to have something new to occupy my mind.

"Carlos lives with his mother and sister," Muharrem said, when we were on the main highway. "He has total financial responsibility for them. His sister plans to marry soon and at that time her husband will take full responsibility for her. That does not mean that she will lose the inheritance she received at her father's death."

"In so many ways, Ankara reminds me of home," I said, looking out the car window. I couldn't imagine why Muharrem was giving me such personal information.

"It is very different in your country, am I not correct?"

I searched for a gentle way to change the topic. "Listen, Muharrem, I want you to understand that my new interest in antique rugs won't replace what we've been doing. My clients will continue to need contemporary rugs. And another thing, I plan to compensate you for introducing me to Mr. Ghazerian."

He slowed the car as we neared an elegant apartment building. Stately cypress trees lined the sweeping driveway.

"Yes, thank you. I understand. Eh-"

"What?"

"There is a challenge."

"I don't think so. There's a valet who can take the car for you."

"No, I mean there is a challenge, a danger, with the antique rugs."

"Danger?"

We stopped and the valet, whose uniform bore more gold fringe than a Christmas tree, rushed to open my door.

"It has to do with proving the age of a rug," Muharrem said, joining me at the entrance where two equally fringed men smiled and pulled aside heavy glass doors.

"Oh, yes, I know. Don't worry. I'm prepared. Besides, you told me we are working with a reputable dealer here."

"Of course. But there is much more money involved and many deceptions. It can be quite complicated because-"

I stopped walking. "Muharrem, have you ever known me to be unprepared – financially or otherwise?" I didn't need another man worrying about my financial security.

Muharrem flushed, but before he could apologize, I told him I had no intention of ever being caught unprepared.

The interior was palatial. Alternate panels of muted green brocade and dark wood covered the walls, and sofas and chairs in deep blue tapestry were tastefully dispersed throughout the area. It was the Kelebek Hotel's wealthy relative, less concerned with history than opulence.

"You are expected, Mrs. Reardon," a man sitting by the elevator said. He had spoken in English and I showed my surprise. Was this the way all guests were greeted or was this the work of Carlos Ghazerian? My curiosity jumped another notch.

We stepped from the elevator and I looked into the deepest blue eyes I'd ever seen.

"Welcome, Mrs. Reardon. I'm Carlos Ghazerian." He offered his hand and bent slightly forward, but his eyes stayed on me until he shook hands with Muharrem. A wave of heat from nowhere pulsed on my face. "Please come in," he said, stepping aside to let us pass.

His skin was the color of coffee lightened with cream. Shiny black hair curled at the nape of his neck, neatly trimmed around his ears. I guessed he was in his late 30s, about six feet tall, but there was no guesswork about the power of his frame, which I noted when he moved ahead of us.

"I would like you to meet my mother and sister." There was excitement in his voice, enthusiasm maybe, but it was well controlled. He moved with the poise and confidence of a man used to being in charge, and I had the strange feeling he had gathered us up in some invisible netting and we had no choice but to follow. I, for one, was more than willing.

The temptation to look at his eyes was strong, but I didn't dare. I'd heard it was considered too bold for a woman. Occasionally I'd done it on purpose, but this wasn't going to be one of those times. Fortunately his mother and sister walked forward to greet us and I saw instantly where the blue eyes had come from – his mother. He surprised me by introducing them by their first names: Elena and Tapis. Both were stunning women and both had long hair drawn back. Tapis' was dark, caught up and spiraled into ringlets around her head, while Mrs. Ghazerian's hair was white and gathered into a roll from one side to the other and anchored with a jeweled comb. Their dresses could have come from any fashion house in New York City and probably had.

"Hello, Mrs. Ghazerian. Tapis."

"Please, call me Elena. We are very happy to have you here. I hope you will make yourself comfortable in our home." Her voice was soft, her hands rested gracefully on the folds of her long black skirt, and she spoke English with just the slightest accent.

We sat down on deeply cushioned chairs, and I was barely conscious of a conversation about the city, the weather, and something about my family. My mind, however, was somewhere beyond.

Elena got up from her chair and asked to be excused. Tapis, rather abruptly I thought, rose and followed her mother, saying something about needing to make some phone calls. The smile on Carlos' face made me think their departure had been planned so we could get on with business.

While he stood and watched them leave, I glanced around the predominantly blue and white room. What struck me first was the Chinese art: an eight-sided pagoda interpreted in gold filigree, statues of dancing figures with elaborate headdresses, and a porcelain platter with red dragons among colorful flowers. Beneath my feet was a pale yellow rug on which two blue dragons circled each other and whose serpentine tails stretched almost to the edges of the rug's border. The size alone told me that this rug had cushioned royal feet at some time in the past.

When I looked back at Carlos, I jumped. He had moved to my side and I'd been so engrossed I hadn't noticed. "This rug...it's so beautiful." I'd intended to ask a question about it, something that would get us talking about the rugs, but my admiration tumbled out. "Mr. Ghazerian, did it, I mean, where...?

"It has been in my family for at least five generations. We have tried to discover its origin, but sadly we do not know. Please, won't you call me Carlos?"

I wondered if he was always so informal, or if he was mimicking his American experience for my sake. He was definitely a contrast to other Turkish men I'd been introduced to. They, it seemed to me, were more concerned with fulfilling rituals than in being friendly.

"Muharrem tells me you are interested in our historic treasures." He nodded to Muharrem, whose head rose a notch. "How can I help?"

"We can help each other," I said.

His eyes widened slightly and he smiled. "Yes, of course, please go on."

"I want to expand my business to include antique rugs. I believe I have a market that is ready for that kind of investment. I'd like your help in identifying at least three pieces, along with background histories, photographs, and costs."

He nodded. "We can begin whenever you like."

The door to another room opened and a maid appeared to say that Muharrem had a telephone call.

"I am sorry. I do not imagine who-" Muharrem frowned and looked shaken as he followed the maid.

While he went to answer, Carlos showed me a few of the rugs on the walls and pointed out their features. Two were from the early nineteenth century in the hanging lamp style. The delicate shades and patterns were rare, as was everything I'd observed, including the Ghazerians.

Fifteen minutes later Muharrem rushed back into the room, looking more upset than when he left us.

"I must return home immediately," he said. "My father has had a seizure and is in the hospital. I have already booked myself on the next shuttle flight. Madam Reardon, I will take a taxi to the airport and leave the car for you."

"That's terrible, my friend. Please go. I'll drive your car back to Istanbul and call you in a few days."

"I will not hear of it," Carlos said. "I will drive you."

"Thank you, Carlos," Muharrem said, heading for the door.

"That's a generous offer, but I'm accustomed to driving long distances alone. I'll be fine."

"May I call you Nora?" His English was flawless, but Nora sounded like Nor*ah*. I didn't correct him; I rather liked the sound. "In my country, a woman driving alone is not a good idea. If by some misfortune your car becomes disabled in the desert, well, I really would be happy to escort you. Besides, if you like, we can use the time to visit a couple of weaving villages where new techniques are being tested. I have wanted to go myself. It is a full day's drive to Istanbul. Except for the side roads, the highway is good. If we leave very early we can make it in one day, even if we make a couple of stops. Is this agreeable?"

"Well, if you're sure you have the time. I'd really like to see the new designs. I've read about them."

"Settled! I will use Muharrem's car and we will leave tomorrow early. In the meantime," he said, glancing at his watch, "will you join us for dinner? We can pass the time until then by visiting the gardens. They are quite nice. Do you like nature?"

"Yes, thank you." He was certainly direct. Decisive too. I liked it.

A gentle breeze accompanied the moon as it rose in the sky. The gardens were lush with trees and plants I didn't recognize. The architecture was classic Moroccan with archways and slender minaret-like towers stretching above the roofline, a darkening silhouette against the red-orange sky. Flowers were planted in waves of color, from pale to bright, bright to pale, and glossy black pebbles formed a precise border.

We turned a corner and I drew in my breath at a patch of hip high golden-leafed bushes. Carlos stopped to look at me.

"Oh, it's nothing. I thought for a moment they were roses, but…"

"Ah, yes, I remember that your country has roses of many colors. They are difficult to grow here – not enough moisture, you see."

"Yes."

"Do you like yellow roses?" He certainly had no problem looking at me directly. It was unsettling.

"Yes," I said and started walking again. "Carlos, may I ask-"

"You may ask me anything. We will be working together. It is important, I think, that we know each other."

"Well, this isn't a question about business. I'm surprised you and your mother have blue eyes."

He laughed with so much enjoyment that I lost any embarrassment I might have felt.

"My mother is from San Sebastian near the Pyrenees in Northern Spain. After so many invasions by Celts and other Germanic tribes, the legacy of blue eyes is common in that region. But beyond my mother's blue eyes, I am hoping you will be in for another surprise when we sit down to dinner."

"I love surprises. What is it?" Any awkwardness I felt was melting away. We were like two old friends, enjoying each other's company. I knew I should be more guarded but I was having too much fun.

"The women from that region on the Bay of Biscayne are noted for their Paella Valenciana, and before we left the apartment my mother asked me if I thought you would like it. Since it is a favorite of mine, I said yes." He laughed again.

At nine o'clock we were seated in the dining room where a Han Dynasty horse of green stone watched over us. The paella was delicious – a mélange of chicken, seafood and fragrant spices. There were Turkish treats too: small triangles of flatbread spread with feta cheese, a spicy grilled eggplant, and a creamy rice pudding for dessert.

Elena explained that she loved to cook and the paella was traditional for all family celebrations, especially Christmas and Easter.

I almost choked on my feta triangle. No one seemed to notice, for which I was grateful. I'd wrongly assumed the Ghazerians were Muslim.

By the time we had small cups of rich, dark Turkish coffee, I was feeling very much at ease with this gracious family. Only Tapis clouded the evening when, after learning she was soon to be married, I asked her where the wedding would take place.

She stared at me for several seconds before answering, her voice taking on an edge of defiance that both surprised and unnerved me. "Mehmet is Muslim. We met at work, but after we are married I will be dedicated to my husband and children and never would I consider working." She maintained the stare and drew herself up in her chair. At the same time I saw Elena and Carlos brace themselves against the backs of theirs. He glanced at me with an unhappy expression and Elena looked downright frightened.

"What kind of work does Mehmet do?" I said, hoping to move to safer ground.

"He is the senior son in his father's investigation firm, Aydin Associates, Inc."

"That must be interesting work," I said. Elena asked if I would like more to eat. I smiled and declined. The conversation never returned to its earlier ease and I soon thanked them for the evening and Carlos drove me home. He spoke the whole way to the hotel about what we would do the next day. I found myself thinking more about the time with Carlos than the sights we'd see.

The next day I watched for him from my hotel window. I told myself twenty-four hours was hardly enough time to know anyone, but that didn't stop me from looking forward to the drive. I spotted Muharrem's sedan pull into the hotel's circular drive, and several minutes later Carlos was at my door, looking comfortable in khaki slacks and a rust-colored cotton shirt. The suit he'd worn the night before only hinted at the powerful build that was evident now. He was handsome, but not by classic standards. He had an angular nose, slightly hooked, high cheekbones and generous lips. Spirit and enthusiasm seemed to spring from his body. The overall effect was magnetic.

It took us an hour to leave behind the city traffic and move into the hilly countryside. Dirt paths fanned out and disappeared into woods all around us. I tried to think of some questions to ask or comments to make – anything to ease the awkwardness. This was not how I handled things - a stranger driving me home, taking me to places I could have managed to see myself. How did I get into such a position?

"Nora, I want to know about you and Oriental rugs," Carlos said.

I jumped at the sound of his voice and suddenly felt foolish. Odd question. But he did say we should get to know each other.

"I learned to love them when I was a child. My parents were born in Lebanon and when they married they immigrated to the United States. Their parents gave them rugs that had been in the family for many years. I believe it was their way of giving them pieces of family heritage. The rugs were always more than just covering for the floors. They were symbols of our closeness to each other." Was I being too familiar? Perhaps he only wanted to know how I got into the business. I looked out the window as an image took shape in my mind, something I hadn't thought of for a long time.

"What is it?" he said. "Something is making you smile."

"I was just remembering a particular rug."

"Tell me about it."

"There was a rug under our breakfast room table that I really loved. It had a rusty brown border with dark hook-like designs on four sides. The center was filled with bright, multicolored flowers on a grass-green background. I called it my play garden. The brown border was a fence and I pretended that every kind of flower in the world grew inside my fence. My mother would cover the table with a cloth that came almost to the floor and I pasted leaves cut from colored paper all over the underside of the table. It was my dreaming place, my favorite place to be."

"I can see you in such a setting. How old were you?"

"It's a little embarrassing," I said. I took a deep breath. Part of me was enjoying the old memories. "I remember playing with my dolls there as a very little girl. But, I also remember being there when I was big enough to take up the whole garden. I guess I must have been eleven or twelve – still fantasizing."

"Don't be embarrassed. I believe if we are lucky we never stray far from our childhood selves. But, you know, you never really answered my question. How did you get started in your business?"

"Oh, I'm sorry, I thought you meant-"

But before I could answer, he pointed ahead to buildings on the hillside.

"That's Usa Dagh, our first stop."

At first I saw only two small buildings among the pines, but as I scanned the forest, I saw several others dotting the area. Some were built with stone, but most were made of wood, and they varied in size from small, one-story, to large, two-story buildings. Smoke curled from chimneys but no one was in sight.

"This is a village with a history of weaving that reaches back centuries," he said. "I hear they are recreating some of the original patterns."

We strolled next to a fire where a large pot was simmering, and close by piles of roots, leaves and flowers were stacked two and three feet high. I recognized the prickly leaves and small greenish-yellow flowers of madder, an herb common to the area. Weavers used the roots to produce a rich red and, with the addition of other plants, also pink, yellow, purple and brown.

When we reached the back of the building, there were children sitting on the ground playing quietly. Nearby a man with stained arms, hands and clothing, ground madder's red roots into a coarse powder using a flat stone. He gave us a quick glance, but went right back to his work. Gradually other men appeared in the doorway. A woman stuck her head through the window of one of the houses and shouted to the children. They jumped up and ran into the house.

Carlos spoke to the man grinding the herb and shortly afterward the man beckoned to another in the doorway. Within a few moments we were escorted inside a long room set up with weaving looms, piles of dyed yarn and fabric stacked in the corners. It appeared they were beginning a new project, giving us the chance to observe not only the rug's infrastructure, but to watch the women's dark fingers grasp three warps, insert yarn, and in one swift motion, knot and cut the yarn, leaving a tuft of pile. Men were painting colored squares on graph paper, and every few minutes a woman would call out to the men to question a color. I yearned to move in closer, but no one had made eye contact with me and I felt unsure of myself. I slowly made my way to Carlos' side.

"This is so exciting. I've seen pictures in books, but I've never seen a rug in progress like this."

"They are recreating a finely-woven Persian floral. That scale-paper method they're using enables them to produce a symmetry that would be impossible otherwise. The headman who brought us in said they use only natural dyes. He says they are very successful because people recognize the quality of their work. I agree with him, Nora; just look at that knotting."

We moved to one of the outside walls so we wouldn't disturb the workers with our whispering.

"This village is a blend of families who have been here for generations and others who were nomadic until recently. It is a phenomenon that is growing in the weaving villages – probably driven by their success."

After about an hour, we left the village, but not the experience. Carlos was excited about the increasing market for traditionally made rugs and the confidence the workers expressed. I agreed they seemed proud of what they were doing, but I told him I had the feeling they were uncomfortable with strangers.

"Not at all. Village people are noted for their hospitality to strangers. Normally they would consider it an honor to ask travelers to eat with them. We left before they had the opportunity to do so."

I didn't press my feelings, thinking perhaps the men felt awkward with a foreign woman in their presence.

About a mile down the main road Carlos stopped at a small store to get drinks and something to eat. I got out of the car to explore a nearby building with a tent next to it. The tent flap was pulled aside and I glanced in. Suddenly an angry voice came up behind me. I turned around to find an old woman shouting and pointing her finger at me. I couldn't understand what she was saying, but I guessed that peeking into the tent had been a mistake.

"Sorry, very sorry," I said again and again in Turkish, but she seemed not to understand. Seconds later more women poured from other tents and small buildings. As the crowd swelled, so did the voices. I backed away toward the car but they followed me. Fear got the better of me and I turned and ran. When I was almost to the car, a woman pulled on my skirt and swung around in front of me. She thrust her wrinkled, dust-colored face within inches of mine and shouted, showering my face with spittle while she jabbed a finger at my head. Suddenly I understood – I'd forgotten my headscarf.

Carlos yelled, "Get in the car." He tossed a package into the back seat and we took off, leaving a billow of dust as tall as a tree behind us.

"Are you all right?" He checked the rear view mirror and slowed down.

"Yes, well, maybe a little shaken. But it was my fault. I forgot to cover my head."

"I am so sorry. I never thought of that. Usually I travel with men. Yes, it is rare but in some villages the women choose to follow strict religious observances. I am terribly sorry, please forgive me."

"It's not your fault." This had never happened with Muharrem. How could I have forgotten?"

"You are shivering," he said, pulling to the side of the road. He reached behind to the back seat and handed me his jacket. "Let's stop for a bit and have something to eat. That small store did not have much, but there is Turka Coke, our brand of Coca Cola, and I will call this a Turkish pizza." He balanced a flatbread topped with tomatoes and other vegetables on his palm.

"I'll have the soda. Thanks."

We got to the Kelebek as the sun cast a saffron glow on the stucco walls. Carlos walked me to my room. He looked crestfallen.

"What can I do for you? Can I order something from the hotel's food service?" He stood by the door with his jacket over his arm. I could still feel where his hands had touched my shoulders.

"No, I'll be fine. Actually, though, I would like a drink. I brought some cognac with me. Would you join me?"

I told him where the bottle was and he poured equal amounts into two glasses.

We sat together in silence. Then, softly, he began speaking of Turkey – inconsequential things like how it struggled to modernize, how it had adopted many Western ways in the cities, and how Turkish storytellers were the best in the world. Mostly, I remember the sound of his voice. Its deep rumble settled on me like a blanket. When my eyes began to droop, he left, and I walked to the bedroom, slipped out of my clothes and into bed.

A ringing phone was not exactly what I wanted for a wake-up call, but there it was. It was Carlos.

"How are you feeling?"

"Fine, really."

"I was wondering, can I come by to see you before I leave for Ankara this morning? I have already returned the car to Muharrem and rented one for my return to Ankara. By the way, Muharrem's father is stable but they will not know anything for a few days."

"Oh, thank you for that news. And thank you for...everything. I enjoyed yesterday very much and I appreciate your concern."

"Yes, me too." There was a long silence and I realized I hadn't responded to his question.

"Forgive me, Carlos, but actually I haven't much time. I was just about to call my brothers to tell them I'm coming home on the first flight I can get."

"I understand, ah-"

"Yes?"

"In a couple of weeks I will be going to New York on business. May I, ah, call you?"

"Of course. Please do. Would you have time to come to Philadelphia? I could show you the City of Brotherly Love."

"What?"

"That's what they call Philadelphia. I'll take you to see the sights and you can meet my brothers and my son." I sounded eager, but rationalized that I needed to learn more about him and this time he'd be on my turf.

"Sounds great. Years ago I drove through Philadelphia, but there was not time to stop to see the historic places."

After we said goodbye, I held my finger on the phone's plunger. I wasn't ready to call my brothers just yet. There was something else I wanted to do, but what? Wait for my heart to reach a normal level perhaps? He was the most exciting man I'd met in a long time. I liked his directness and his curiosity. He'd asked me lots of personal questions and usually I hated that, but this time I didn't mind.

So why was I hesitating to call my brothers? Then I remembered. It was because of the last conversation I'd had with them. Philip had called the morning after we argued.

"We'll take care of Skipper while you're gone. My God, Nora, we'll take care of him whenever you need us. You know that, don't you?"

"Yes. I'm sorry I talked to you the way I did. But, please, you've got to accept that I can take care of myself and stop pampering me."

"We don't think of it as pampering. It's more than that. We're worried about the effect your absences are having on Skipper."

"Now, see, I don't get that, I really don't. When I leave, he's with you and Val and you love him as much as I do, right?"

"Yeah, but-"

"Stop worrying, will you? Everything is fine. I wish you had more confidence in me. Sometimes Val makes me feel like some kind of monster."

"Oh, no. He's excitable, that's all. The doctors told him to let go, but…"

"Doctors? What doctors? Is Val sick?"

"Of course not. It's water over the dam. Long time ago, you know. He's just excitable."

"Well, try to trust me, okay?"

I released the plunger and dialed Philadelphia. Skipper answered.

"How's my big boy?" Music was playing in the background and I could hear my brother laughing.

"Hi, Mommy. We're playing Blockhead." Skipper had been playing this game of stacking blocks since he was two and he still enjoyed it. Players took turns stacking oddly shaped blocks until someone caused the stack to fall. At that point they became a "blockhead."

"I beat Uncle Val two times already. Are you coming home now?"

"That's why I'm calling. I'll be home very soon. I miss you. Can I talk to Uncle Val, please?"

The phone thumped and thumped again. "Baby sister, how are you?"

"Fine. I've finished my business so I'm getting ready to make travel arrangements."

"That's good. About time too. Call when you have the details and we'll pick you up."

Someday it would be nice to have a conversation with Val without getting mad. "Is everything okay?"

"Sure, but Philip and I are glad we decided to come to your place instead of taking Skipper to our apartment. He needs an extra room just for his cars and trucks."

"We have to face it, Val, they're Skipper's buddies."

"So, how'd the buying go? Were you successful?"

"Very, and I've got lots to tell you."

Would I tell them about the incident in the village? I didn't think so. Would I tell them about Carlos? I wasn't sure. After all, what did I actually know about him other than the way he made my pulse race?

4

Three weeks later Carlos called from New York. It seemed longer.

"I have finished here and I would like to see you," he said.

"I look forward to seeing you again too." How stupid. I sounded so formal, like I was conducting business.

"Are you free tomorrow afternoon, about three? I would like to see- what did you call it, the city of brother's love?"

"Brotherly love. Tomorrow at three will be fine. Do you need directions?"

"No, my friend recommended a global positioning system. It is amazing; it talks to me. Your home is near the Belmont exit of the expressway, am I right?"

"Exactly. I'll ask my brothers to watch Skipper for me."

"Can he come along? I enjoy children and there are not many opportunities for me."

"Why don't you stay for dinner? It won't be Paella Valenciana, but perhaps something from my family recipes. I'll ask my brothers to join us. Then, you'll meet the whole family."

I hoped I wouldn't regret it. I had no idea how my brothers might react to Carlos, particularly because he was part of my work.

Philadelphia delivered one of its clear, brisk winter days for our touring. Skipper showed no reluctance with Carlos. Within minutes he was bubbling over, eager to share things he'd learned at school about Independence Hall.

"Come see the crack in the Liberty Bell. It broke when somebody died. My teacher said it weighs more than two thousand pounds. I weigh forty-six pounds."

"And you are not cracked," Carlos said. Skipper laughed.

At the Port of Philadelphia, we walked along the docks, found a bench and watched the longshoremen unload the cargo of a large commercial ship. Skipper found some stones and moved closer to the water to toss them in.

"Finish telling me about how you got interested in the Oriental rug business," Carlos said.

I stared out on the river seeing Aunt Georgina's kitchen. It was two months after Mama died. My brothers found a small apartment for themselves and I moved in with Mama's brother, his wife and kids. Usually their kitchen was a chorus of banging pots, the voices of their four young children, and although nobody ever listened, a radio playing in the background. On this day it was quiet. Aunt Georgina was bent over the white Formica table stretching strudel dough. She moved slowly around the four sides, her fingers coaxing the dough into a paper-thin sheet. A bowl of freshly cut apples coated in sugar, raisins, nuts, tapioca and cinnamon sat nearby. I began to cry.

"Darling, what's wrong?" she said. She wiped her hands on her flour-streaked apron, put her arms around me, and sat me next to her on the window bench.

"Mama made wonderful strudel, Aunt Georgina."

"Ah, yes, the best, my darling. She taught me. What did I know? I was not Lebanese, only a poor Italian pasta-maker."

"You make great pasta."

"It's only natural that you miss your Mama and Papa. Uncle Nitu and I love you very much, but we can't take their place."

She held me. Her body was like a pillow and she smelled of nutmeg and cinnamon.

Three days later Uncle Nitu told me the rug store in the neighborhood was looking for someone to help out.

"It's the perfect job for a high school girl. Shall we talk to them? We've known Sam and Esther Bezdikian for years – nice people."

I looked back at Carlos. He was watching Skipper's antics at the water's edge and seemed unaware of my daydreaming. I told him how we'd moved into my uncle's home after my parents died and how they introduced me to the Bezdikians, owners of a gallery nearby.

"They were like another family to me. They taught me about the rugs and the business. I remember being thrilled to have my own bank account."

Carlos never took his eyes from me.

"I liked being around the rugs. To me they are much more than floor covering. They represent a whole culture, my family's culture. I was lonely in those days, and when I was around the rugs…" Something caught in my throat. "The more I learned the more the Bezdikians increased my responsibilities. When I graduated from NYU with a degree in marketing, they offered me a full-time job. Soon after that I married, but I'd already decided to become an Oriental rug broker."

"I wish your husband could have come with us today. Will I meet him at dinner?"

"Oh, I thought you knew. My husband was killed in a car accident."

He stood up and fumbled with his jacket. "I am so sorry. You spoke of your son. I don't know what to say. You are very brave."

It was the first time I saw him flustered. For my part, I was beginning to feel transparent.

I got up and walked toward Skipper. Carlos fell in at my side.

"I have my son to think of and I really love my work. What choice do we have but to carry on with life?"

"Of course. Do you take Skipper with you on your buying trips?"

"I did once, but he's in school now. My brothers look after him for me."

"Your brothers, they are very close to you."

"They love Skipper like he was their own."

"I understand. It is the same responsibility I feel for my mother and sister."

It wasn't the same, but before I could say anything Skip turned around and waved. "Mommy, is that the kind of boat that brings your rugs from Turkey?"

"Yep, exactly."

"Daddy said we shouldn't say yep or yeah."

"Right, I remember." I called his attention to the parking lot behind us. "See those big trucks over there? Trucks like those take the rugs to my warehouse. Then I deliver them to the people who buy them."

Carlos lifted Skipper. "I am glad you came today. I have learned many things from you."

Skipper glowed and he didn't mind being picked up, something I was no longer allowed to do. Carlos was learning everything about me; unfortunately, I couldn't say the same about him.

Dinner was an exercise in diplomacy. My brothers were more reserved than usual, but were genuinely interested in the stories Carlos told about his family, particularly about the family's Armenian background and how they related to the Turks.

"As a boy I was unaware, but my parents said it had been a struggle since Armenia was conquered by the Turks in the late 1800s. We maintain our own language and religious traditions despite the fact we are surrounded by another culture."

"Yeah, we know how things are in the Middle East," Val said. "Our parents came from Lebanon. Nora tell you this already?"

"We have talked a little about it."

Later that evening I stood at the curb with Carlos next to his rental car. "I enjoyed being with your family," he said. "Are you free to have dinner with me tomorrow? I am told the Bellevue Stratford Hotel, where I am staying, has a fine dining room."

"It does. That'd be nice. Eight o'clock okay? I can meet you in the lobby."

"We can discuss a little business too. I brought photographs and information about two rugs, as you requested."

Some business talk would get my mind off other matters. Maybe.

Dinner at the Stratford exceeded everything I'd ever heard about the hotel's food and service. The dining room itself was a history lesson. On the walls were paintings of Philadelphia as a burgeoning English colony, and there were portraits of the men who shaped the laws that later became a standard for the nation. Carlos peppered me with questions about them, and between bites of food I chewed through at least a century of history.

When it was time for coffee, Carlos suggested we have it sent to his suite along with dessert. "I am in love with New York cheesecake," he said, raising a hand to catch the waiter's attention. We met him midway to the elevators and Carlos placed the order and gave him the room number, while I glanced around the room. Several women were looking at Carlos. I lowered my head and casually touched my hot cheek.

We finished our coffee in the sitting area of his suite, a large space with two sofas, two chairs, coffee table and desk. The cherry wood glowed and brass fittings glittered on the crystal chimney lights. Carlos cleared the table and said: "Have you heard the term *'sigheh'*?"

"No."

He placed two photographs of rugs on the table. "These were made at the end of the eighteenth century and given as a gift for *sigheh*." He shifted in his chair. "*Sigheh* is a Shiite tradition, an agreement between a man and a woman and sanctioned by a religious cleric. The agreement can last for as little as a few minutes or as long as ninety-nine years."

I opened my mouth to ask a question, but Carlos held up a hand. "You will understand in a minute. *Sigheh* is an agreed sum of money in exchange for a temporary marriage."

"That sounds like prostitution."

He chuckled. "That is what Westerners would say, and undoubtedly the motive is sex, but the difference is that the couple must go before a cleric to record their contract. This contract settles any questions that might arise later, say, regarding legitimacy of children."

"Oh."

He reached over and ran his thumb across the frown on my brow. A small smile curled at the edges of his mouth, while my brow burned where he touched.

"The reason I tell you this is because it is the history of these rugs. The Ayatollah Mahoud, a well-loved and respected man, gave these rugs to Hafsah, the twenty-one-year-old daughter of his closest friend. The Ayatollah's wife, whom he loved very much, had not been able to give him children. With her full consent, he made a *sigheh*, which lasted many years. The result was three sons and a daughter."

"Interesting." What could I say? Here was another cultural difference between our two countries I needed to absorb, no matter my discomfort. I concentrated on the photos while Carlos explained that each rug was a ten-by-eight-foot silk Heriz, made in the city of Tabriz near the Caspian Sea. One was an unusual tree of life design in pale yellow, soft red, blue, ivory and brown.

"How much do they cost?"

"The tree of life design is $98,000. The other is $86,000. You will no doubt be able to sell them for at least $350,000. Is that acceptable to you?"

"Do you really think they'll sell at those prices?" Once again my words had spilled out too quickly. "I'm sorry, Carlos, I don't mean to doubt you. It's just that I'm surprised at the value these old rugs accrue."

"You said it yourself, Oriental rugs are more than floor covering. Are you ready for the magic carpet ride?" He was smiling broadly.

My head was spinning, dizzy with the prospects, dizzy with the moment. "I'm ready. I'll contact the clients I have in mind and we'll arrange for shipment."

There had to be more questions I should be asking, but I didn't feel like discussing business anymore. What I was feeling had nothing to do with business. I walked to the window.

"Are you all right?"

"Yes, I'm fine." But I wasn't. An avalanche of sensations was beginning to cascade and I couldn't stop it. My heart was racing, my cheeks burned. When Jared and I first became intimate, I remember thinking of it as an adventure. I was swept up in Jared's pleasure, pleasure I was giving my new husband. It made me happy to know that my body could give it to him. But this...

"Whose statue is illuminated there?" Carlos said, moving to the window and standing behind me. I could feel his breath moving my hair.

"That's, uh, William Penn, the Englishman who founded Pennsylvania. The word means Penn's Woods."

His face was buried in my hair, the full length of his body pressed against my back. His breathing became shallow. He lifted my hair and kissed the back of my neck.

I turned and faced him, resting my head and hands on his chest, not sure whether I would push him away or pull him closer. Wasn't it too soon to feel what I was feeling? I didn't care. My skin was screaming to be touched. Ultimately, Carlos answered my ambivalence. He wrapped his arms around me and held me tightly.

"I have felt drawn to you from the day you came to my home in Ankara." He sighed, dropped his hands to his sides, shrugged his shoulders and looked flustered. "I need to know how you feel."

In all the years of my marriage to Jared, I'd never felt included in our lovemaking. I came to him with no knowledge and it seemed natural to follow his lead. He told me what to do. Now

Carlos was asking and suddenly all my questions were irrelevant. I lifted my face to kiss him. There was no pressure, just the warmth of his lips. The touch started a wave of heat from my head to my toes.

"Nora?"

I unbuttoned my blouse. His hands reached for me as one by one our clothes fell to the floor. He eased me down onto the thick Oriental rug at our feet. The rug's pile was deep and soft against my skin, and Carlos' hands explored my breasts until I tingled where he touched and ached below. I wasn't thinking anymore, only floating on the waves of building excitement. Sensations I'd never felt before were rushing with an urgency I couldn't check, didn't want to stop. What I wanted was Carlos, and it thrilled me to feel his desire as he held me.

At that moment, liberation and submission were one and the same. Carlos was everywhere, touching me with his hands, his lips, his tongue. Our bodies danced to an internal music and rhythm that flowed to a perfect ending – pleasure shared.

After Carlos returned to Turkey, I missed him so much I found myself trying different ways to recapture our time together. I ran our conversations through my head. Sometimes I lingered in bed imagining Carlos' hands on me. On one of those mornings the phone broke my reverie. It was Claudine Caldwell, the principal of Wister Academy. She wanted to see me in her office as soon as possible.

"Is Skipper okay?" I pushed away the bedcovers and stood to clear my head.

"For the moment," she said.

Skipper had been in first grade for only three weeks. "I don't understand. Is he ill? Has he hurt himself?"

"No, nothing like that. Can you come in later this morning?"

I didn't like her evasive manner. If this was how she approached problems, she was going to find me a difficult parent.

I arrived at the school an hour later. The office looked like an ant colony under attack. Phones were ringing and children and adults jostled each other as they rushed in every direction. A bell, sharp and loud enough to be heard in New Jersey, clanged on the wall next to me. I moved away to another area of the counter that separated the mad masses from three secretaries who alternately listened to requests while plucking papers from piles and holding telephones to their ears. There was something comical about the entire scene, and by the time I got my turn and was escorted into the principal's office, the mayhem had lightened my mood.

Ms. Caldwell gave me a warm smile, though we'd met only once when Skipper was admitted. Now she was closing the door, transforming sight and sound completely. My light mood was replaced by heaviness in my chest. Bookshelves muffled the sounds on the other side of the wall and dark wood furniture sank into the thick carpeting. The principal had created a refuge for herself – an eye in the storm that raged just outside her door.

"Please don't be alarmed by what I'm about to tell you. Children do things sometimes for no apparent reason," she said, after we'd sat down on two chintz-covered chairs in a corner of the room. "Skipper has been giving expensive pieces of jewelry to several children in his class. This morning I questioned him about it and he pulled these from his pockets. I have no idea how many pieces he gave out before his teacher noticed and reported to me."

I gasped. Jared's school ring, some cuff links, a pair of tiny pearl earrings my mother had given me on my twelfth birthday, and more, were spread out on the table between our chairs.

"These are my earrings."

"I know this is upsetting," she said, "but as I told you earlier, it may mean nothing at all. I'm so glad your first reaction isn't anger. So many parents become enraged when something like this happens. Talk to him, of course, but don't blow it out of proportion."

I looked around the book-lined room thinking about the improvement in Skipper's behavior in the last few weeks. Now I imagined Skipper's face, his defiant eyes, and his demanding voice. I shivered just thinking about the inevitable confrontation.

"I'll talk to him."

She handed me the jewelry. The chill increased as each piece of cold metal struck my palm.

"One more thing, since you're here. Skipper's teacher says he's very much a leader in class. I thought you'd like to know."

I nodded but held my response, especially since the look on her face warned there was more.

"Sometimes, though, he tends to force his opinion. He has difficulty accepting the ideas of others. His teachers have noticed that some of the children avoid working with him. Maybe you could mention that relationships require give and take, that sometimes we must be followers too. I'm sure you'll know the best way to handle this."

At midday I poured myself a hot cup of coffee and sat in the kitchen to wait for Skipper. All day long I practiced what to say. It hadn't helped. When I heard the front door open, I braced myself and glanced at the wall clock – a silly cat face I wanted to punch right then. I never wanted animals in the house and the clock had been Jared's joke.

"I'm in the kitchen, Skip."

He walked to me. His face had changed since we returned from Turkey. No more little boy, he was developing a strong jaw line that matched the willfulness in his eyes.

"Skip, Ms. Caldwell spoke to me today." No reaction. "She told me that you've been giving our jewelry to your friends."

He shrugged his shoulders and looked at the wall. I set the pieces on the kitchen table.

"These things were not yours to give away. These are things I want to keep for our family." I walked to the sink with my coffee mug.

"They're nice things, aren't they?" he said.

"What's that got to do with it?"

"You always said we should give nice things to our friends." His voice was rising and his eyes had that defiant look I hated.

"Of course, but-"

"Well, I wanted to give my new friends presents," he said, like that was the beginning and end of it.

Jared argued this way – taking my words, twisting them, throwing them back at me. I struggled to check my growing frustration.

"Skipper, look, I know you thought you were doing a good thing, but you didn't think about how I would feel if you gave these things away, did you?"

His face remained expressionless except for the coldness in his eyes. Now it was my turn to stare at the wall and remember the principal's comment not to blow this out of proportion. I sighed. I knew I wouldn't accomplish anything once he got angry.

"I don't want you to do this again, okay? If you want to buy presents for your friends, just ask me and we'll go shopping." I waited for a response, but didn't get one. "I want you to ask your friends tomorrow to give the jewelry back."

Suddenly he was agitated, his face contorted in anger. "No, I won't. It's not fair. I'd be an Indian giver and that's bad." He stamped his feet, turned away from me and headed up the stairs.

I followed him and heard the door slam. From behind the door, I heard: "You're mean. You don't want me to have any friends."

"Listen to me, Skip. You don't need to give presents to have friends. Why do you think that?"

"Daddy said he was my friend and then he went away."

I was confused. What did Jared have to do with his friends?

"That's different. Daddy couldn't help it."

"He's never coming back because he didn't really like me. You don't like me either. That's why you're mean to me."

This was bouncing all over the place. I leaned against the wall. Jewelry? Friends? His father and I didn't like him?

"Will you let me come in, please?" Without waiting for an answer, I opened the door. He was sitting in the middle of the floor surrounded by his trucks and cars. Now that I was in I couldn't think of anything to say. He bosses his friends around so they don't want to play with him. He thinks his father left him on purpose. What could I say to that?

Finally I sat next to him on the floor. "You must like your friends at school very much."

"I like them but they don't like me."

"That's not true. They came to your birthday party and had fun, didn't they?"

He bounced up and faced me. "That's only because we had cake and ice cream. They don't play with me at school."

"Do you know why?"

"They're dumb." He picked up a green tow truck, hooked up a small, red convertible car and drove it in the air. He had relaxed again. He was focused on his cars and the anger had vanished. I wished I could dissolve my feelings so easily.

"They're dumb?"

"I tell them what they're supposed to do but they're too dumb to do it. I'm the smartest boy in class."

"I know you're smart, Skipper, but smart people know it's important to be kind too. Try thinking about other people's feelings, will you?"

"Okay." He was on the other side of the room, completely caught up in his toys.

"How 'bout if we go shopping now? Then you can give your friends new presents when you ask them to return the jewelry. That'll make it easier, won't it?"

"What if some won't give it back to me? Can I tell them they can keep it?"

"I don't think it would be fair if some kept the jewelry and some gave it back. You want to treat your friends equally, don't you?"

"Will they still be my friends?"

"They will if you remember to think about their feelings." I stretched out my hand to him and we went downstairs together.

We spent about an hour at the toy store buying things he thought his friends would like. But when we were finished, I wondered what we had accomplished. There was no way to be sure he really understood what I'd tried to tell him about friendship, no way to know if he believed I wanted him to be happy, and no way to explain why people die and leave us.

When we got back home, a florist's truck was parked in front of the house. The driver had flowers for me from Carlos – yellow roses. The sight of them brightened my mood, and when the driver left and Skipper had gone to his room, I sat down to open the card tucked inside. It said: "Life is beautiful."

The urge to speak to Carlos overwhelmed me. He would welcome my voice, listen to my concerns and offer me, if not solutions, his confidence. I reached for the phone, but stopped mid dial when I noticed the time. It was too late to call.

But at three in the morning when I was still awake, I dialed his number.

"I called to thank you for the flowers. They're beautiful."

"Not nearly as beautiful as you are. I miss you. Why are we so far apart?"

I rested my head on the pillow and let his words blanket me. "I miss you too. In fact I wish you were here right now."

"Is something wrong? Are you having difficulty locating clients for the antiques?"

"No, it's nothing to do with business."

"Well, then, everything will be fine. I just realized it is the middle of the night for you. You mustn't worry. It is only that you are beginning a new market. The rugs are at the packinghouse and will be shipped very soon. I must go, my driver is here."

"Yes, of course. I just wanted to thank you for the flowers and for remembering they're my favorite."

It was good to hear the encouragement and to know he missed me, but I felt suddenly alone and insecure. I shook off the feeling, blaming it on the late hour. My clients would love the antiques, and as for Skipper – he was a child and children do things for no good reason. Weren't those the very words the principal had used?

5

Carlos shipped the two Heriz to The Persian Rug Gallery in downtown Philadelphia's exclusive Chestnut Street shopping area. The owners, Sylvia and Jacob Gordon, were not only my friends but also clients, and from time to time they let me use their display area. My antique rugs were hung in an alcove at the back of their gallery, awaiting my first client.

Huang Wei arrived early for his appointment. We'd met years ago when he was beginning his rug collection, and over the years I'd helped him to increase the value and variety of rugs.

"Why have you decided to sell antiques?" he said, walking toward me.

"That's a surprise question coming from you." His eyes registered mild irritation, but I ignored it. "You're a businessman, Mr. Wei, you understand new ventures very well."

"I also understand risk."

"You don't take risks when you deal with me. After all these years, I think you know you can trust me."

His mouth stretched almost imperceptibly and the fine lines around his eyes relaxed.

"Let's see what you have," he said, looking beyond me to the back of the gallery. I led the way, rehearsing what I knew about him as we walked.

He'd been born in New York's Chinatown and rarely left it. I'd never seen him in Western clothes, and today his gray braid hung down the middle of his back on a heavily embroidered, emerald green tunic. Since inheriting his family's restaurant in New York City, he'd expanded throughout the state and was about to open his first in Philadelphia.

We walked to the rear to a large, circular alcove where the two silk Heriz hung, bathed in soft lighting. I began to describe the history.

"Have you heard the term *'sigheh'*?"

"No," he said, examining the underside of the rug closest to him.

"It's a term used by Muslims for a temporary marriage contract." There was no reaction from him so I continued. "These contracts are arranged for many reasons, and these rugs were involved in a contract for the purpose of procreation. They were given as a gift to a young woman who agreed to a *sigheh* in order to have children for an influential man."

Mr. Wei licked his lips and busied himself again with the silky fringe, drawing it through his bony fingers. His nails, overly long for Western tastes, were buffed to a high sheen.

"How much?"

"The tree of life design is $196,000. The floral is $172,000."

He was impassive, but I knew him well enough to understand that the abacus beads in his mind were flying furiously back and forth.

"I offer you $350,000 for both."

"They are exquisite, aren't they? Considering their history, it would be a pity to separate them." I saw his back stiffen. "I want to sell them together, but I believe the other clients who will see them today will offer me more individually. May I call you later in the day?"

He worked his jaw from side to side but never took his eyes from mine. "$360,000 for both will be my last offer," he said.

"Mr. Wei, they are yours. Thank you."

After he left I cancelled the other appointments, telling them that the rugs had been sold, but assuring them I would soon have others for them to consider. That should whet their appetites for the next time.

Carlos was ecstatic when I called him the next day. "Congratulations. You have sold your first antiques and gotten even more than I thought."

"Mr. Wei was thrilled and there was genuine disappointment in the voices of the clients I cancelled, so I'm certain I have a ready market for others."

"I have always thought the hands that make these rugs give their spirit to the threads. It seems the spirits are happy with you."

I didn't answer him, but I wondered if he thought the spirits were at work between us too.

"Well, what is your next step?" he said.

"You're looking for another rug, correct?"

"Oh, yes, I am working on something unique."

"Do you think you could find a fourth?"

There was silence for a long moment. "You are talking about a lot of money."

"I know. Call me when you have something." I wasn't ready to share the ideas that were exploding in my head.

A few weeks later, I had a call from Sam Bezdikian, the gallery owner who'd given me my first job. He and his wife had sold their gallery a number of years ago and moved to New York City. Sam was restless in retirement and made it a point to call me regularly.

"I want to make sure you're doing things right."

"How could I go wrong? You taught me everything I know, didn't you? Or did you leave some things out so you could still teach me a few tricks?"

He laughed, a high-pitched wheezing sound. "Well, it's the first of the year. When was the last time you paid a personal call on your customers?"

One of Sam's Sacred Rules of Business was at least one in-person visit each year.

"Actually, I was in the middle of making a list of the galleries I serve," I lied.

"Excellent. January is a good time. Supplies are down now that the holidays are over. It's the perfect time to introduce them to something new."

For a fraction of a second, I thought perhaps he'd read my mind. But Sam wasn't one to "beat around the bush." If he wanted to know something, he'd ask.

"I'll let you know how I do. Give Esther a hug." I hesitated. "Sam, maybe there's something you could help me with."

"Sure, anything."

"I've been thinking about opening up my own gallery and getting into the antique market."

Sam sucked in his breath. "Why'd you want to do that? Have you any idea how much more work is involved in owning a gallery? And antiques? I don't advise it, not for a minute."

"I'm not asking for your permission. Obviously you've forgotten what you said when I started brokering on my own. You said you had confidence in me, remember?"

"Yeah, yeah. What I remember is a hard working, smart young woman."

"Oh, and I'm not hard working or smart anymore. Is that it?"

"Of course not, but you didn't have a kid then and you had a husband making a good living. You shouldn't be taking risks now."

I felt a rush of heat – not anger at Sam but at my own stupidity. Esther had never worked. She kept home and hearth for Sam and their kids. Still did.

"Think, Nora, think. Why take chances? You have a nice life and you're good at brokering. You should be thinking about protecting Skipper and yourself for the future."

"Exactly," I said.

"Exactly?"

"Listen, my dear friend, I don't need reminding that I'm responsible for my son and myself. You said it yourself - I'm willing to work hard. But you're forgetting something about me. I like a challenge. Are you going to help me or not?"

There was silence on the other end. One of the reasons I felt close to Sam was that he'd always taken me seriously, always considered my opinions, even when I was a kid. But this was asking him to leap into another culture. I didn't know how he'd respond.

"Okay, okay. But what do you know about antiques, huh? They're tricky. I never wanted them in my shop. And a gallery? Now you're talking real estate and real headaches."

He was coming around, getting to specifics and I was ready for him. "I've checked out a dealer in Ankara who has integrity and good credentials. Just last week I sold two antiques he got for me and I did really well, so I know I've got a market. As for the gallery, I've been working on that and I have two locations in mind: Chestnut Street or the Main Line. You know the areas, right? There are galleries in both locations now, but they don't handle antiques."

"Well, listen to you. Okay, you've been hustling. But you're talking about a huge investment. You'll be in hock up to the top of your pretty little head."

"This is where I need your help." I swallowed and took a deep breath. As far as I was concerned, I was on solid ground. Insurance money had come through to cover my loss on the Ysilada order. I was debt free. Still that hadn't been enough for the banks, and they turned me down for a loan, told me my collateral wasn't adequate. "I was wondering if you could recommend a venture capitalist. I figure I'll need about three million as a start up figure."

Sam's hair was gray, but he was as shrewd as an alley cat. He'd understand immediately that I hadn't passed the conservative qualifications of the banks. He was slow to answer me.

"You're sure you want to do this?"

"Very sure."

He sighed. "Abdullah El Ramil. We've been friends for years, ever since he moved to New York and consulted with me about carpeting for his hotels."

Sam went on to tell me that Abdullah's family still lived in Saudi Arabia, where they were powerful, financially and politically. He said Abdullah was charming and adventurous, so much so that his family tried to sate him with travel. But when he hit New York City, he didn't want to leave. Sam said he was fascinated with capitalism, with how people master their own destinies and compete with each other.

"He's bright too – quickly understood how companies jockey to find customized markets for their products. I can't tell you how many times he's mentioned American women. They shock the hell out of him, but he loves them."

"Sounds like I'm the perfect client for him," I said.

"Well, if you're sure it's what you want. I'll call him."

"Yes, please. And thank you, Sam."

"Just promise me you'll go slow."

"Don't worry."

I turned back to my desk feeling another piece of my new plan fall into place. Perhaps my speed limit exceeded Sam's but it felt right to me. And I wasn't abandoning my current business needs. Planning a trip to visit my clients had been in the back of my mind, just a little bit farther back than I let on to Sam. The trip would take only four or five days since my best clients were closely clustered on the East Coast and all were in major cities. I could use the train. It'd be more relaxing than driving and safer if it snowed.

Skipper walked in and stood in front of my desk. His eyes had that impertinent look and I braced myself.

"I'm going to Marty's house."

"It would be nice if you asked permission instead of telling me."

"You're busy and I have nothing to do." He was dressed in his brown corduroy pants and a brown shirt and looked like a little dictator.

"Skipper, I won't have you talking to me like you're the boss. It's already dark outside and you should visit friends only if you've made arrangements with the parents first. You know this."

He screamed and came at me with his fists clenched. I flinched but he stopped just in front of me. "Marty told me at school he wanted me to come over. He's my friend and we have fun. You don't want me to have friends or have fun. You hate me." His hands were still balled, fused to his sides.

"That's not true. Of course I want you to have friends."

"Then let me go to Marty's."

"Well, let's call the Denbys first, okay?" His hands uncurled and I walked to the phone.

Carloyn Denby answered. "Of course, we'd love to have him. I think they can play for an hour or so. And if you're not busy, why don't you come too and have some coffee with Jack and me? We haven't seen much of you since you and Skipper came back from Turkey."

What she meant was she hadn't seen much of me since Jared's death. For weeks after the funeral, Carolyn or Jack called repeatedly. How was I doing? How was Skipper coping? Wouldn't it be good to go out to lunch? No. No. No. I just wanted to be left alone to adjust on my own. It didn't matter how many times I was told it would take time, the message was received but fell short of my gut. Keeping busy was what was best for me.

Carolyn and I used to be close. She became pregnant just a month before me, and we saw each other often then, particularly after the boys were born. As toddlers you couldn't say Marty and Skipper played together, but they seemed fascinated with each other. Sometimes it was comical. Carolyn and I used to play at guessing what their conversations might be like if they could talk.

Skipper: "So, Marty, what do you think of your new diapers?"

Marty: "Well, old chap, they're highly absorbent, but I predict these bowlegs will need attention some day."

We'd laugh at our silly humor. Looking back on those days, I think we were both a little scared of our new responsibilities. Now, as I sat in the Denby's bright kitchen, it felt surprisingly good, and I regretted the awkwardness that had settled over our relationship. It would be good for Skipper if I spent more time with them.

Jack and Carolyn were an odd personality mix. He was outgoing and funny. His fleshy face could change in an instant and his arms and legs seemed attached to strings that jerked him into almost constant motion. In contrast, Carolyn was sober and slow moving. She had a dry wit that hinted at her keen intelligence, and for the most part she was quiet and observant.

Carolyn brought a steaming cup of coffee to the table for me. "How are things going for you? We love seeing Skipper and Marty together again."

"I'm fine."

"Are you still working?" Jack said.

"Yes."

"Are you still traveling?"

"Yes, when I need to. You know, I can't stay after all. I've got calls to make. Sorry about the coffee. Will you call me when Skipper is ready to come home and I'll walk over?"

Sadness registered on Carolyn's face. "Jack will take him. You go make your calls. It was good to see you."

"Thanks for having Skipper over to play and, well, thanks. See you later."

I walked back to the house. The cold evening air added to the chill I felt in my heart. Each time I settled a crisis with Skipper, he'd hand me another. The jewelry incident was settled. All of the pieces had been returned and Skipper said his friends liked their new presents even better. Still, he was sullen and disrespectful and nothing I did seemed to help.

Several days later, I finished working out a schedule to visit my clients and called my brothers.

"Val, can you take care of Skipper for four days or so while I visit my clients?"

"Sure, that'll be fine. When do you need to leave?"

"I was thinking of next Monday."

"Tuesday would be better. Philip and I have an appointment with a new client. We've given them a competitive bid for an electrical system and they want to talk over a few details."

"Fantastic. I'll be eager to hear how it goes. Good luck."

"We'll firm things up with you over the weekend, okay? I'm just glad you're not going back to Turkey."

I braced myself for the usual lecture, but it didn't come.

"Listen, you may as well know. I'll need to go sometime soon. When I visit my clients, I'm sure they'll place orders and my inventory is barely adequate. I can't afford to let them down."

"Well, we'll talk about Turkey another time," he said. I hoped my sigh wasn't too audible.

Two weeks later I was in Atlantic City on the New Jersey shore wrapping up my client visits. My agenda with each client had been twofold: to update them on the newest trends in weaving and to learn from them the latest movements in retail sales. I was hearing some common themes all along the coast.

"You wouldn't believe how the interest in tribal rugs has grown," the gallery owner said. His words confirmed what Carlos and I had heard at Usa Dagh. The tribal rugs – those made in the small villages – were seen as "purer," distanced from commercial taint.

"In a way I'm glad. We both know the synthetic dyes might be more resistant to light and water, but the colors can't compare to the subtlety of the earth's natural gifts. Is the higher price a deterrent?"

"No, and that surprised me too."

"I'm finding this return to the old authentic ways has opened up an interest in antique rugs, and I'm offering them to my galleries now. Would you be interested?"

"They're awesome, but they've got price tags to match. I don't know."

"I've got an excellent wholesale contact in Ankara who can provide me with outstanding rugs at good prices. You could begin with no more than two and see what the response is. If after six months you can't move them, I'll take them back at the same price you paid."

"Same price?"

"Gladly. The only question is: Do you have a market for them?"

"I can't lose with an offer like that, Nora. I'd like to look at a couple."

"Give me a few months. In the meantime you can spread the word among your clientele."

That evening in my hotel room I tallied my successes. Three galleries out of the dozen I'd visited were interested in antique rugs. I should tell Carlos, but, as I stood at the window of my beachfront hotel, I began to daydream about my own gallery.

The moon, surrounded by a pale halo, was almost full, and its glow was reflected on the ocean foam gliding across the sand. I knew I was jumping ahead of myself, but I could actually picture my gallery. I'd definitely have a special alcove like the one at The Persian Gallery. In the street-facing windows, I'd hang room-sized antique Orientals. Next to each rug would be an easel where information about the rug's history would be written in script. It would slow the shopper down and let the rug work its magic. Inside the gallery I'd have a few pieces of sculpture, tile work, or jewelry. My customers should feel the culture of the countries where the rugs originated.

I was completely caught up in my vision when the phone on the bedside table rang. It was Philip. I shivered, knowing it had to be a problem with Skipper.

"Val and I thought it was important to call you."

"Of course. Is it Skipper?"

"He's acting so strangely."

Why couldn't Skipper let me have a moment's peace? Just once it would be nice to have the cooperation and affection he gave Jared. Why was I his punching bag?

"What's he doing?"

"He went to play with Marty after school, and about an hour later came home and went straight to his room. He's still there. He won't talk to us and he won't come out, even to eat. We don't know what to do."

"Let me talk to him."

Minutes passed. I heard Philip's soft coaxing and then Skipper's screams, banging and a crash.

"He won't come to the phone. He says he wants everyone to leave him alone. Can you come home?"

"I'll leave immediately. I just have to pack up my things, but I think I'll call Carolyn first. Maybe she can shed some light on Skipper's behavior."

I hung up, dialed the Denbys and got Jack.

"Hey. I didn't think you'd be back until the end of the week."

I recounted what Philip told me.

"Oh, he and Marty had an argument. No big deal. They're kids. Kids have fights all the time."

"But Skipper won't come out of his bedroom, not even to eat. Do you know what they quarreled about?"

"Not really. Marty hasn't said anything and we didn't take it very seriously. All I remember is Skipper slamming Marty's bedroom door and Marty shouting that he wouldn't be Skipper's friend ever again. Kid's stuff."

He offered to speak to Skipper, but I didn't want Carolyn or Jack to see that part of my boy – the part even I didn't understand and couldn't handle.

Skipper was on the sofa in the den wrapped in his blanket when I arrived home. Val and Philip met me in the hall.

"We got scared when we discovered he'd locked the bedroom door so we forced it open. He hasn't spoken to us or moved from the sofa since then. We had to see him, you know, to make sure he was all right," Val said.

"Of course. You did the right thing. I'd have done the same."

"He didn't come willingly though. He was like a crazy person – more than temper, Nora, he was wild," Philip said.

"I've had the same experience with him a couple of times."

"And you didn't do anything about it? Get him some help, for God's sake."

"Don't you think I've been trying? Most of the time he's fine."

"I'm sure you have, but sometimes we aren't good enough and we need help," Philip said.

"I'll handle it. Jack Denby said he and Marty had a quarrel, but nothing serious. He said it was just a normal spat between kids."

"Do you want us to stay with you?" Philip said.

"I'd rather be alone with him. I'll call you later. Thanks."

"It doesn't matter what time it is," Val said. The hall clock was striking midnight.

I walked them to the door, took a breath and returned to the sofa. Skipper didn't resist when I gathered him up in my arms. Almost instantly, he asked, "Do you think Daddy's happy in heaven?" The sound of his voice startled me. I was preparing myself for a long wait before Skipper would open up to me. I planned to ask him about Marty and why they fought. Why this question?

"Heaven is sort of...I think of it as a place of wonder where everyone is happy."

He seemed calm. This had to be a good start.

"Does he have lots of friends?"

I felt relief and began to relax.

"Daddy has everything he wants, Skipper. I'm sure of it." The only sound was our breathing. It was quiet, peaceful, and I snuggled closer to him.

"Then I want to be dead with Daddy."

His words hit me like ice water.

"What did you say?"

He turned away, got up and went back to his room. I was too stunned to follow. My mind raced. I had the urge to call Val and Philip, to go to my room and scream into my pillow, to go to Skipper and tell him – what?

Philip was right. I needed help. Skipper must be sick to say such a thing. I glanced at the time and saw that it would be hours before I could call anyone. Ms. Caldwell at the school would be able to recommend a psychologist. There was nothing I could do until morning when the school opened.

Waiting was agony. I rested on the sofa, walking every half hour or so to check on Skipper in his room. He was still fully dressed but asleep on his bed. Back in the den with my scary thoughts, I didn't even try to hold back the tears.

At seven the phone rang. I snatched a tissue from the coffee table and mopped my face, coughed and blew my nose while it jangled four times. It was Philip calling to ask if Skipper had said anything.

"I'm really scared. I never expected anything like this. He told me he wants to be with Jared."

"What does he mean? I don't understand."

"I'm not sure, but I think it's all about wanting friends. He asked me if Jared had friends in heaven and when I said yes, he said he wanted to die and go to heaven."

"Oh, my God. You have to do something."

"I know. In a few minutes I can call the school. I'm sure they can give me the name of a psychologist or a counselor."

"Good. Should I go with you?"

Didn't they think I could do anything on my own? "No, but I'll keep in touch."

Ms. Caldwell was calm and reassuring when I spoke to her. Her stomach wasn't churning like mine. She said the school had a psychologist on staff – a Dr. Rosemary Fiori. She put me on hold while she called, and moments later she said Dr. Fiori could see me at one o'clock.

When Skipper wandered into the kitchen, I set a bowl of cereal on the table. He nibbled at it but wouldn't look at me and didn't want to talk. I'd never seen him like this. Anger, defiance, indifference, even aloofness – these behaviors were common. But this was none of those. This was suspension. He was present physically, but removed at the same time, like he was waiting for something.

The morning dragged on. When the phone rang, I resisted answering. I didn't want to talk to anyone and didn't want to let Skipper out of my sight, though he'd made no move away from me. Finally, I lifted the receiver and heard Carlos' voice. He was excited about a rug he'd found.

"I know you want two rugs, and I'm still working on another, but wait until you hear what I have. It's a 1745 Regence Aubusson pile carpet just released from a private collection in London. It is selling for $300,000, an unbelievable bargain. The owner needs to generate cash quickly. It will bring well over half a million once the word is out among private collectors."

"Aubusson sounds French. Is that where it was manufactured?" Carlos had my full attention. I glanced at Skipper. He was staring at his plate.

"Yes." Carlos explained Louis XIV commissioned the Savonnerie to make large quantities of carpeting exclusively for the Louvre and Versailles Palaces. He died before all the work was completed, but the monarchs who succeeded him carried his plans forward.

Skipper had shifted his stare to my face and he looked angry. I changed my position to face the window.

"These rugs were huge," Carlos said, "and the few that remain are partially restored fragments of the originals. All of the designs from this period imitate Orientals, particularly Turkish patterns. This one is roughly eighteen-by-sixteen feet, and for its age has amazingly bright colors. It is pieced together in some areas, which is typical for rugs of this age, but it is in remarkable condition."

Skipper's movement caught my eye and I turned to look at him. He was standing, arms folded, chin jutting. I turned my back to him. What possible reason could he have to be angry?

"What evidence do you have of the rug's age," I said.

"There is no question about the date. It is woven right into the edge – 1745 in Arabic symbols."

"That seems strange. Why is the date woven in Arabic if it was made in France?"

"Ah, Nora, you are as fascinated by the details as I am. As I told you, the design imitates the Orientals of the time. Can you imagine such dedication to authenticity?"

"Oh, that's so interesting," I said, watching Skipper walk out of the kitchen and into the den. I followed and saw him stretch out on the floor on his stomach, his usual sleeping position.

"We can be sure of the date on this rug, but you know there can be many complications regarding dating."

"I know."

He continued in his excitement. I caught fragments: "the symmetry of a rug requires some sets of numbers to be written backward…the dating from the birth of Christ or the beginning of the Hegira, Mohammed's flight from Mecca…the conversion factor."

"Conversion factor? What's that?" Skipper hadn't moved. I thought he'd fallen asleep so I moved back to my chair in the kitchen to concentrate on Carlos' complicated explanation. "The lunar year is shorter than the solar year so the lunar system gains one year every 33.7 solar years," he said. Then he began to recite other qualifications and my head reeled.

"I'm sorry, Carlos. You're making me dizzy. You have my total confidence."

6

Dr. Fiori requested I go alone for the first session. She'd see Skipper later, she said. That meant at least two sessions just to help me reassure Skipper he had friends? How much time could that take? As I walked to the school, I imagined endless questioning, long explanations, twists and turns around irrelevant topics. I dreaded the whole process. She'd probably want my life history too.

Her office was at the rear of the school's first floor, overlooking the grassy playground. She rose to greet me with a smile. Her light brown hair was shoulder length and her wire-framed glasses enlarged her green eyes to the point of giving her a perpetual look of surprise. She wore a simple tan cotton shirtdress and by the time I got to her Birkenstock sandals and socks, I was even less inclined to high hopes.

There were plants everywhere – on her desk, in the corners, on the windowsills – and somewhere in the room a fountain made the sound of water flowing over stones. When she introduced herself, I felt I was meeting Mother Earth in her own green forest.

"I knew your husband," she said as we took seats on opposing sofas. "We both attended the University of Pennsylvania. My degree in sociology required one course in ethics, and your husband had the same requirement for his law degree. It was the only class we shared, but it was enough to tell me he was very bright. I'm so sorry about the accident and your loss."

Off course already. God help me. If she continued in this vein, I'd find some way of getting out. What did Jared have to do with anything? Staying on track – that's what gets things done. If her office was meant to relax her clients, it wasn't working for me. The trickling water seemed louder. I turned my head and saw water flowing over a bowl of stones on the table at my side.

"Well," she said, "why don't you tell me what happened."

I told her about Skipper's behavior while I was away on business, about the argument he had with his friend, and how frightened I was when he said he wanted to die.

"I'll wager that was a shocker, eh?"

Her question didn't need an answer as far as I was concerned, but she seemed to need one so I nodded. I wondered if I could reach the off switch on the fountain.

"Look, I'll need to hear much more," she said, "but I can tell you this right now: Children Skipper's age are tough and resilient. They may say they want to die, but if you're thinking he means to commit suicide, relax. It's not likely, so don't worry about it."

This time my nod was sincere. I pressed back into the cushion and felt the ache between my shoulders recede.

She wanted to know if there'd been other unusual behavior in recent months. Was he sleeping well? Was he eating normally? Was he generally a happy boy?

I described the temper tantrum over having his birthday party on Val's sailboat, and how shocked I was because he'd always loved sailing with his daddy.

"Ah," she said. "I'll bet Skipper wasn't really reacting to the birthday party on Val's sailboat."

"Yeah, he was." I ran my fingers through my hair and looked up at the ceiling.

"No, he wasn't. I believe he was missing his dad. The next time you think his anger might be triggered by his grief, I suggest you tell him he has every right to be angry. No little boy should lose his daddy. And even if you're not sure why he's acting up, it wouldn't do any harm to tell him anyway. At the very least it'll let him know you recognize his loss."

Maybe she was more solidly rooted than I'd first thought. I had an urge to tell her I was angry too – angry that my son's behavior often came from nowhere, angry about my husband's death just when my work was becoming successful. No woman raising a child should lose her husband either.

At the end of the hour, my feelings were mixed. She made me feel I should have understood Skip's reaction. But on the other, she seemed to have good instincts. Time would tell.

That night I called my brothers to report.

"It was good. We discussed Skipper's behavior mostly," I said to Val.

"Did you tell her about the long periods of time you spend traveling?"

"Val, you're so out of touch with how things are today. She didn't ask about my work because she knows lots of kids have working mothers."

An awkward silence floated between us. "She told me six year olds may talk about wanting to die, but they don't act on it. She told me not to worry."

"Glad to hear it," he said. "But if you think that's all there is to it... When's she seeing Skipper?"

I took an early morning train to New York to keep an eleven o'clock appointment with Abdullah El Ramil. He lived in a large suite on the top floor of his hotel, and when I stepped out of the elevator, a distinguished, gray-haired woman introduced herself as his housekeeper.

"He'll only be a moment. Come into the library and I'll bring you some coffee, if you like."

Before I could answer, brisk footsteps sounded outside the door and a tall, lean man stopped at the threshold.

"I am Abdullah El Ramil. Please call me Abdullah because Sam has made me feel I already know you. I am sorry not to be the first to greet you in my home. Thank you, Clara. She is my excellent housekeeper. Nothing functions without her." He placed his hand on her shoulder as he spoke to her.

Clara smiled her response and asked again if I wanted something to drink. I declined and she left, closing the door behind her.

A vase of red roses on a carved stone pedestal filled the room with sweetness, a soft touch in an otherwise masculine room. And in the corner, looming over a mahogany desk, was a lamp that looked like an umbrella fashioned from bamboo. Lighting for the room came indirectly from a ledge about a foot below the ceiling, otherwise the room was dark overall. While Abdullah pulled a chair from his desk, I couldn't resist assessing the rug at my feet. It was black or very dark brown with semi-abstract yellow-orange stripes, reminiscent of a Tibetan Tiger Rug, although I couldn't be sure. When I looked up again, Abdullah was smiling.

"You have identified it as a Tibetan Tiger Rug, yes? Do you like it? I like the fact that it is mysterious, not definitely a tiger, you see? It keeps you guessing, yes?"

Although he was very different from Carlos physically, he had the same candid attitude and confident personality. His taupe suit had a subtle sheen and his tie was as vivid as a church window. I was starting to relax but quickly checked myself. This meeting was going to determine my future.

"Sam tells me you are successful in everything you do," he said.

"Sam is a family friend. He feels responsible for my career because he was the one who introduced me to Oriental rugs when I was just a high school student."

"I believe this is only partially true." He paused and crossed his legs in the other direction. "Sam and I have been friends for many years. He is a wise man and I trust him, but his confidence in you is not just an old man's pride. I have studied the business plan you sent to me. You have excellent judgment and I am intrigued by your – What do you Americans call it? – guts."

"Ah, thank you." His candor was disarming, which made it difficult to remember that the purpose of a venture capitalist was to make money. Just below his well groomed black hair had to be a highly tuned analytical mind and I'd better not forget it.

"Tell me how you wish to grow in your business," he said.

"I want to acquire an inventory of antique rugs, open the largest gallery in Philadelphia, and become the only gallery to sell new and antique Oriental rugs."

Again he shifted his legs and drummed his fingers on his knee. Each time he lifted his index finger, a gold ring flashed. His other hand rested in a relaxed curl over the arm of the chair.

"How much capital do you need?"

"Three million dollars."

The drumming fingers stilled and I imagined my request was settling itself among his thoughts, lining up in straight columns under as many headings as venture capitalists maintained. Then, just as slowly, intensity poured from his eyes, eyes that had never left mine since I stated my needs. Somewhere in the room the pendulum of a large clock marked the passing seconds. I counted fifty-four strokes before he spoke again.

"I have confidence in your abilities," he said, "and I'm going to provide your full request."

A rush of heat moved from my neck to my face. "Thank you," I said. The two words slid from my mouth on the breath of a sigh. I hadn't expected it to be so easy.

"I know I am going to enjoy being a partner in your new venture," he said.

We exchanged smiles and I was ready to discuss details when he said: "Now, for the use of my capital, I will need a fifty-one percent interest in your business."

Why hadn't I anticipated this? I should have discussed the methods of venture capitalists with someone before coming. I was furious with myself and looking at his calm, relaxed pose didn't help. This was unacceptable. I wouldn't allow anyone to control my business.

I took a deep breath, gearing up to tell him his arrangement was not what I wanted, knowing our interview was over. But his face was so relaxed, so approachable. I reminded myself he liked boldness. What did I have to lose?

"Abdullah, I'm interested in a loan only. I prefer to keep full control of my company."

Perspiration had begun to form on my upper lip and I swallowed involuntarily. His demeanor, on the other hand, didn't change. He sat motionless. The swinging pendulum became my companion again, this time in counterpoint with the faster tempo of my heartbeat.

"What will you do if I refuse you?" A smile rippled across his face.

"I'll seek a loan elsewhere," I said.

"Well, Sam warned me. He said your determination was amazing, and so it is." Another pause. I discovered I was holding my breath so I forced a cough and inhaled slowly.

Finally he slapped his knee. "I want to see if you can pull this off. But," he said, "the percentage of return on my loan will need to be twenty percent, and I would like a one third payment at the end of the first year." The smile was gone, replaced by a poker face while he waited for my reaction.

I swallowed again. In twelve months I would have to pay him $1,600,000. Could I do it? What would Carlos say? What would my brothers think of such debt? But as the questions zipped through my mind, confidence interceded.

"You'll have your payment, and, yes, you're going to enjoy watching what your money can do."

Towns and trees flashed by my peripheral vision as I drove the corridor between Philadelphia and New York City, sights I normally enjoyed. Today was different; I was different. Scarcely more than three hours had passed since I took Skipper to school that morning. I was a broker of Oriental rugs then. Now I was the owner of Philadelphia's most prestigious Oriental rug gallery. Well, almost. A quivering sensation in my stomach that began when Abdullah and I shook hands was accelerating, a mix of excitement and apprehension.

Carlos shipped the Regence Aubusson to The Persian Gallery and I alerted a network of antique collectors. Responses came swiftly. Some, I knew, were just curious to see this rug, but there might be a buyer among them. I decided on a higher than 100 percent markup - $625,000. The price was not beyond market expectations and, once I saw the rug hanging in a color-enhancing spotlight at The Persian Gallery, I was sure of it.

The Aubusson was a Mamluk-inspired design. The Mamluks, originally a group of mercenary soldiers of Central Asia, founded a significant rug industry. Their rugs were complex and innovative and as I examined the Aubusson, I saw it bore the same trademark features. There was a central medallion of red, blue and gold which incorporated the coat of arms for Cardinal Armand-Gaston de Rohan-Soubise, Prince-Bishop of Strasbourg. Crosses of various styles were sprinkled throughout the carpet.

My first visitor, however, was disappointed to learn that the rug was a fragment of a larger piece.

"This rug covered the reception hall of the Palace at Versailles, an area larger than many of today's public spaces," I said. "Since the rug was quartered, it has found interested owners all over the world. One fragment, for instance, is in the Chateau de Rohans, another is in an American private collection, and the other fragment is in the Al-Sabah collection of the Kuwait National Museum." Still, he rejected the rug.

The second caller represented a prominent Southern family. He explained his clients recently purchased a mansion in New Orleans built by a French consulate at the turn of the century, and their hope was to furnish the home in French antiques. However, after a quick glance at the Aubusson, he rejected it on the basis of its motif. "Entirely too informal," he said, dismissing it with a wave of his hand. Informal? The Palace at Versailles?

The third customer flew in from Chicago. Claire Mason Teawood was curator of a Middle Eastern Cultural Center, a new endeavor financed by several Saudi families. She spent two hours with me discussing the Aubusson, particularly its history and special attributes. Carlos would have enjoyed her expression as the facts piled up.

"What verification do you have of the rug's 1745 date of manufacture?" Teawood asked.

"It's woven into the rug." I flipped the corner to show her. "In addition, I have a numbered Certificate of Authenticity, signed by a representative of The Museum of Ottoman Treasures of Ankara, Turkey," I said. I handed her the certificate.

"Carlos Ghazerian? I don't recognize his name."

"He's a board member for the museum which authenticates rugs from all of Asia and the Middle East. The original French papers, of course, are gone, lost over time. However, you needn't worry. I have worked very successfully with Mr. Ghazerian on other purchases. In fact, I recently sold two eighteenth century silk Heriz, which I acquired from him. His reputation is well established."

"One more question: I'm somewhat puzzled that the authentication comes from Turkey when, in fact, the rug was made in France."

"That's an interesting question, one I asked myself. The original paperwork, as I mentioned, has been lost over the years. When the rug was last sold to a collector in England, it was decided to have the rug carbon tested and authenticated in Turkey because the rug is of Turkish design."

She asked to use the phone to confer with her Acquisition Committee. I left her and busied myself with checking the inventory of rugs I didn't own. A few minutes later she joined me in the main showroom.

"We'd like to offer you $600,000."

"I'd like nothing more than to see this rug in your museum because I wholeheartedly support your mission, but I cannot accept less than $610,000."

Teawood gazed up at the Aubusson. The longer she looked, the stronger I felt she would submit to its beauty. Finally she said, "I believe the committee would be willing to increase our offer."

A week later I received a wire transfer of $610,000 and called Carlos from home. I chose my favorite chair in the den and settled back, hoping I'd find him amenable to a long conversation. More than sharing news, I needed to hear the sound of his voice.

"Tell me, are all antique sales so easy?"

"Absolutely not."

"Well, so far it's easier than negotiating for new Orientals in your country."

He chuckled. "Middle Easterners love the challenge of bargaining. It is part of our culture. We suspect everyone of a hidden agenda, and we have a passion for catching the unaware." He was as eager to talk as I was.

"Like the spider and the fly," I said. Suddenly, I sat forward. Was that how he thought of me? An easy catch? Maybe I'd been too quick to give myself to him. Perhaps he sensed my need. I'd never been with anyone before or after Jared until he came along. He was experienced and intuitive, capable of... My flesh felt clammy and I became aware of pain in my hand from clutching the receiver.

"Yes, you could say that," he said. "But because of this it is also true that we have immense respect for those who know how to play the game. A worthy opponent is a treasure."

What was my game score? Was I a worthy opponent? "Do you think Americans are naïve?" I asked.

"It depends. Once stung, I'm told Americans are quick and ingenious in their ability to recuperate and retaliate. Rarely are they caught unaware again. Reminds me of a Turkish saying: 'A man who burns his lips on boiled milk will blow on yogurt.'"

And a woman snared by charm is a fool and a loser. "We're quick studies," I said, vowing to make it so.

"When are you coming back to Turkey?"

"Soon. I need a container of new rugs to supply my clients." Who was I kidding? I ached to be with him. "My inventory is lower than it's ever been, and…"

"Yes?"

"Well, I…" My inner thoughts were taking me off course. "Actually, I've been making plans, big plans, but I'll discuss them with you another time, hopefully in Turkey."

"Can't you tell me now? I want to know everything about you."

"I've been having problems with Skipper and I can't leave him now." I got out of the chair, the comfort of my body suddenly in conflict with my mind.

"Is he sick?"

"No, but he's upset. It's just a common childhood problem. I'm seeing a child psychologist. He'll be fine."

"You are like…yes, Donna Reed. She is the perfect mother in 'The Donna Reed Show.' We have this on television in our country," he said.

"Yeah, we have the same fairy tale."

The school playground looked melancholy without its riot of running, jumping children. I'd been waiting near the swings for only moments when Skipper walked through the school's side door. It was his first session with the psychologist and I was anxious to know his reaction.

"She was fun," he said when we reached the sidewalk.

I reached for his hand, but he began to swing his arms. I balled my hands and stuck them in the pockets of my coat. Maybe affection would never be on my boy's agenda, but at least he'd had no outbursts of temper lately. His face was animated as he walked just slightly ahead of me. His jaw moved like he was holding a conversation.

"I'm glad. What did you talk about?"

He ran ahead. We were walking the path he took everyday to school and he seemed to have a routine. He zigzagged in and out of the trees along the sidewalk and jumped up to grab leaves from the lower branches. After he tossed them in the air, he walked back to me.

"We played games."

"Games?"

"Uh huh. We played make-believe. I was the mommy and she was my little boy."

"I see." What was she going to accomplish by playing games? Skipper's improved behavior was all the proof I needed to know he was okay. The next time I saw Mother Earth Fiori, I'd tell her the visits were over. As if to confirm my decision, Marty showed up with Skipper after school. They ran off to play upstairs in Skip's room just as though nothing had happened between them. Jack had been right after all. It was kids' stuff.

I arrived at Fiori's office the following week to find the door propped open. She was carrying a large tin watering can, and I watched her move from plant to plant, plucking off yellowing leaves and poking her finger in the dirt around a drooping rubber tree in the corner. When she saw me, she waved me in and asked me to sit while she cleared away the wilted leaves and washed her hands in the adjacent bathroom. She was back in moments and asked me how Skipper was doing. She smiled broadly when I told her that Skipper and Marty were playing together again, but it quickly disappeared.

"That's good, but don't jump to conclusions. I've had only one session with him, and it's been my experience that it's too soon to know for sure if we've done him any good. He could be in trouble."

"Why? Do you have to dig until you find a problem?"

She pulled a chair closer to me and sat down. "Because I suspect your son is doing an exceptional job of covering up his true feelings, and so are you."

"This isn't about me."

"I'm afraid it is, and I suspect your husband as well, and the sooner you face it the better it will be for your son." She leaned back, a punctuation mark more than a move.

"Just tell me what I need to do for Skipper to make him happy."

"Ah, yes, you want a happy boy. That's a good place to begin."

She was so smug, so sure of herself. She knew just how to handle this, to handle me. I stiffened. I couldn't believe that my first impression of Rosemary Fiori had been of a soothing, nurturing, Mother Earth type. She was more like a blight of grasshoppers. I didn't care what she did in her own backyard, but I wanted her out of mine.

"Please relax. Can I call you Nora? I'd be pleased if you'd call me Rosemary." She softened her voice. "Would you tell me what you think makes Skipper happy?"

"Cars and trucks and more cars and trucks." She gave me a half-hearted smile. "He's happy at school and he has fun with his friends." The smirk remained frozen on her face. "Well, you already know about the little episode that brought me to you was over friendship. But as I told you, he and Marty have begun playing together again."

"How about his interaction with other children, say, at school?"

I wondered if the principal had been talking to her.

"Skipper's a leader, I'm told, but his teacher says he tends to be bossy and some of the children don't like to work with him."

She dropped the smirk and shimmied forward in her chair, making her skirt bunch up and showing the tops of her woolen socks. She was getting into something; I could feel it.

"You mentioned in our first session together that he has a temper."

"He's always been strong-willed. And when he doesn't get what he wants, he can be a challenge." I pictured Skipper's eyes and felt a chill.

She sat back again. What did that mean? Was she satisfied somehow? I hoped so because the conversation was having the opposite effect on me. Jared's words popped into my head: *You never deal with him.*

"I don't think arguing with a child is a good thing. I usually try to find a way to take the heat out of a situation," I said.

"Can you give me an example, a recent situation, perhaps?"

I told her about the jewelry and how we solved the problem by buying small gifts for his friends.

"I see. And did Skipper understand that stealing was wrong, do you think?"

"He's a child. All he was concerned about was making his friends happy. It all worked out fine." Damn her. I stood up and faced the door to her office.

She quickly moved in front of me and smiled. "I think I understand your impatience. You probably don't think we've accomplished much today, but we have. Think about this: As a parent, your job – and mine too – is to help Skipper deal with life. That means we've got to have a clear understanding of why he reacts as he does. To begin with, we need to find out where his anger comes from. I have some suspicions, but I can't be sure yet. And just because he and Marty are together again doesn't mean we've found the answer to how he reacted in that situation or that we understand why he's carrying around so much anger. These are serious questions that need to be addressed. I can help, if you'll let me."

"I'll think about it, but to be honest I think you're making more of this than necessary."

"Sometimes minor behavior problems are just symptoms of other things."

If they were minor, why should it take so much time? I sighed and agreed to meet with her again.

A few days later, Philip and Val stopped by. They'd secured the electrical contract and wanted to tell me about it. I hoped it would be my chance to tell them about the new plans I was making.

They walked to the den. It was the coziest room in the house, furnished with two loveseats, a Shaker-style rocking chair – my favorite – and a big recliner. Jared and I picked varying shades of tan, brown and taupe for the entire space because we thought those related colors gave the room a quiet feel. Large and small ferns filled other spaces in the room, and along with the bookshelves that covered one wall we had the look we wanted.

Skipper appeared out of nowhere and climbed into the recliner to join us. Val launched into the details of their new contract and I expected Skipper would become bored and leave. He didn't, and after a few bemused glances from my brothers, I began to tell them about my hopes to open my own gallery.

"That's just what we've been hoping for," Val said.

He caught me off guard and before I could respond, Philip said, "It's a great idea. A gallery here in Philadelphia will give you a solid presence in the Oriental rug market."

"I'll bet your business doubles in the first year," Val added.

I hoped he was right. I'd need a huge increase to make the first payment to Abdullah on time.

"You know, this is fantastic," Val said, "because it shows you're determined to…" He glanced at Skipper. "It will center your activities here, here at home."

I had the feeling my brothers had been secretly planning this for me and in some subliminal way I'd "caught" the idea.

When I followed up with my need to go to Turkey for a couple of weeks, I expected the usual objection. It never happened. I think they saw it as my final trip and agreed immediately. There was a trap out there somewhere, but I wasn't sure who was going to step into it.

We started to talk over the details when Skipper walked out of the room.

"Are you going to say goodnight, Skip?" I called after him, but he was already upstairs and we heard his door slam.

"I guess he's had a tiring day," Philip said.

That night I lay in bed wrestling with my conscience. What if I gave up traveling to Turkey? No, I couldn't. How would I stay current with changes? Each trip exposed me to new brokers, new weaving techniques, and the never-ending twists of Middle Eastern culture. My job made me feel alive in every sense of the word. Then there were the antique rugs, more money, and Carlos. Carlos.

I couldn't wait to see him again. I ached to be in his arms, feeling those sensations again. Since meeting him, I'd discovered emotions I never knew I had. What kind of cage had kept such passion trapped in me? I couldn't imagine. I only knew I liked it and wanted more.

It had been so different with Jared. I followed his lead in everything, even when we made love. Sometimes he'd take my hands and place them where he wanted me to touch him. Carlos and I came together on an altogether different level. Another level? It was another planet and as soon as another spaceship could be launched, I wanted to be on it.

7

The steady drone of an airplane engine is good for two things: sleep and thought. Barring turbulence, a change in the flight pattern, or a seatmate hell-bent on conversation, there are no intrusions. I settled back for the long stretch between New York City and Frankfurt, closed my eyes and waited for peace to descend. Instead, I was ambushed by thoughts of Skipper, Fiori and Jared.

By the time I boarded a shuttle to Ankara, I'd have given anything for a trapdoor in my skull so I could dump my broodings. Rosemary Fiori and I were worlds apart. I wanted to help Skipper with his friends so he'd never again have thoughts of death. She, on the other hand, was heading off on tangents and playing games. I should have cancelled the sessions, but when my brothers took her side, I relented and let her finish up while I traveled.

Carlos was waiting at the gate inside Esenboga Airport. He looked wonderful in a blue tweed sport jacket. Turkish custom frowned on public displays of affection, so throwing myself into his arms was not an option. But seconds after he closed the car door, he kissed me long and sweet.

"You feel just as I remember," he said. "Would you like to have a light supper before I take you to your hotel, or perhaps a walk to stretch your legs after the long flight?"

My answer was another kiss. We drove to the hotel and when I told Carlos I wanted a hot bath he gave me a sly look.

"A Turkish bath?"

"Huh?"

"Have you had a Turkish bath?"

"You mean in one of those bath houses? No, I don't-"

"In all the time you have been coming to Turkey, you have never been to a Turkish bath?"

We parked the car and gave my luggage to a bellboy. I requested my key from the desk clerk and we stepped into the elevator. Its polished mahogany walls and shiny brass railing reminded me of old Philadelphia.

"I know your bath houses are very popular," I said, walking into the room.

"They are more than popular; they are a Turkish custom. Even the smallest towns have at least one or two."

"Public baths? I don't know. I enjoy the privacy of my own bath...speaking of which-" I placed my handbag on a nightstand and opened my suitcase.

"Really? I wonder."

"Carlos, it's what I'm used to. It's my American custom." I threw my robe over my shoulder and extracted a small toiletry bag.

"Are you curious enough for a small demonstration?"

I set the items on the bed, turned to face him and shrugged my shoulders.

He dictated instructions in a serious tone, but the curl of his lips sent another message. I was to remove my clothing while he prepared things in the bathroom. He'd let me know when to enter. I waited several minutes, watching steam seep under the door. Then he called.

The room was thoroughly misted and warm. Carlos, a towel tied around his waist, stood over a large towel spread on the tile floor. The tub was filled with hot water but he directed me to lie on my stomach on the floor. He knelt by my feet and I watched him dip a cloth into the bath water and lather it with soap. He started with my toes – each toe, massaged and soaped, one foot and then the other. He gave the same attention to my hands, fingers and arms. Later he moved to my head and began to massage my neck, shoulders and back with his strong slippery fingers. I moaned with pleasure. The slow, rapturous movement cancelled out time. I closed my eyes and concentrated on the feeling.

"Will you turn on your back?" His whispered words didn't register immediately, but I turned by myself when I felt his arms reach beneath me. At some point my bones had been massaged away.

"Well, what do you think so far?" he said.

"Hmmpf," was all I could manage.

He was at my feet once again, rubbing each toe, the valley between each foot bone, then my legs, and finally my thighs. He circled my stomach again and again while I imagined the wave of lather moving ahead of his hands.

"Now, this is not part of the Turkish bath," he announced, and his warm hands moved on my breasts.

I pulled away his towel and his body became part of mine.

"I've missed you so much," I said, as he dried my hair at the edge of the bed.

"Me too." He put down the towel. "I will tell you the truth – I don't want you to leave, ever."

"That's how I feel too. But Skipper? School?"

"Yes, I understand."

In the silence I imagined Carlos thinking of his own obligations while I thought of mine. My eyes stung.

Suddenly he sucked in his breath. "Our relationship is worth whatever we have to do. We'll work it out."

Did he mean he'd be content with alternating trips to Turkey and the United States? I wouldn't be. Could either of us change the course of our businesses? I'd worked too hard to just let go. So had he.

"I want to believe that," I said and pulled him closer. I didn't want to think about what separated us, not just then.

After Carlos left I dragged myself to the phone to call Muharrem in Istanbul to tell him I'd be in Ankara for the next four days.

"This is good. Since your last visit, I have found new brokers to meet you. Maybe three days are needed. Now that I know your schedule, I will make the appointments." His voice conveyed his eagerness.

I sat upright against the headboard of the bed and listened to his litany of details, items I would pluck from memory during negotiations. This was our routine and Muharrem had never disappointed me. By the time we concluded our conversation, I melted into the mattress, sated with efficiency and love. I couldn't imagine a better sleeping potion.

Carlos picked me up in the early afternoon. He wanted to show me two newly acquired antique rugs at his warehouse, and then we were going to have dinner at his favorite restaurant. I wondered what his idea of "favorite" would tell me about him.

We drove through Ankara, a bustling city like Istanbul, yet different.

"I can't put my finger on it, but Ankara has a look unlike Turkey's other cities," I said, recalling those I'd visited. They were poorly planned, a hodgepodge of streets and buildings with no sense of separation between commercial and residential areas. Ankara, on the other hand, had broad avenues and an obvious downtown.

"That is because Ankara was torn down and rebuilt," Carlos said.

"An earthquake?"

"No, a man."

He told me that in 1930, President Kemal Atatürk, a most charismatic leader, inspired the people to Westernize. Ankara became a model city for his vision.

"He wanted Turkey to be recognized as a progressive country, not like the stubborn backwardness of other Middle Eastern countries. He encouraged the people to dress in Western styled clothing, which I believe you have noticed in Istanbul and here in Ankara."

I was about to agree when he suddenly pulled off the road and stopped.

"Last night you distracted me – not that I minded one bit - but you said something in our last telephone conversation about big plans. I want to know about them and they must include me, yes?"

"Yes, you're included. I'd never be so daring without you." I took a deep breath. "I want to open my own gallery and offer antique as well as contemporary Oriental rugs. I want to have the largest, most exclusive merchandise on the East Coast of the United States." Just saying the words sent shivers through my body.

Carlos looked stunned. "That is big. And it will take big capital, but you must know that already."

"I do. I've taken a loan from a venture capitalist. His name is Abdullah El Ramil. He was recommended by an old family friend."

Carlos' eyes widened. "I know Abdullah. Our families have been together on social occasions since we were small boys." He began to shake his head. "The family is Saudi, very well connected. They were large contributors to the museum my father managed." He frowned. "Abdullah is a risk taker. Have you thought this through?"

His question stung and I bit my lip. These were my decisions to make and I was sure they were the right ones. He still had some things to learn about me, and I imagined my silence might be better than a verbal defense. I looked at him and he was smiling. A quick study.

Carlos started up the car again and for a time neither of us spoke. I mulled over the words "risk taker," and I imagined Carlos was testing the term out on me.

He pulled into a paved space next to a modern, one-story building. A dozen red and white trucks with Ghazerian painted on the sides were lined up against the wall at the back of the lot. Another truck was backed up to a loading dock where several men were filling it with rolled up rugs.

We walked through a cavernous space past rows of inventory to an area separated by a locked metal gate. I glanced at the workmen scattered around the room and saw I was causing a stir. A guard greeted Carlos and moved the doors aside for us. He didn't try to hide his head-to-toe inspection of me. I raised my chin as I walked past him.

"Two of the rugs I want to show you are extremely rare and very expensive. I have been thinking since you told me about your future plans that perhaps you should look at some smaller, less valuable antiques while you are here. A broader range of prices will appeal to a larger clientele, yes?"

It seemed he was still thinking about my news, already considering the practical applications of what I said I wanted. I liked that.

Once inside with the gate secured behind us, Carlos called to two young men with broad shoulders and muscular arms. Carlos directed them to a stand of rolled rugs of various sizes. "Take a look at these. You'll get an idea of the varieties and styles I have. Later you can decide how many you want and how much you want to spend, and I can choose a selection for you, if you wish. All of these are at least one hundred years old."

If you wish – didn't that tell me everything? He wanted to help me reach my goals. I took a deep breath and turned my attention to the process going on in front of me. For the next hour the two young workmen lifted carpet after carpet, unfurling them at my feet like they were cotton tablecloths. I soon understood how they got their physiques. At the same time I visualized Abdullah's investment passing from my hands into Carlos'.

"Now, let me show you the two rugs I have been saving for you."

We moved to the outer edge of the room where two rugs hung on the wall in front of us. I was particularly drawn to one of them – a unique octagonal rug about twenty-by-twenty feet with three red medallions parading across the center and stylized flowers clustered at the top and bottom. The background was a soft gray, accented with golden wing-shaped forms sprinkled throughout. It also had an unusually deep outer border in which miniatures of the larger medallions were interspersed with small golden wings.

"They are both nineteenth century, made in India. The wholesale figure for each is $180,000. What do you think?" he said.

"Extraordinary." I was too busy looking at the details to say more, but I didn't need to. Carlos could talk endlessly about any carpet and I loved the sound of his voice when he described the rugs. It took on a quality of wonder, not unlike his whispers when he loved me.

"The octagonal is an Agra carpet, made in northwest India. In some places it has been rewoven, but the work is very fine I think."

"I can't tell where it's been repaired," I said. The rug seemed in excellent condition – the red and gold colors were still brilliant.

"The other rug has some minor moth tracks," he said, pointing to an area along the bottom edge of the second rug.

The second rug was very different. The center was filled with a tight cluster of multicolored flowers, the largest blossoms in blue. Delicate vines looped around the cluster, filling the remainder of the rug, and everything rested on a subtle background of cream and tan geometric shapes. The pattern might have been too busy except for the fine texture of the vines and the sprinkling of tiny flowers along them. The combination of dense background pattern and delicate vines was beautifully balanced. The narrow border pattern repeated the vines but they were on a base of blue, which accentuated the blue flowers in the central medallion and others that blossomed along the vines.

"This one is magnificent as well but smaller by several feet and yet the price is the same. Why is that?"

"I guess it's because of the moth damage." We laughed.

We left the warehouse long after the sun had set, satisfied that we'd put together an adequate shipment of antique rugs for the opening of my gallery. He agreed to store them for me until I was ready. That meant I'd better start hunting for a property as soon as I got back to Philadelphia, but for now other things occupied my mind.

We drove to a restored villa on the outskirts of town. Carlos asked for a table in the greenhouse. "This home was owned for generations by one family. Many of the furnishings are original, including some of the tableware," he said.

Portraits of the original owners hung on the walls, framed in intricately carved, gilded wood. There was an elegant sideboard with large copper serving platters, and the rugs on the stone floors were colorful Turkish kilims.

We followed the steward through several rooms until we reached the farthest corner of an oblong greenhouse. Our table was completely obscured by lush plants, perfect for conversation and hidden kisses.

The three outer walls were glass, divided by wide columns of native stone and covered with thick neon-green moss. Water trickled down the wall and glistened in the candlelight, then gurgled along a stone trough at the base of the wall. "Carlos, I love it here. It's like being in a garden."

I let him choose our dinner. Though he spoke rapidly in Turkish, I gathered we were having some kind of fish and vegetables. After the waiter left we picked up our earlier conversation about the rugs, only this time he told me stories about the people. He said the Bedouins, desert wanderers for thousands of years, were adding an interesting mix to the village dwellers. Even after the Bedouins chose the easier life of the village, it often took years before the two groups learned to trust each other and work together in the weaving rooms, he said.

Several men swarmed around us with platters balanced along their arms. The aroma made my mouth water.

"This fish is *hamsi*," Carlos said, placing a small portion on my plate. "We call it the prince of all fish. Here in Ankara we are lucky because we have the best of four seas: the Black, the Marmara, the Aegean and the Mediterranean. The people in the Black Sea area know forty-one different ways to cook *hamsi*."

I reached for the vegetables. "Let me do this. Zucchini, tomatoes, green peppers and, and..."

"You missed the onions," he said.

"I'm hungry." I pulled a large piece of warm wheat bread from another platter.

"Here in Turkey bread is the main part of the meal, vegetables are the second most important, and the meat or fish is the least."

There was no butter on the table and when I bit into the bread I understood why. It was moist and flavorful.

"I think most Americans would reverse the order of importance. And some would say dessert is the highlight of any meal. This tastes great."

The waiter returned with tea. He poured from a serving pitcher two feet above the glass, sending the soothing smell of mint wafting all around us.

We ate in congenial silence, helping ourselves to more from the platters. In the quiet I reminded myself to ask Carlos how he got into his business, and when the eating slowed I did.

"It was a natural evolution for me, but to be totally truthful, it was a bit of a rebellion too."

"You? Rebellious?"

"Yes. Abdullah and I have this in common. My father's work as a curator acted as a kind of bridge across ethnic lines. Turks, East Indians and Chinese – every artist in the Middle East befriended us. My parents wanted me to have that kind of stability and acceptance.

"When I insisted I did not want to follow in my father's footsteps and I wanted to go to school in the United States, they protested. I went anyway."

"I know what it's like to go against the wishes of family."

"The pressure was unbearable when my father died. My mother insisted I return to Turkey to take my father's place. Our relationship was strained for many months, but I wanted to make my own way."

"Your mother is proud of you."

"She is an exceptional woman. I hope you will get to know her. In the end she accepted that I would take care of her and Tapis, but I needed to do it in my own way."

The waiter returned. *"Çay istermisiniz?"* His question was followed by another rapid Turkish exchange - evidently a request for tea since seconds later another mint mist filled the air around us.

"Your degrees are in law, specifically international law and economics?" I said.

"Yes. At the time I wasn't sure I was on the right track, but now I realize I benefited tremendously. There are often complications when I deal across international borders and my background helps with solving problems. I like that almost as much as meeting collectors around the world. So you see, we receive pleasure from the same things."

"I like the money."

Our table was cleared of all but the glasses of tea, which were filled once more. Then another waiter appeared with a shallow pottery bowl.

"Oh, I'm not sure I have room for anything more," I said looking into the bowl. "It's so beautiful."

"This is called bride's pudding and it is rarely offered other than at very special occasions. When the waiter told me they had it…well, this is a special occasion isn't it?"

"Very special."

Pale orange apricots spiraled around the bowl. "Their centers are filled with ground walnuts, grated carrots and rice, and syrup is poured over it before baking," Carlos explained.

I accepted a tiny portion and nodded appreciatively as it flowed over my taste buds.

"A moment ago you said you knew what it was like to go against the wishes of family. Is it because of your work?" Carlos said, pushing aside his empty dish.

"Yes. My brothers don't understand my need for independence, my need to support my child by myself. They want to help me so I can stay at home with Skipper."

"And you disagree with them."

"Of course. They have their own business. You've seen that I'm capable of taking care of myself. I like it this way. I'm excited about what I do and no one is going to stop me." I realized my voice was getting urgent. I sat back and allowed the flush to pass.

"I see." I had the feeling he wanted to say more but he stood and placed lira on the table. "How about a short walk around the villa?"

The estate was on the side of a hill. We stopped to admire the city lights and enjoy the minarets piercing the skyline from one edge of the city to the other. Wild pink oleander was everywhere, lit by small lights on the sides of the restaurant. There also were several grape arbors and tall Aleppo pine trees.

"Tomorrow I have a surprise for you," he said, stopping under an arbor.

"Not more work, I hope."

"No, this will be pure fun. I want to be sure what happened to you in that settlement, when you forgot your headscarf, isn't your most memorable Turkish village experience."

"I'd like to put that behind me," I said. A wave of panic shot through me again thinking of the old woman's anger.

"I have just the thing to purge your memory. The mother of one of my friends, a weaver, is celebrating her one-hundredth birthday. The whole village of Zolve will honor her. I want you to see it."

The next day we drove north from Ankara for about fifty miles. Although Turkey's roads were excellent between major cities, the small towns and villages were strung out at the ends of ancient trails. Zolve was on a high hill, surrounded by a conifer forest and the only access road was narrow, rutted and winding. Even though the sun blazed directly overhead, it was cold when we arrived. I was fastening my jacket when Carlos reached into the glove compartment and pulled out a small package.

"This is a gift for you from my mother," he said.

I drew a pale yellow, hand-woven cotton scarf from the package. It had tiny embroidered amber flowers connected by a moss green vine along the edges.

"She said the amber would match the highlights in your eyes. Let me put it on for you."

He placed it on my head, wound the ends loosely around my neck, and brought them together again in the front, just as I'd seen on many Turkish women. It felt secure, but light as gossamer.

"It's lovely," I said. "Will I have a chance to thank her personally?"

"You have been invited to dinner whenever you can make it."

Before I could respond, a short, rotund man came running clumsily toward us, his body undulating beneath his loose-fitting clothes.

"*Merhaba, arkada şim.*" Hello, my friend, he said. Two young girls and a woman followed shyly behind him.

Carlos bent low to put his arms around his friend's girth and kissed him on both cheeks.

"Nora, this is my good friend, Selim Aksu, his wife, Sera, and their beautiful daughters, Nursel and Güldan." They wore headscarves like their mother, skirts that reached almost to their ankles, and jackets buttoned to their necks.

I tried my Turkish and asked the girls how old they were. They giggled and said they were twelve and nine. I smiled, partly because I was happy they understood me.

Nearly a hundred people filled a large room inside the long stone building. There were no looms or drawing tables in sight, but I suspected it was a weaving room. For this event the walls were lined with pillows and the smell of cinnamon and cumin filled the air.

Selim took us to his mother, seated in the center of the long outside wall directly across from the entrance door. Her chair was decorated with strips of bright fabric, her cheerful face deeply lined, a map of years of laughter. It took a few whispered words from her son before she recognized Carlos. Then her smile burst and she raised her arms to him. When I was introduced, she shook her finger at Carlos and gave him a sly look.

Nursel and Güldan took our hands and led us to the food-laden tables. There were juicy lamb kabobs, grape leaves plump with rice and raisins, tomatoes, olives, green beans and pistachio-filled *baklava* dripping with honey. At each end of the long table, platters were heaped with bread. I sampled everything.

We threaded our way through the crowd, balancing our plates, until we found a spot to sit. Just in front of us some children were practicing what looked like a dance, but they sat down on the floor when some men and women began to tap out a beat with wooden spoons. Then others joined in playing wooden flutes. Every child in the room got up and raced through the crowd forcing people to clear the center of the floor.

"You are going to love this," Carlos shouted over the voices and music. I plucked a piece of tomato from his chin.

A woman approached the center of the room doing a lively barefoot step. She tied a large shawl around her waist.

"What will she do with the shawl?"

He shrugged his shoulders. "I have no idea, but they always do that when they dance."

A moment later the lone dancer was joined by a dozen women of all ages. That seemed to be a signal for the children and they poured out onto the floor until it was filled. Those who weren't dancing were singing and clapping. Carlos and I licked our fingers, put down our plates, and joined in.

The highlight came when Selim gently guided his mother onto the dance floor. A way was cleared for them and they circled the entire room while people shouted their love and good wishes.

Hours later when the music and dancing ebbed and the families began to drift outside, we made our way to Selim to say goodnight. I bent to tell Güldan how much I enjoyed her dancing – straining to remember the Turkish word for dance – and I noticed a small pin of colorful beads on her blouse.

"This is beautiful. Just the right color for your dress," I said.

Güldan smiled, but her mother quickly snatched the pin from her blouse and handed it to me.

I started to protest, but Carlos whispered, "Take it," and hustled me off to the car while he smiled and waved to his friends. Once we were inside, I told him I felt terrible taking Güldan's pin.

"Yes, I knew you would refuse and to do so would have been a problem for Güldan."

"Why, for heaven's sake?"

"It is an old superstition. By having something others might envy, they believe one can attract the evil eye."

My mouth dropped open.

"The evil eye is motivated by envy and they believe it will bring bad luck."

"Can't you even admire someone's baby?" I said, remembering a beautiful infant I'd seen at the celebration, but never managed to get close to.

"Yes, but in that circumstance, a mother might sew a blue bead on the child's clothing, believing it would cast back the evil influence and protect the child."

"Amazing. So the safest thing to do is admire things in silence?"

"Well, no, not necessarily, but for the superstitious, it must be very circumspect. 'Whatever God wishes' is an acceptable praise for a beautiful baby or a precious possession," Carlos said.

"My education continues. Thank you."

For the rest of the drive home, we couldn't stop talking about the celebration. The circle of family and acquaintances I had in Philadelphia couldn't compare to what we'd just witnessed. Skipper would have loved it and so would my brothers.

"I won't forget this day. I've never experienced anything like it. In many ways my life in Philadelphia pales by comparison."

"Ah, yes, it is true. The small villages have a closeness people in the cities rarely attain. I certainly do not have it in Ankara. But you and I are lucky to have close family relationships, and I will admit I would miss what Ankara offers."

I spent most of the next day making a financial plan for my purchases. There was so much to think about: the search for a gallery, the rug inventory, the ratio of antiques to new rugs, the portion of the loan that had to be paid in less than twelve months. I felt paralyzed by the pressure of it all. But I'd made a choice; I'd make it work.

At eight o'clock Carlos picked me up for dinner at his apartment. His mother met us at the door in a full-length, loose-fitting gauze dress in the same shade of blue as her amazing eyes. Her silver hair was wound artfully at the crown of her head. It suited her dignified bearing.

"Tapis is visiting with Mehmet's family tonight. She apologizes for her absence," Elena said.

"It's important to spend time with his family. There must be a hundred things to be discussed," I said as we sat down in the living room with those same engaging blue Chinese dragons stretched out under our feet.

"Yes, particularly since Mehmet's family is not Armenian, there will be adjustments for his family and ours," she said.

"He is Muslim," Carlos said, "and we've been concerned this may be a problem, but several weeks ago Mehmet explained that he is Alevis."

"Alevis?" I said.

"They are a branch of Islam but, as in the case of many religious beliefs, the pressures of modernity bring about a wide range in understandings. Alevis believe their religion to be a true form of Turkish Islam, evolved from the shamans of the early Turks in Central Asia.

"According to Mehmet, the Sunnis borrowed their beliefs from the Arabs, and although the Sunnis are a Muslim majority, the Alevis are a substantial minority," Carlos said.

"What is important to us is that Mehmet's family is happy with their son's choice, and we're happy as long as she is," Elena said.

"Of course. Oh, Elena, forgive me for not saying this sooner – thank you for the beautiful scarf. I love it."

"She looks fabulous in it," Carlos said. I felt my cheeks flush and both Elena and Carlos laughed. Was it possible to feel such a bond with this family so soon? Luckily, the feeling seemed mutual. I had a new love in my life with a wonderful family and a new business venture. It made my head spin.

Each time I said goodbye to Carlos it was harder. Before we left the hotel, we made love again, and I tried to lock every kiss and caress in my memory. What made the parting more difficult was that neither of us knew when we'd see each other again. For now, our love would travel on telephone cables.

Four days later Muharrem drove me to the airport for my flight home. We'd had a wildly successful negotiation with the brokers in several villages, and I had a full cargo container for the next commercial ship to Philadelphia. When I was ready, he would meet with Carlos in Ankara and make preparations to ship the antiques.

As the plane pulled away from the gate, there was a commotion near the cockpit. A garbled message blasted from the intercom and I leaned to the woman next to me to ask in careful Turkish if she understood what the captain had said.

"He apologized because we are returning to the gate." The flight attendant reopened the cabin door and a piercing female voice asked all passengers to keep their seats. There was to be a routine inspection, she said, and should take only a few minutes. Seconds later four uniformed men pushed their way down the aisle, shoving aside passengers who tried to get up.

They stopped at my seat, checked the number and asked me to stand. One of the men shouted my name to the flight attendant, still standing by the open cabin door. She nodded her head, but her fear and reluctance were obvious. The woman sitting next to me increased the space between us and would not look at me. It was like I'd suddenly come down with bubonic plague. One man pulled me into the aisle while another yanked my arms behind me.

"What are you doing? Leave me alone," I said in Turkish. "I am an American citizen here on business. I have a license and a Turkish agent. I have done nothing wrong."

They pushed me down the aisle toward the open door. I looked from side to side at the passengers, hoping that someone would stop what was happening. All eyes were averted until, almost at the door, an elderly Turkish-American – someone I'd chatted with before we boarded – stood and blocked the doorway. He faced the uniformed guards and spoke in a loud voice.

"What are you doing? This woman has the right to know why she is being taken in such a manner," he said in Turkish. The guard let go of my arm, pushed past me and punched him in the face. Blood spurted from his cheek and he fell backward into his seat. On the other side of the aisle, a small child screamed and her mother gathered her up and turned to the wall to shield her. Fear and disbelief was on the faces of passengers and attendants alike, and I knew no one was going to help me.

8

Two men grabbed my upper arms and hauled me into the airport terminal. I searched the crowd for Muharrem, but couldn't see him, and when I tried to look behind me, I was pushed forward. Just as we were ready to descend the steps to the street, Muharrem came running in front of us.

"Stop, please. This is Nora Reardon. She is an American," he said to the officer in charge. "There must be some mistake. Where are you taking her?"

We never stopped moving. Muharrem continued to keep pace along side, protesting until I was shoved into a car and we sped off with sirens wailing.

My heart raced, desperate to know why this was happening. Thank God Muharrem had seen me, and he would know what to do.

The men were dressed in official-looking uniforms, but I didn't get a good look at their arm patches until the man next to me leaned forward to speak to the officer in front and I read *polis*, police. None of it made any sense. Why were the police arresting me? I had a legal passport. I didn't break any of their customs regulations. I wasn't a criminal.

We drove for at least an hour before the car slowed and we entered a wide, winding drive. Up ahead I saw a one-story stone building stretching as far as I could see. Razor wire topped the high metal fencing around the building. A prison? My heart was hammering.

"Where am I being taken? What have I done?" I said to the policeman nearest to me. My words poured out in English – at that point I couldn't remember a single Turkish word. It didn't matter. The words hung in the air as if I'd never spoken. No one even looked at me.

Once in the building a woman in a black uniform and the policeman exchanged a few muffled words. Another woman came forward, took my arm, opened a locked door, and pushed me into a small, empty room.

I barely had time to look around when a dark-skinned woman in a gray jacket entered. A heavy club hung from her wide leather belt. She walked around me slowly. Her black hair, divided by a streak of white, was twisted in a knot at the base of her neck.

She pulled my purse from me and removed my jewelry, including my watch. I was too stunned to react. She looked at me with black marble eyes for so long I felt she was waiting for me to say something, but I was so shaken no words came.

She rifled through some papers she'd been holding, looked up and said in excellent English: "Do not expect that because you are American you will not be treated like any other evildoer."

I found my tongue. "I've done nothing. Why am I here? I want to speak to someone at the American Embassy."

"Bah! You show no respect for Turkey, why should we do anything for you?"

The door behind her opened and two female guards dressed in the same gray jackets took my arms in the same bruised spots made by the police. She saw me wince and smiled.

We walked through several hallways. Rusting pipes hung from the ceiling and the walls looked wet. We went down two flights of stone steps and through doors that protested when they were pulled open. With each step into the prison's bowels, the air became more fetid. The only sounds were our pounding shoes and the keys bouncing on the guard's hip.

We stopped at a flaking metal door with an eye level, barred opening and a small rectangular slot at the floor. One of the guards opened the door to a room the size of a closet. The heavy door slammed, separating me from their fading footsteps. I steadied myself against the door and looked at my cell in the dim light of an overhead bulb. A cot with a filthy mattress and a blanket was against one wall. A sink with an overturned metal cup in the bowl and a three-legged stool were along the opposite wall. Gray stones formed the third wall – an outside wall. Outside. Underground.

My body suddenly begged for relief, sending me back to the door. I shouted, but my words merely echoed. Then I saw the hole in the floor near the outside wall and when I stumbled closer I heard the faint movement of water far below and recognized the foul smell of a latrine. There was no escape from the smell or the surroundings.

I marked time with the sound of footsteps, the scrape of a tin plate in the door slot, and thoughts of someone coming to take me home. Each time I closed my eyes I hoped for change, any change. There was no outside light, no sound of human voices, nothing. I was wet with perspiration and shivered even with the blanket wrapped around me.

I walked in a circle until my legs ached. When did I begin walking? The cot showed the shape of my body, but I didn't remember sleeping. I saw a face in a black stone, touched the eyes, and put my finger inside the moist mouth. Were they watching me? I screamed at the face and waited for an answer. Silence. Suddenly angry, I threw myself on the cot and closed my eyes. When I opened them, there was light in the corridor. No one was watching. I slipped through the bars, traced my steps backward through the hall, up the stairs, and out the front door. I saw myself fly in the sweet open air, follow the highway to the airport and sit safely buckled in my seat awaiting takeoff and home.

I woke on the cold floor facing the door. As I looked at the door, it soared beyond the ceiling, and the barred opening stretched long and thin. All I needed to do was to reach the door and I could slip through the stretched bars again. But I heard footsteps in the corridor and a woman's face appeared in the opening.

A plate of food slid through the slot on the floor. "*Ye!*" Eat, she said. I reached for the plate and watched her walk away, terrified to see her figure stretch tall and thin like the bars. She was suddenly small, yet her footsteps thundered. Something was wrong with my eyes.

"Wait," I said, but the door at the end of the corridor clanged shut.

I grabbed the food and pushed all of it into my mouth. Moments later I lunged for the hole, vomited, and rolled onto my back.

There was something moving at the hole. A dark stain spread out from the opening. The darkness divided into individual pieces. Roaches. Thousands of black, clicking roaches. I lunged for the cot and pressed the blanket to my eyes.

I woke on the floor, feeling something tugging at my lip. I flailed at my face and jumped onto the cot as roaches swarmed through the cell. I heard a voice and saw things coming through the slot - soap, a towel, a roll of fabric.

I sat on the stool and turned each of the items around and around in my hands. I moved to the sink, removed my clothes, and as I pulled the dress across my face, a sour smell fouled the air. My smell. I heard screaming and saw words fall from my mouth. They crashed, littering the floor with rubble and sending the roaches retreating into the latrine. I slid to the floor and tried to gather up the pieces, but they vanished in my hands.

I took the soap and rubbed my wet head until it hurt, scoured my skin, inch by inch, until it burned. I filled the cup, poured the cold water over my breasts and back, feeling each rivulet slide over my body. When I pulled on a black cotton dress, it felt strange against my skin. I fell exhausted onto the cot.

I saw Skipper playing Blockhead with Philip and Val. I stretched my body with pleasure feeling Carlos at my side. I saw Muharrem meeting with officials.

A guard opened my cell door, led me through the hall and up two flights of stairs. Spasms of coughing bent me in half. She grabbed me around the waist and wrestled me along. I tried to keep my feet on the floor. When we stopped, I was wet and shivering, my teeth banging together. The guard unlocked a room.

"I'm Bradford Temple from the American Embassy." The voice came from a man seated at a table with two chairs. A cot with no blanket was against the wall. Where was my blanket? The guards placed me on a chair and left.

The man got up and came close to look at me. "Mrs. Reardon, ah, do you need to lie down?"

I shook my head.

"We had a call from your agent Muharrem El Habashy three weeks ago when you were picked up at the airport."

Three weeks? The room began to spin. I felt myself sliding sideways. When I opened my eyes, he was standing in front of me, holding onto my shoulders.

"I'm so sorry," he said. His brown eyes, behind horn-rimmed glasses, were shiny and he shook his head from side to side. "I know what the conditions are here. All of Turkey's jails are like this."

"Get me out of here. I don't feel well," I said.

"We're doing everything we can, believe me." He sighed. "The bureaucracy here is unbelievable. It's disgraceful it took them three weeks to arrange my visit. I assure you we contacted the department head immediately after hearing from Mr. El-Habashy.

"I will insist on a doctor for you before I leave. But, can you listen for a few moments? I want to explain the charges against you in the States so you'll know what to expect when you get there."

"Charges?"

"Our communications from the States say you've been charged with fraud. Allegedly you sold an antique rug to a museum in Chicago?"

"Yes, but-"

"They're saying the rug is a fraud."

I slipped forward and rested on the table, tacky against my cheek. Other hands were on the table, clutching and banging. I looked beyond the man and saw people filling the room. Then they faded into the wall. "Where did they go?" I said.

"Who?" He followed my eyes to the wall. "Please, Mrs. Reardon, I want to tell you what's going to happen. There will be an American officer at the-"

"I want to go home now. Please get me out of here."

"We will. You'll be out soon. You're being held illegally. They have absolutely no right to hold you. We've registered a strong complaint."

He leaned close to me and lowered his voice. "It's pure arrogance on their part. They say they are offended that a rug of Turkish design has been misrepresented. My understanding is the rug was woven in France so none of this makes any sense to me, but we've struggled with their justice system for years and it never improves."

Then, in an even lower voice, he said, "They might be hoping to make money by holding a rich American. There's corruption in the system."

I wanted to scream, make him listen, but there was no strength in my voice. "Take me with you now if I'm not supposed to be here."

"It's only going to take a few more days." He stood up.

"I don't feel well. This is all wrong. Please, take me with you." I pounded my hands on the table and sobbed. The others were back, pounding along with me.

He began walking to the door. "I'll be back very soon, I promise."

I coughed, a deep strangling cough that wouldn't end. A heavy weight pressed on my chest, making it hard to breathe. I wanted to lie down, close my eyes and think of nothing.

Back in my cell, I wrapped myself in the blanket and thought about the man from the American Embassy. He promised to come back.

Dark eyes looked at me as I lay on the cot. "I heard what the American Embassy representative told you. You think he will be back? He doesn't know what he's talking about." She laughed. "We Turks are proud of our country and its art, and you have made us look foolish. For this you will be punished and our justice is not soft like yours. American pig."

She swept her eyes around my cell and licked her fleshy lips until they shone like the moisture on the walls. "Enjoy our hospitality. You will be with us a long time and your misery will make me happy." When she turned away I saw the white streak in her hair.

I pulled the blanket tighter, and closed my eyes.

9

Unfamiliar sounds surrounded me and a thick blanket cradled my arms. The light was so intense it hurt to open my eyes. A soft voice was calling my name.

"Nora? Nora? You're okay, you hear? You're gonna be just fine."

The surroundings came into focus – tubes, hanging plastic bags bulging with clear fluid, windows bright with sunshine, and the face that belonged to the voice.

"Where am I?" I said.

"You're back in the good old USA, sure enough."

She had pale green eyes and a sprinkling of freckles on her fresh, young face.

"How did I get here? I was in Turkey-" I sucked in my breath. "I was in prison."

"That's what they told me and it sure don't sound like a trip to Disneyland. For now, honey, you just think of me as your tour guide, you hear? My name's Georgia," she said, tucking the blanket around my body. "You don't go anywhere or do anything unless I issue the ticket, you hear? Your first trip is to a place called Healthy and I promise to get you there as fast as I can."

"What's wrong with me? Can't I go home?"

"Whoa. Let's start with you telling me how you feel."

"Not very well."

I heard other people in the room and tried to get up, but she placed a hand on my shoulders and eased me back. "Did I issue you a ticket to get up? No, I didn't," she said. "Where do you hurt?"

"My chest and, and my head."

She pulled on the stethoscope looped around the neck of her pink tunic, placed the black tips in her ears and listened to my chest.

"We've been treating you for pneumonia, a doozy of a case if I ever saw one too. You had a high fever for a long time, but antibiotics have taken care of that." She tapped the hanging plastic bag over my head, held my arm, peeled off some tape and removed an intravenous drip. It burned.

"The doctor said you don't need any more of this. You'll still need plenty of rest and some watching, but you're gonna be just fine. In a day or so we'll move you out of ICU, but as long as you're here, don't forget I'm the boss. Do you get my meaning?"

"How could I miss it?"

"Good. I like a patient with sass." She flashed me a set of white teeth and left.

"Wait," I said. "What hospital is this?"

"University of Pennsylvania – the best."

I tried to remember how I got from the prison to the hospital. There was a man from the American Embassy, but I didn't remember going with him or getting on a plane. My stomach twisted remembering he said I was accused of fraud. Was I still under arrest? With all my heart I wished for Carlos. The best medicine for me right then would have been to have him by my side. But he was thousands of miles away. Did he know what happened to me?

I pressed the button hanging on the rail alongside my bed. A few minutes later Georgia came.

"Do you know if I'm under arrest?"

"I was just on the phone with your brother to tell him
how well you're doing, and we expect to release you to a
private room in a few days. I'm sure he can answer all
your questions."

For two more days I was poked, prodded and x-rayed.
Midmorning of the third day I woke to a flurry of activity
around my bed.

"Nora, we're moving you to your own room," the freckled
face said.

Two men lifted me onto a gurney.

"You're no longer critical, but you're not out of the woods
yet, you hear? The pneumonia has been cleared, but we still
need to keep an eye on some of the secondary infections."

"Infections?"

"They're not serious. Some are a result of malnutrition,
okay? Don't worry about them; they're easily fixed. The
doctor'll discuss them with you, and when she feels you're
strong enough, you'll go home. My guess would be a few more
days."

She walked around the bed, tucking and pulling at the sheets
and blanket. Then she nodded to the men and the bed was
rolled to the doorway.

"Now, you be good, you hear?" She waved to me the entire
length of the hall until they wheeled me into the elevator.

I waved and mouthed a thank you.

Philip was waiting for me when the elevator doors opened
several floors above. I cried in his arms. I didn't even mind
when he greeted me with, "How are you, baby sister?"

He held my hand as we moved down the hall, past the
nurses' station, where people hung over the counter, talking on
phones and working at computers.

"They tell me I'm much better and I should be able to go
home in a couple of days," I said when we were alone.

He gave me a look of surprise. "It might be a bit longer. Be
patient."

"How's Skipper?"

"He misses you. He wanted to come to the hospital and I told him I'd ask the doctor."

"That'd be great. I miss him so much. How long have I been gone? I'm so confused. I don't remember very much. Do you know if I'm still under arrest? They wouldn't tell me."

He set his overcoat on the chair next to the bed and moved a floor lamp aside so he could stand close to me.

"Take it easy. It will all come back to you in time," he said.

Philip said Muharrem had called them first and then the American Embassy.

"We got no information about your treatment in the prison, but we imagined the worst. Val and I told Muharrem we wanted to come to Turkey, but he discouraged us. We felt helpless."

He walked over to the bedside tray table on the other side of my bed, changed its position, and shifted the tissue box from one side to the other.

"The first piece of information we got came from the officer who accompanied you on the flight from Turkey. She called us from the plane to request an ambulance. She said she had no idea you were so ill or they would've sent a doctor or nurse to accompany you on the flight."

He turned to look out the window and pulled on the cord of the blinds to change the angle of the light.

"She said you were unconscious and hallucinating most of the time on the plane."

He sat on the bed and took my hand. "We were here at the hospital when you arrived."

"I don't remember - not any of it."

The door swung open and two women came into the room.

"Mrs. Reardon, I am Dr. Blanchard." She spoke so slowly I wondered if she thought I was impaired in some way. "This is Phoebe Bennett, your nurse. You will be seeing Phoebe every day until your release. I will see you tomorrow morning to check on your progress," she said.

"When?"

"When what?"

Was this woman dense as well as slow?

"My release."

"Let's slow down shall we?" she said.

I bit my tongue.

"You have just left ICU. Let's take one day at a time. I want you to get a good night's rest. I will be here in the morning to check you over." She gave me a smile that flicked on and off so fast I'd have missed it if I'd blinked. Slow-motion voice, fast-speed smile. Strange woman.

"My ICU nurse mentioned I have some secondary infections. What are-"

"Tomorrow. I'm late for a meeting now." Then to Philip she said, "Can we agree on a fifteen-minute visit?"

I started to protest, but Philip squeezed my hand and nodded to them. They left the room.

"Nora, you're dead tired. I can see it in your eyes and you've lost at least twenty pounds."

"Am I under arrest? Tell me. I need to know."

"Yes. There's a guard posted outside the door. But try not to worry. Everything's going to be all right."

"It's just that I remember so little of what's happened. A man from the American Embassy came to the prison – or was it a dream? I had so many dreams."

"You've had a terrible fever."

"He told me I'd been arrested for fraud but that can't be true. Everything I did in Turkey was handled legally." I was going to cry and never stop, never. Damn, I hated crying.

"Listen, for once in your life. Give yourself a break. It's going to take time for you to heal."

I checked my tears when I saw the sadness in Philip's eyes.

"Don't worry about anything. We have Simon Carrington handling your case. He said you'd be arraigned before a judge as soon as you're able to leave the hospital, and he's certain you'll be released on bail. Once you're well, we'll make sure the blame is placed where it belongs – on Carlos Ghazerian, that son-of-a-bitch."

His words took my breath away, but before I could respond Phoebe came in to tell Philip I needed to rest. He patted my hand and they left together. Rest? What a joke. I hated the empty room. When no one was with me, everyone was there – that horrible prison guard, the man from the Embassy, the roaches. Philip was wrong to think Carlos deliberately sold me a fake. He'd never do that to me. I turned my face to the wall.

The doctor wouldn't let Skip visit. I pleaded with her but she pronounced all children "germy" and in my weakened condition they were off limits. My brothers were my only source of information, welcome distractions from the quiet times when all I had were ugly thoughts. When I put them aside, the void quickly filled with worries: the new gallery, the money I owed, and the trial. I broke out in a cold sweat.

On one of Val's visits he told me about taking Skipper to Comp-tech on a business call and how he was fascinated with the electronic devices. Both he and Philip thought it was a sign that my boy might follow in their footsteps and become an electrical engineer. He also reminded me of Skipper's continuing sessions with Rosemary Fiori – something else I had to attend to.

"One more thing," Val said as he was leaving, "when you're ready to come home, would you mind coming to our house? You're going to need rest and our work is so busy right now, it would be easier for us."

"Sure. It'll only be for a few days."

During the next three days I learned the doctor was concerned about ulcers and bleeding gums, both the result of poor nutrition. I had recurring reminders. One day, beans were served and when I raised a spoonful to my mouth, the brown mash on my prison tin plate appeared. I couldn't eat them and probably never would again.

"We'll release you as soon as your lab work indicates you're absorbing nutrients the way you should," Dr. Blanchard said.

"How long will that take?"

"A few days."

It was not the answer I wanted. I took short walks around the hospital corridor to pass the time. The room swayed wildly the first time my feet hit the floor. It made me angry, and I couldn't find a specific target for what I felt – a mass of Turkish faces, a stone building, tin plates of indescribable food, and roaches. And there was Carlos' face. I had to hate him too, didn't I?

The day before I was released, Simon Carrington came to see me about the arraignment. He entered the room like a general ready to address his men before battle, expecting complete attention, total respect. I focused instead on the impeccable clothes topped by his shiny head, fleshy jowls and missing chin. For some perverse reason his physical flaws placated me, acted as a buffer to his arrogance somehow. Simon was a senior partner in Jared's law firm. I hadn't seen him since Jared's funeral, and unless he'd had a personality transplant, I didn't expect pleasantries.

"Are you feeling strong enough to go to court tomorrow when you leave the hospital? It won't take more than an hour."

"I'm ready," I lied. The whole process scared me to death. An arraignment was one step closer to a trial. I could lose everything I'd worked for.

"Okay, then. We'll see a judge in the afternoon tomorrow. He'll state the charges against you and ask you how you plead – not guilty, of course – and he'll set bail. There won't be a problem. Leave everything to me."

I'd been to several company parties with Simon when Jared was alive. His ego siphoned off every bit of air in the room. In fact, he was no different from any of the other five partners in Jared's firm. It's a wonder they didn't asphyxiate each other. Nevertheless, Simon was an excellent lawyer. I didn't have to like him.

"Tell me about Carlos Ghazerian."

"He's a board member of the Museum of Ottoman Treasures. My Turkish agent recommended him as an antique rug broker. We've had several successful dealings."

"I know all that. He sold you the Aubusson rug, correct? I've been doing some research." He pulled down on his vest and thrust his puny chin forward.

"Yes."

"Did you verify the date of the rug's manufacture?"

I paused to exhale. "I have a Certificate of Authenticity." Did he think I was an amateur, or worse, stupid?

He pulled a paper from his bulging briefcase. "Signed by him, I see." He replaced the paper and squared his shoulders. "What was your relationship with this man?"

"I've already told you."

"Come on, Nora, you get it. Don't pretend you don't."

I resented his haughty voice as much as his impertinence and considered telling him to leave.

"I've been professional in all my dealings in Turkey, including those with Mr. Ghazerian. No one can say otherwise."

"I'm not passing judgment on you, I just need to be prepared for any possibilities the prosecutor may throw at us. Were you sleeping with him?" His pitch was higher and the volume of his voice louder. Together they were sandpaper on my nerves.

"Where are you going with this line of questioning? I've been in this business for more than five years, and I've purchased hundreds of rugs. I know what I'm doing." I was on my feet, steadying myself against the bed.

"I'll tell you exactly where I'm going. If the jury feels that you were negligent in your responsibility to your client, then you were partly to blame, and we've got a problem."

I felt a cold chill. This was moving into unwelcome terrain. Had I been virgin territory for Carlos? Was it possible he'd planned this from the beginning?"

All I remembered of the rest of my conversation with Simon was he'd call in the morning to find out the time of my hospital release. The minute he left I pulled on my coat and went outside to a courtyard near my room. The air was cool and moist and smelled strongly of overturned earth. Green shoots were breaking through the snow-soaked garden and overhead there were fat buds on the tree's branches – all signs of continuance, of hope, of shedding the old and giving way to the new. I needed that.

Later I flipped from one side of my bed to the other, trying to sort out what might have happened, and by the time light filtered through the window, I'd processed more questions than answers. Perhaps Carlos disapproved of a woman doing business. Was he like Jared, feigning support and approval, while harboring other thoughts? Jared came roaring into my head. I saw him standing at the street-facing window in our bedroom, his back to me as I entered the room.

"Glad you finally managed to pay us a visit."
"Come on, Jared. The plane was only a half hour late."
Facing me now with ice pouring from his eyes, he continued.
"You haven't a clue what it takes to be a wife or mother. I think it would be best if we separated and I took custody of Skipper. You and your career will be better off without us."

I pushed the memory away. I didn't want to think about Jared. The spot where I kept him was numb and that suited me just fine. But I couldn't forget him either, not because he'd been my husband and Skipper's father, but because I didn't understand why he changed his feelings for me. Now he was gone and I'd never know.

Philip picked me up the next day, and we drove directly to court. Simon was waiting inside the door. I couldn't meet his eyes when he greeted me. Things progressed as he said they would. The judge heard my plea and accepted it. Bail was set at \$125,000 and I was free to leave. An hour later I was wrapped in a comforter on my brothers' living room sofa and Skipper, just home from school, came flying into my arms.

"Mommy, guess what? I can read," he said.

I pulled him onto my lap and buried my face in his sweaty smell. The tears started flowing again. I couldn't help it. Almost two months had passed and Skipper looked older.

"Can I read to you?"

"Yes, I'd love that. As soon as I get settled, okay?" Satisfied, he ran off.

Over the protests of my brothers, who wanted me to go to bed immediately, I said I wanted to see their house. The truth was I wanted distraction, anything but an empty room, and I hadn't seen the house since the day they made settlement. Now it was furnished and appropriately masculine. When we reached the bedroom area, one was cluttered with toy cars and trucks.

"Let me guess; this is Skipper's garage," I said.

Val's hand was on my back, providing gentle pressure to move me down the hall. "We've set this one up for you," he said, "and I really think you should rest now."

I couldn't believe my eyes. They'd brought the coverlet from my own bedroom to cover the bed and my pillow with the embroidered case our mother had given me. I turned back to Val to thank him and saw a vase of yellow roses. I was crying again, but thankfully Skipper arrived with his book tucked under his arm. We climbed into bed and he began to read. Listening gave me a reason not to think about the last time someone gave me yellow roses.

Skip came to my room each day after school to give me an earful of the day's happenings. I wondered if the closeness would continue when we got home.

"Can I play with my knights in here?" he said.

"Knights? That's new, isn't it?"

"Uncle Val bought them for me and a castle too." He gathered up his school papers and left. No answer had always been a "yes" to Skipper, and in a few minutes he was back on the floor to set up a long line of silver armored knights, some on horseback.

"I like this better than my room because the rug is blue and I can pretend it's a moat around my castle," he said.

"And the brown rug in your bedroom is a highway, right?" But he wasn't listening. He was moving the knights around the room, shouting orders, making plans for battle. Suddenly he tore one of the knights from its horse and threw it under the bed.

"Was he hurt in battle?" I said.

"No, he's too dumb."

"Dumb?"

"He didn't do what I told him to do. Now he has to stay in the dark and think about it."

Carlos was in my thoughts every day, thanks to my brothers. They brought up the trial at dinner every night.

"In a couple of months Simon will take care of it," I said, hoping to close the discussion.

"But you'll have to discuss it. You'll have no choice but to tell them you bought the Aubusson in good faith. You were given a Certificate of Authenticity, right?" Philip said.

"I'll testify when the time comes. Do I have to do it here, every single night?"

I pushed away from the table and stood. Anger, frustration and hurt were forming words I didn't want to say. My brothers didn't deserve another outburst from me. They'd been wonderful to Skipper and me. I took a deep breath and pushed aside the coffee mug that was still full. My brothers' faces appeared braced, waiting for my anger.

"I love you both, you know that. And there are no words to thank you for how you've cared for me and Skipper, but it's time for us to go home. Please understand."

Before they could protest, I left the kitchen and climbed the stairs to the bedroom. My things were scattered around, no more at home than I was. I set my suitcase on the bed, snapped open the lock and saw a note I'd written to remind myself to call Muharrem and thank him. But it would have to wait. I couldn't bring myself to think of anything or anyone Turkish yet. Getting home was enough for now.

A few hours later Philip helped me carry my things into the house while Skipper ran straight to his room.

"Skipper, come back downstairs and help Uncle Philip carry our suitcases."

He was down the stairs again, jumping the last four steps in one leap. He took two of the smaller tote bags and followed Philip up the stairs, while I went to the office on the second floor to retrieve telephone messages. It surprised me to see there were none. I guessed that my brothers had picked them up on their frequent visits to the house. As I walked away, the phone rang. I picked up the receiver. It was Carlos.

10

I lowered the receiver slowly. His was the last voice I expected to hear. My hand shook and when the rest of my body followed suit, I found the nearest chair. Carlos? Did he think I didn't know? I shook my head and walked away.

Skipper bounded down the stairs, talking to me before he reached the den.

"Mom, did I tell you I have a new book? It has lots of hard words, but I can read them." He waved the book in my face. "Do you want me to read to you?"

"You bet I do," I said, pulling him next to me on the sofa, glad to think of anything but Carlos. But the phone rang again, and before I could restrain him, Skipper ran to answer.

"Hello, Dr. Fiori. Yes, we just got home. Mommy is all better now." He shifted from one foot to the other as he spoke, full of energy, enjoying conversation with an adult. "Okay, here she is." He spun around and handed me the receiver.

Rosemary wanted to see me and we agreed on the following afternoon. It would be refreshing to work on the parts of my life I could control, or at least improve. I also was curious to find out what had happened during her two months with Skipper. I could say with confidence that he and I were closer. Maybe she'd helped or perhaps it was just the passing of time.

The question now was whether or not she could improve his relationships with other children.

Thoughts of Carlos were already fading, albeit leaving a trail of questions. Why had he called? To apologize? I could never trust him again. I had to try to stop thinking about him. For now, even Fiori and her endless probing would be more acceptable than poking around in my bruises.

Philip joined us saying he was ready to leave. Skipper and I said our goodbyes and I thanked him for taking such good care of both of us. His final hug came with an admonition to rest. I assured him I would. I pulled the plug on the phone and sat on the sofa with Skipper.

"You're going to like this book, Mommy. It's about an alligator that lives in a house just like ours. He takes a bath in his own bathtub."

I filled up with new sensations listening to him. His patience amazed me most of all. That certainly wasn't characteristic. Only once when I tried to help he shot me a sharp glance and made it clear he didn't want my help. I understood where that trait came from.

"Skipper, you're doing really well. I'm so proud of you." I leaned over to kiss him, but he slapped the book in his lap and sighed loudly.

"I want to finish. You just listen."

I made a mental note to work on rudeness another time.

Rosemary Fiori greeted me warmly. She had shortened her hair, but otherwise, her unadorned face, long cotton dress – lilac, this time – and plant-filled office told me I was getting back to nature again.

"I'll bet you're glad to be home. It must have been terrible for you. Do you think you'll ever go back to Turkey?"

"I haven't thought about it. There are other things to deal with," I said.

"That's smart. It'll take time to heal physically and emotionally after what you've been through."

She motioned me to a chair across from her desk while she slipped in behind it, leaned back and waited.

"I want to know what you've learned about Skipper," I said.

"I believe I've discovered some important things. But, first, do you mind if I ask you some questions about Jared that will help me confirm what I believe is going on with Skipper?"

The hair on my arms and neck prickled.

"Would you tell me about Jared's relationship with Skipper?"

She may have cut the length of her hair, but she still preferred the long way around the issues.

"Jared was a wonderful father."

"How?"

Unbelievable. She'd just spent two months with Skipper. Surely it was obvious his qualities were the result of his upbringing and the relationship he had with his father and me.

"Jared loved being a father from the moment I brought Skipper home from the hospital." I told her how Jared had been concerned about Skipper's education, and how he wanted his son to be exposed to the wider world. "When Skip was old enough, Jared worked with him on manners and courteous behavior. Does that give you some idea about the kind of father he was?" I knew I sounded testy.

"Absolutely, and Skipper's teachers confirm he's bright and discerning. He also challenges opinions and he is not easily swayed once he makes up his mind. I'd say that's unusual for a child his age."

It appeared she thought these were good traits. I did, too, except defiance was closer to the truth than challenge.

"But you haven't really answered my question," she said.

"What do you mean?"

"I want to know about their relationship? How did Skipper interact with his father? What was he like when he was with Jared?" She got up from her chair and transferred her gaze from me to some papers on her desk. All she did was shift one pile of papers to another spot and it made me edgy.

"They got along well together," I said. "Skipper never argued with Jared, if that's what you mean. He seemed eager to please."

She came around to the front of her desk, leaned against it and faced me. I felt the urge to put more space between us, but she had effectively corralled me in the chair.

"Was his attitude toward you the same?" she said.

A long moment passed as I pictured how Skipper's blue eyes would turn cold and steely and I remembered his anger. I swallowed.

"Because of my travels, Jared was Skip's main caregiver."

"Yes?"

"He often questioned me. I think he did it because I wasn't his authority figure."

"And I believe you've mentioned tantrums. Did he have tantrums with Jared?"

"No, just with me." My energy was draining and I hoped this would be over soon.

"Physically and mentally alert children like Skipper are always challenging, but let me assure you they turn out to be adults who make things happen," she said, but it sounded like she was throwing me a bone. "Can you stay for just a few minutes more? I'd like to tell you some things that may surprise you and maybe upset you some. Are you okay?"

"I'm fine – maybe a little tired, but I want to know everything you have to tell me."

"Here it is: In role-playing situations with Skipper, I've learned Jared was often overly harsh, even cruel. Did you know that?" She didn't wait for a reply. "I'll be clear, he was abusive."

I gasped.

"When Skipper made mistakes," she continued, "wasn't quick enough, or showed poor judgment, he was made to spend time in your bedroom closet, or under the bed, where his daddy said he wouldn't be distracted. He was told to think about his infraction and to come up with a solution before he was permitted to come out. Did you know this?"

"No." Goosebumps formed on my arms. I saw Skip throw the knight under my bed. With horror I remembered all the times Skipper spent playing in his room in the dark. I swallowed again. It hurt to think that my child knew how to find comfort in the dark. I'd been staring at my hands, feeling anger and embarrassment.

"What do I do? I don't understand what this means."

"Skipper's going to be fine," she said. "He's still reacting to his past and he may for some time to come, but do you remember the first time you came to me, when he was upset about not having friends?"

"Yes. He wanted to go to heaven with his father." I shuddered remembering.

"I told you then how resilient children are. Skipper's a lucky boy. He has you and his uncles who love him." She sat again, facing me and leaning forward with an earnest expression. "You love your work, don't you?"

"Well, I want Skipper to be secure. It's frightening for a child when the family has no security. He needs to know I will always take care of him." I realized my voice had risen and perspiration was forming on my upper lip.

"That's interesting, but money isn't the only way to give a child security," she said.

Mother Earth and a touch of fantasy too. "Listen," I said, "when you can't pay the bills and your parents are more worried about finances than they are about you, it hurts."

"Of course it does. You're right, and we should talk about that sometime." She made a note on a tablet in front of her.

I took a deep breath and looked at my hands in my lap. I saw my mother's face and she was staring at her own hands.

Rosemary changed her position in the chair, then leaned, and smoothed the fabric of her skirt. I didn't know how she did it, but I could feel the pressure to speak.

"To answer your question, yes, I do love my work, but all that may be changing."

"How?"

There was my mother's face again. My thoughts were slipping back to the time after Papa lost his job. How he suffered with worry. It killed him and Mama too. Tears filled my eyes remembering the look on her face in the weeks after he died. She was lost without him and then she was gone, and I was lost. Deep in my chest I felt the same fear and panic I felt then.

"You may as well know. In a few weeks I will be on trial for fraud." I turned my face and spoke to the wall. "An antique rug I bought in Turkey and sold to a group in Chicago turned out to be a fake." I fought to control the trembling but I couldn't. I held my head and sobbed. "I'm so embarrassed. I seem to cry over everything lately."

Rosemary handed me some tissues from a dispenser on her desk. "Can't one of Jared's partners help you?"

"Yes, but if things don't go well…"

"Look, you've enough to think about. I feel I've kept you overly long today. Just mull over what we've talked about. Skipper will be okay. About his anger, well, I believe I understand why he directs his anger at you. We'll talk about it next time."

"He's been better lately, but there've been times when I thought he hated me," I said.

"No, he doesn't. In fact, it's because he loves you."

I left her office feeling puzzled. I didn't understand her last comment and I wanted to pursue it, but I suddenly felt exhausted. It was a common problem lately whenever I overextended myself. I wanted to get home and close my eyes. What she told me about Jared had shocked me, but I couldn't dismiss it. In fact, something inside me resonated.

I stopped in the entrance to Rosemary's office to steady myself. It took a few minutes before I was ready to walk to the bus stop. The bus had been a good choice. Philadelphia's inner city streets – narrow, cobbled and congested – were a gauntlet for a distracted driver. I knew I fit the category.

A bus whined to a stop in front of the small group that had formed and we filed on, paid our tokens, and found seats before it lurched into the stream of cars. I sat on one of the red, plastic-covered seats near the rear and rested my head against the window.

Would Skipper have emotional scars? Rosemary didn't say he would. She said he'd be okay. I wondered if she knew why someone like Jared could do such things. I'd ask her next time. Surprisingly, I looked forward to our next session. I guess I'd come around to believing she could help – at least with Skipper.

I wondered why Rosemary questioned me about my work. Did she think, like my brothers, that I should stay home with Skipper? She hadn't asked about our finances, but she was too smart not to know Skipper and I were well cared for. But that wasn't the point. I wanted to work.

The bus approached my corner. Just in time. The levee that held back my tears was weakening and I yearned for the privacy of my bedroom. I reached up to pull the cord to alert the driver to stop at the next corner and worked my way to the exit door. Advertising posters were lined up end on end across the tops of the windows on both sides of the bus. I didn't read the messages, but the smiling faces mocked me. All they had to deal with was toothpaste or insurance carriers.

March winds were having their last say, and a cold blast of air hit me as I stepped onto the sidewalk. I leaned into the wind and walked the fifty yards or so to my door. At the steps I glanced up and saw Simon Carrington.

"I was just about to leave. I'm so glad you're here. Wait'll you hear the wonderful news I have for you," he said.

"I could use some good news," I said, fitting the key in the lock.

Inside, I hung our coats in the entrance closet and motioned Simon into the den. He didn't budge. Instead, he stamped his foot and looked like a child impatient to be heard.

"Nora! I mean very, very good news."

"What?"

"We have the evidence to prove your innocence."

My legs buckled and Simon helped me to a chair before parking himself in another.

"Early this morning I received this package of information." He patted a thick FedEx envelope balanced on his knee.

"Remember I told you our first move would be to locate a Turkish investigating firm to gather evidence," Simon said.

"No, not really."

"Doesn't matter. Well, the best turned out to be Koray Aydin and Associates."

"That means nothing to me," I said.

"Yes, yes, but it will in a minute. When I called to discuss the case with them, it seems they'd been working on it for weeks and had just uncovered the felons."

I sank back into the chair, unable to grasp the full meaning of what Simon was telling me. "But, I don't understand. As far as the Turkish government was concerned, the felon had been captured – me."

"Does the name Mehmet Aydin ring a bell?"

The name sounded familiar, someone I'd met in Turkey I supposed. Then I remembered. Mehmet was the name of Tapis' fiancé. She'd said he worked in his father's criminal investigation firm. That was where his sister met him. But I was still confused.

"Here, read this," he said. He handed me a single sheet from his briefcase. I read slowly. It was a translation of a contract between Koray Aydin and Associates and… The sheet slipped to the floor and I looked up at Simon's raised eyebrows.

"Carlos Ghazerian," I whispered.

It took several minutes before I could put the question to Simon.

"Does this mean that Carlos hired investigators as soon as he heard I'd been arrested?"

"That's how it looks."

I jumped up from my chair. That was why Carlos was calling.

"Simon, I know this is rude of me, but I need to make a phone call right away. Do you mind?"

I dashed to the closet, pulled out his coat, thrust it at him, and opened the front door.

"No, I believe I understand perfectly well. I just want to tell you I will meet with the judge tomorrow. He'll dismiss the charges against you."

"Do I need to do anything?"

Simon was already on the doorstep, his coat flapping in the wind as he wrestled his arms into it. He shook his head and I closed the door. I'd apologize next time I saw him. I reached for the phone, calculating it was early evening in Ankara.

11

It took the Ghazerian's housekeeper only moments to deliver the phone to Elena.

"My dear, how are you? We have been very concerned," she said.

"I've just been given the good news that they've found the ones responsible. Is Carlos there?"

"Isn't he with you?"

"No." Shivers traveled under my skin.

"He left Ankara right after Mehmet called to say they were sending their report to your authorities. That was early yesterday. He should be there by now."

My heart jumped. Carlos was coming here. All the time we were separated, I was in his thoughts. He was working on my release. He loved me, oh, thank God, he loved me.

Skipper came in and tugged on my sleeve.

"Excuse me, Elena. Skip, can't you see I'm talking to someone."

"But, Mom, Carlos wants to know if he can come in. I said he could, but he wants you."

"Oh, Elena, he's here. He's here now."

"Well, then, I am happy you are together. Goodbye."

I loved that woman. She understood everything. I ran to the front door. Carlos was standing outside, looking unsure.

I held out my arms to him as much to feel him close as to support my weak limbs. Neither of us could find words of greeting. Relief and joy rippled through me, carrying three months of despair away like an outbound tide.

"My lawyer left just moments ago after giving me the news about the evidence Mehmet found to clear me. I can't believe it," I said.

"I have been so worried about you. Are you well? You are very thin. Did they hurt you at *Izmir Buca* – the prison? The Minister of Justice assured me you would be shown every courtesy."

"Oh, let's not talk about it. Everything's fine now. I don't want to think about that place. I'm feeling stronger every day. You're the best medicine I could have."

He hugged me again and I closed my eyes and cried. There was a noise behind us. We both turned and saw Skipper standing with his coat. If he thought it strange to see me in Carlos' arms, he gave no indication.

"Can I go out?"

"How about if we all have some milk and cookies first? Carlos?" I grabbed a tissue from the kitchen counter and blew my nose.

"Are substitutes allowed?"

"You'd rather have tea, right?" I turned on the flame beneath the kettle, reached in the cupboard for the teapot and set out mugs and a glass for Skipper's milk.

We sat on stools around the kitchen bar area, and I listened while Carlos bombarded Skipper with questions about school. Between sentences he glanced at me. I was eager to talk to Carlos, but their conversation was flowing so easily, I was awed. They were talking about soccer. Carlos was telling him he'd played in school and he suggested a game with Skipper.

He looked at me. "After school tomorrow?"

"Sure," I said. I'd have agreed to anything.

"Now, can I go out?" Skipper said. It was his after-school routine to drop off his backpack, have a snack, and then go outside to play with neighborhood friends, usually Marty.

I nodded and he was off.

"It must be a male thing. You two seem to have so many things to talk about. I have to tie him down to have a conversation of any substance."

"You should start playing soccer," he said with a twinkle in his eyes.

I poured a second cup of tea for both of us.

"Is it really okay to play with him tomorrow? I do not wish to intrude. It is just that kids are such fun and I have few opportunities."

I stared at his face, and then grabbed his hands, remembering. "Thank you for what you've done for me." I couldn't go on. We managed a kiss through my tears.

"I love you, Nora. I would have turned the country upside down to find a way to set you free. You are my family."

"And I've loved you for months, but until now I don't think I realized how much. I need you to be a permanent part of my life."

He pulled me close. "I intend to be."

We separated, but not before I registered the profound security I felt in his arms. I became aware of how alone I'd been – not just in prison, but long before, during the years spent with Jared, and in the years after my parents' deaths. There were unresolved questions and problems to be worked out, but this moment with Carlos was happiness and I wanted it without reservation. I gathered up the cups while Carlos put the milk back in the refrigerator.

"It is cold outside," he said, "but would you be willing to take a walk? My legs are cramped from the trip."

Outside I waved to Skipper and told him we were taking a short walk. The boys were playing tag under the watchful eye of one of the boy's fathers.

"I'll be back in about half an hour," I shouted and received a nod.

The air was brisk. I led Carlos to a densely wooded area at the far end of a neighborhood park where we hoped the trees would block the stiff breeze. The ground was covered with a cushion of dead leaves. Overhead a canopy of soft greenery was emerging. Next year at this time they'd be part of the mulch.

"What are you smiling about," Carlos said.

"I was just noticing the leaves, last autumn's remnants under our feet and the green ones just starting to unfurl. Sort of like our lives."

"You are in a philosophical mood, yes?"

"Maybe. I've certainly had a brush with death and now I feel reborn." I resolved to sweep the last three months of dead leaves out of my mind. At least I could try. I squeezed his hand.

The street lamps cast pale round moons on the brick pavement. In the fading light, the rows of white marble steps glowed, spotlighting each home.

"These brown homes are part of Philadelphia's history, yes?"

"They're Italianate brownstone, built in the late nineteenth century. Of course they've been extensively remodeled over the years to add modern conveniences. Just in the last few years, this Spring Garden area was designated a historically certified neighborhood. Now someone is looking over our shoulders when we make changes."

"You call that 'big brother,'" he said.

"Exactly, but, you know, I'm glad because I want to see these wonderful homes preserved."

We got back to the house with our cheeks burning from the cold wind that hurried us along. Skipper was still with his friends. He'd come home reluctantly when the light faded to a point to make playing difficult.

"Can you stay?" I said.

He looked at me but didn't answer, and realized I hadn't been clear.

"Can you stay for dinner?" I pulled off my jacket and placed it in the closet. I reached for his and hung it next to mine, enjoying the look of them together.

"Yes, I'd like that. Can I help? I can make a salad."

I pulled greens from the refrigerator.

"Actually I feel relatively confident making a tomato salad. I don't want to fail my first cooking test."

I laughed and gave him the materials he asked for. He bent to his work, chopping tomatoes, parsley and olives.

"Do you have business in New York?" I said between tomatoes.

"No, I came only to see you." He stopped, put down the knife, and faced me with tears in his eyes. "When Muharrem called to tell me you had been arrested, I became a madman."

He told me he was ready to confront the authorities and demand my release. Elena had stopped him.

"She had not lost her head like me. She said it might not be in your best interest to make demands." He said she reminded him that his father had donated a rug for the office of the Minister of Justice, and she suggested Carlos offer the same courtesy to the current Justice who had recently moved into a new office. Once he made contact, she said, he could explain that I was a friend.

"Perhaps that's what paved the way for the American Embassy to see me," I said.

Carlos sat on a kitchen stool and wiped his eyes with a patterned handkerchief and looked sheepish. I couldn't say anything, didn't want to remember those dark days. Instead I leaned into the comfort of his chest and arms.

The front door slammed and Skip, glowing from the cold air, asked when dinner would be ready.

"In about an hour. Why don't you read for awhile?" I said.

"Do you want to read with me?" he said to Carlos.

"Oh, no you don't. Your teacher said to spend time reading alone. It's just as important as reading aloud. If you still want to read with Carlos, you can do it before your bedtime, okay?"

He set his jaw and gave me a cold look, but then looked at Carlos and agreed. I wondered if he expected reinforcement. Getting none, he turned and stomped up the steps.

"You seem quite comfortable in the kitchen," I said.

"Sharing meals is the best part of any day as far as I am concerned. It is a ritual I enjoy."

"I'll admit I like having a man in the kitchen with me. My brother Val is a good cook. When he comes for dinner, he always has his hands in the pots. Sometimes he insists doing it all himself and I move aside and watch. I've learned from him. "Oh, I haven't told my brothers the good news." I reached for the phone. Carlos walked to the den.

Several minutes later I joined him. He was looking at my collection of jazz CDs – Dave Brubeck, Charlie Parker, Louis Armstrong.

"What did they say?"

"I'm surprised you couldn't hear Val all the way in here. He was overjoyed with the news. Philip wasn't home. They'll come for dinner tomorrow to hear all the details. Is that okay with you?" He smiled. Then I bit my tongue. Maybe it wasn't a good idea to have the three of them together. My brothers didn't let go of anger easily. Perhaps they'd still be suspicious of Carlos. Why did life have to be so complicated?

"By the way, have you registered at a hotel yet? You can stay with us if you like," I said.

Carlos flushed red so suddenly I had to laugh. "We have a guest room," I added.

I understood how he felt. My own inclination was to skip dinner in favor of feeling his skin against mine, but it seemed awkward with Skipper nearby.

"My luggage is…ah, I thought I'd go back to the Bellevue," he said.

"To a room with an Oriental rug?"

Carlos and I were finishing up with the dishes when Skipper called from upstairs to say he was ready for bed.

"That's our signal to report for a reading session," I said.

We read propped up on pillows in Skip's bed. When I declined Skipper's request for another story, I was expecting a protest, but it didn't come. Instead he tossed his Lion King pillows on the floor in his special arrangement: Simba had to be in the middle, flanked by Pumba, Timon, Mufasa and Lana. Then he wiggled under his comforter. He shook hands with Carlos and gave me a hug and kiss. My boy was unpredictable – this time in a nice way.

Carlos and I walked away from Skipper's room hand in hand.

"He reads well. Is it unusual? He has not started formal schooling, correct?"

"Yes he has. He'll be in second grade in the fall, but he reads at a higher level than most. His school has a progressive program that challenges children to move ahead at their own pace."

Carlos glanced at his watch.

"You can stay a little longer, can't you?" I said, leading him into the den. I couldn't give him up yet. Three months ago I thought I'd never see him again. I wanted to revel in his presence for as long as possible.

"We should not be left alone together for too long," he said.

"Hmmm, you're probably right, but, please, just a little while."

We sat close together on the sofa. I leaned back against him, finding a sanctuary that felt custom-made. His arms wrapped around me. He kissed the top of my head and his moist breath seeped through my hair. Contentment flowed through my body, warming me in ways I hadn't felt since the last time we were together. Passion was just below the surface but this was softer, more like a down comforter that takes your body heat and gives it back to you.

"Did they mistreat you in prison? I imagined the worst," he said.

"Don't ask me to talk about it. I can't, really. I remember only bits and pieces. I was sick." Cold crept through my veins like a transfusion of ice water. In seconds I was wet with perspiration and beginning to shudder. Scenes flashed in front of me – the flaking walls, the guard's face at the barred opening, a hand in the slot. I sat up straight.

"I'm so sorry. It is just that I keep thinking about it. I thought if I heard your words, I could somehow take them on myself. I cannot stand the thought of someone hurting you."

He took my hands in his and brought them to his lips.

"I'm safe now and the memories will fade, but sometimes they're so real, I think I'm still in that cell."

The quiet wrapped around us, sealing in the good feelings. I relaxed.

"Tell me what happened with the Aubusson?" I said.

"It was my warehouse supervisor. Someone I had trusted for many years."

I sat up again, eager to hear every word.

"Throughout the Middle East and Asia there are networks of gangsters who manufacture copies of Oriental treasures. They monitor the movement of rugs, jewels, art - anything of great value. When they learn about sales, trades or transfers, they use elaborate methods to steal and replace them with fakes. It is a very lucrative business," he said. "Fortunately, Mehmet's firm was already in pursuit of these gangsters when I called to tell him what happened to the Aubusson."

"But didn't you send a security guard to accompany the rug from your warehouse to the port?"

"Of course, but he also was a gang member. These people are as patient as they are corrupt."

"I can't imagine reproducing the Aubusson. It's so unique, so intricate."

"The operation is very sophisticated. They have their own weavers, sculptors, jewelers, and potters. My guess is that in the case of the Aubusson, a reproduction was made long ago and stockpiled for the future."

"Amazing. I'm just so grateful to you, and Mehmet, and to Muharrem too. Tomorrow I must call, but right now I want to enjoy being with you."

I turned again to rest back in his arms and I closed my eyes. "You know what the worst part was? Not knowing why I'd been arrested." I told him what I remembered about the policemen who took me from the plane, and how I worried that no one would know what happened to me, and how relieved I was when Muharrem came running. I knew he would find a way to help me. I explained what I remembered about the man from the Embassy, but I was so sick by then the memories were vague.

"He told me I'd been arrested because the Middle Eastern Cultural Center reported I'd sold them a fake. I was sure there was a mistake, but they wouldn't listen. It was worse later in the hospital, after I was better. I was devastated just thinking you had deceived me, that somehow you didn't really love me, that you were only using me."

I felt Carlos' body stiffen behind me. His arms dropped to his sides and he edged away from me. I turned to look at his face. It was cold, hard, distant.

"What's wrong?" I said.

He looked away, rising. His jaw was moving, but he didn't speak. He walked toward the closet near the front door. I reached for him but he pulled away.

"Carlos, what's wrong?"

He pulled his coat from the closet and slipped his arms into the sleeves, looking over my head like I wasn't there. He opened the door and stood facing the street. The wind carried his words back to me: "Perhaps our cultures don't mix after all." He pulled the door closed behind him and I was left facing the wood panels.

12

What did he mean our cultures didn't mix? He must have misunderstood something I said. The clock ticked off the passing minutes while I paced back and forth. When thirty minutes had passed, I called the Bellevue, believing he'd reach his room by then.

"Yes, Mrs. Reardon, he was here, but only to pick up his bag," the hotel clerk said. "He asked me to book him on the next available flight to Ankara and he left. That was about ten minutes ago."

The room spun and my legs buckled. I fell backwards and hit my head on the ball and claw of the entrance table leg. A warm trickle moved down my neck and the chandelier above sparkled and faded to black.

When I opened my eyes, Skipper was shaking me.

"Mommy, get up. You have blood on you. What was that loud noise?"

His image blurred and the room spun when I pulled myself into a sitting position.

"Where's Carlos?" he said.

"I'm all right. I tripped on the table. Maybe that's what you heard, or maybe you heard the door slam."

The back of my head felt swollen and sticky. I resisted the urge to touch it, not wanting to alarm Skipper. It wasn't like him to show fear, but I read it on his face.

"What time is it?"

He ran to the den and shouted, "Thirteen minutes after nine."

"Can you call your uncles and ask them to come over?"

While he rushed to the phone, I stood slowly, holding onto the table, waiting for my eyes to focus. A dark spot on the parquet floor slowly became red blood. I used the wall and the furniture to steady myself and made my way to the kitchen sink, pulled a checkered dishtowel from the drawer, wet it and dabbed at my head. The white checks turned pink.

"Uncle Philip said he'd be right over." He stared at the blood.

"I feel okay now. Don't worry. Let's just sit here and wait for Uncle Philip," I reached over and patted his hand, but he pulled it away and balled his hands in his lap.

Philip let himself in fifteen minutes later and helped me into the den. He looked at my head and sent Skipper to the bathroom for bandages and aspirin.

"You shouldn't have come home so soon," he said, the minute Skip disappeared up the stairs.

"If you're going to lecture me, just leave now. Everything I do is wrong in your eyes, isn't it?" I was on the verge of tears and my head was hammering.

"I'm sorry. But it's obvious you needed more time to rest. What happened?"

Skipper rushed back into the room and handed him the bandages and a bottle.

As Philip struggled with the package, I saw Skipper standing at the entrance to the den. He hadn't said a word since Philip arrived. The panicked face I saw hovering over me under the table was gone.

"Come here, Skip," I said, reaching out to him.

"No, I'm going to bed now." He backed away toward the stairs.

"Please, I want to tell you something."

Philip moved into the kitchen as Skipper stood in front of me, his eyes avoiding mine, and his body poised to bolt.

"Thank you for taking good care of me, Skip. I'm so lucky to have someone in the house who knows what to do in an emergency."

"Okay. Can I go to bed now?"

I nodded. He said goodnight to Philip, who lifted and kissed him on both cheeks like he always did. "Want me to tuck you in?"

"No, I want to go by myself." He walked up the stairs, taking one quick glance at us before he moved out of view.

I sighed and rested my head in my hand.

"Are you dizzy? You might have a concussion. Maybe we should call the doctor."

"No, I feel okay. The aspirin's working. It's Skipper I'm worried about. And something awful has happened between Carlos and me. I feel like everything's falling apart."

"Skipper seems fine."

"I wonder. Don't you see how he avoids me and how he hides his feelings? How he can't say what he thinks? I saw how upset he was, but he wouldn't let me comfort him."

"That's just his personality."

"There's more to it than that, Philip, lots more."

Philip moved next to me on the sofa and pulled off his sweater. I rested my head on his shoulder.

"I learned some things about Skipper from Dr. Fiori this morning, some things that are beginning to make sense to me."

"Like what?"

"All I wanted from her was to know how to help Skipper make friends and control his anger, but she started asking me about Skipper's behavior around Jared. She didn't come right out and say this, but I'm beginning to think that Jared needed to have complete control of Skipper and me, and that in some way this relates to Skip's anger toward me."

Philip looked confused, but I was feeling more confident by the minute. "Do you remember when I told you Jared wanted a divorce?"

"He thought you were neglecting Skipper because you spent so much time in Turkey."

"I don't think so. I believe he thought he was losing control of me."

"What's that got to do with Skipper?"

"Dr. Fiori told me Jared was cruel to Skipper."

My brother's eyes widened, and he moved back sharply as though I'd hit him. In a way I had.

"I don't believe it. How can she know that? She's wrong."

"No, she isn't." I got up and paced from the window to the bookcase. "I didn't believe it myself at first, but after awhile what she said answered questions I'd been carrying around since Jared's death – some even before his death. Like, why was Skipper so defiant with me and so well behaved for his father? I think Skipper was angry at his father and, out of fear, he was directing it at me."

"Nora, sit down. What did Jared do to him?"

I explained how Jared made Skipper sit in our bedroom closet or lie under the bed for all kinds of behaviors Jared felt needed correcting. I told Philip about the incident with Skipper and his toy knights while I was recuperating at their house.

"Do you see how this fits together?"

"What did Jared do to you? Did he hurt you?"

"Not physically, but now that I've begun to reexamine our lives together, I believe Jared needed to be in complete control of Skipper and me. He wanted me to follow his directions in my business, in our... He turned against me when I found success on my own. Does all this sound crazy?" I settled back on the sofa again.

"I'm not sure what I think. It's hard to believe Jared would do that to you and Skipper."

"I'll admit I'm still a little confused, but I'll tell you this: I don't miss Jared. Since he's been gone, I feel freer. I know I have problems, things to work out, but I can manage. I know I can."

Philip walked to the other side of the room and back, shaking his head. "What about Skipper, Nora?"

"I'm not sure just yet, but the next time I see the doctor, I'll be better prepared to sort it out. She told me to think about my marriage as a first step.

"It's really helped me to tell you this. Can you stay a little longer? There's another problem – with Carlos."

He sat down again. "I can if you can. How do you feel?"

"Strange. Even after you arrived, my strongest urge was to go to bed, pull the covers over my head and cry myself to sleep. I feel physically sore, like I've been battered. So much emotion has been hurled at me the last few months, I can't take much more."

"Let's have some tea," he said, slipping his arm around my waist and guiding me to a stool at the kitchen bar.

Was it just hours ago Carlos and I were fixing dinner? Tears blurred my vision, melting the blue platters and mugs on the cupboard shelves, while Philip placed two mugs of water in the microwave.

"I'm in love with Carlos."

"That's no surprise. We thought so the last time he was here." He dropped bags of Earl Grey into the hot water.

"He doesn't love me." My eyes filled, as I swirled the dark liquid.

"It didn't look that way to us."

The cat clock on the kitchen wall struck midnight before Philip left. I explained my conversation with Carlos, but in the end my brother had no answers. "If he loves you, he'll find a way to understand without your explanation," was all he said.

There was nothing I could do but wait. All I could be sure of was I'd seen a part of him I'd never witnessed before. My thoughts turned steely and I felt a twinge of anger. Could Carlos be like Jared after all?

I pushed him from my mind and thought of my work. There were the plans for my own gallery and the looming payment deadline for Abdullah. Work was the best patience-maker I could think of. I slipped out of my clothes and into bed.

Late afternoon the next day, I called Muharrem. My hands shook as I made my first contact with Turkey, but Muharrem's eager voice chased away the boogeyman and I found myself responding to his upbeat voice.

"Mrs. Reardon? I have been worried."

"I'm well, my friend, and ready to work again. But first I want to thank you for everything you did for me. You have no idea how relieved I was that you saw the police take me from the airport."

"It was good fortune. I hear someone say the police are arresting an American woman. I ran fast and saw you."

My knees felt weak. I sat down on the edge of the sofa.

"I called Carlos first and he told me to contact your brothers and then the American Embassy. He said he would find out why you are arrested and he will take care of everything."

"Yes. Thank you. Everything is fine now." I never thought talking about Carlos, hearing his name, would have such an effect on me. It was an effort to keep my focus.

"Muharrem, I need your help. I'm going to open a gallery of my own in Philadelphia. The last time I was in Ankara, I purchased an inventory of rugs from Carlos and I'll need you to make arrangements to have them shipped here when I'm ready. Can you do that for me?"

"But-"

"It won't be right away. I must make arrangements here first."

I slumped to rest my head on a pillow.

"Yes, of course, but-"

I knew he didn't understand why I was asking him to make the contact. He was aware of my deepening relationship with Carlos, but I also knew no amount of curiosity would allow him to ask me about my personal life. Neither could I wait for my relationship with Carlos to straighten out before pulling my gallery plans together. Perhaps we'd never be together, but I wasn't going to think about that now. Making sure the rugs I purchased would be ready when I needed them was crucial. As things were, Muharrem had to make the arrangements.

"I'll call you within the next few weeks."

He sighed, obviously giving up on clearing his confusion. "Mrs. Reardon, will you come back to Turkey?"

Part of me wanted nothing to do with Turkey, but I couldn't deny the lure. It was a world of beauty and mystery. Still this was not the time to make any decision about future buying trips or – dread the thought – the need to find another rug broker with Carlos' contacts. I liked the way I was thinking. It proved to me I could be totally rational when I needed to be.

"Right now I must concentrate on opening the gallery."

When I finished talking to Muharrem, I turned immediately to my next task. Where should my search for a gallery location begin? I decided to talk to my old friend Sam Bezdikian, but as I reached for the phone, it rang.

It was Rosemary Fiori. "I'm glad you're home. Since I hadn't heard from you I was afraid you'd left on another buying trip. Have you thought about the things we discussed?"

The front door slammed and Skipper came in chatting, but he stopped quickly and settled on the floor next to me. He was doing exactly what he'd been taught to do, but I didn't want him in the room listening to my conversation with Dr. Fiori. I asked her to excuse me for a moment, held my hand over the mouthpiece, and asked Skipper to go to his room and I'd join him as soon as I was finished. When he was out of earshot, I continued.

"Yes, and you were more helpful than you know. I realize now there were some issues relating to Jared I'd never faced. You made things fall in place for me and I'm grateful."

"Oh, I'm so glad. It's only a beginning you know. Skipper needs-"

"He's doing very well. I think he's feeling happy and his schoolwork is excellent. I'll call you at the first sign of a change, but right now I have so much to do, I don't have time to make an appointment with you."

"Nora, we've only begun to understand what's going on with Skipper. It's a mistake not to follow up on his anger, for one thing, and-"

"Have you forgotten the reason I came to you in the first place? Look, he's okay. I'm his mother, I should know. If there's any change, I'll call you."

She wasn't happy with me, and I was just as convinced she could keep the sessions going for years. My life needed tending if I was going to support my child and myself, and I wasn't going to be sidetracked by Rosemary Fiori. She could find another garden to dig around in.

I put her out of my mind and dialed Sam Bezdikian to discuss ideas about a location for my gallery. Predictably, he had some words of warning.

"Location is primary, of course, but if you choose the Chestnut Street area where the Gordon's gallery is, you'll be cutting your own throat," he said.

"You mean I'd be competing, right?"

"Don't the Gordon's buy rugs from you?"

"Oh, I see where you're going. You think I'll be competing with myself."

"Glad you see that."

It was my turn to show off. "I'm also considering the Main Line, west of Philadelphia, but right now I think Chestnut Street is the better of the two locations. If it turns out to be my best choice, I'll discuss everything with Sylvia and Jacob at The Persian."

"They won't like it."

"Sure they will when I tell them it will increase their business." I stifled a chuckle.

"What? I'd sure like to know how you figure that."

"Well, I'm not ready to spell it out yet."

Fact was, I'd been reading some marketing studies that showed similar or related businesses benefit from clustering when properly executed. If I decided on Chestnut Street, I'd make sure it was and the Gordons would agree. I wrapped up our conversation and climbed the stairs to Skipper's room.

Three-dozen yellow roses dominated my entrance hall the following day. The attached card said, "I am a fool. Please forgive me, Carlos." Four days had passed since he turned his back on me and returned to Turkey. It still hurt to think about it. Now here he was with loving words and my favorite flowers. I decided to wait before responding to him, but by the next morning I found I couldn't wait.

"Thank God," he said. "I wasn't sure if you could forgive the stupid way I acted."

"I'll admit I was hurt."

"I was wrong, but please let me explain. When we are apart from each other, I tell myself it is only temporary, that being together is our normal state. Does that make sense to you?"

He didn't wait for my response and for several minutes the words kept coming. He explained his reaction had to do with loyalty – loyalty to family. Even though we were not yet an official family, that's how he thought of me. When I considered he might do anything to hurt me, the thought was inconceivable to him. It meant I didn't love him.

I told him I understood, but doubted my own words. There were things about his culture that were beyond my grasp, maybe always would be.

Carlos was sure we'd find the answers to the things that separated us, but while he talked my mind wandered to Skipper. Carlos had no idea about Dr. Fiori's revelations and what possible problems might be ahead. This was an aspect of my life Carlos barely knew about. They were fond of each other, but how would it be if Carlos were an equal partner in parenting? Would he be any help at all?

I wasn't holding up my end of the conversation, and finally Carlos said I should concentrate on the new gallery and call him if he could help.

"I will fill my mind with good thoughts for the future," he said.

The next day I called a commercial real estate agent to begin the search for a gallery location.

13

A few weeks later I was in trouble, working every day and sometimes well into the night. The demands of seeking a gallery location, maintaining my business, organizing inventory for the new gallery, and tending to Skipper's needs was unbearable. Since I never knew when I could get home, I decided a boarding school for Skip would be an ideal solution. I sought a recommendation from Claudine Caldwell. She was reluctant, but when I explained my problem, she proposed Baderwood Boarding School for Boys in Vermont.

Minutes later Rosemary Fiori called to tell me boarding school was a bad idea. There obviously were no stoplights along the school's information highway.

"It's a temporary fix, Rosemary. Bottom line is I can't give him the attention he needs right now, and I think being away from me will be good for him," I said.

"How do you figure?"

"He'll learn independence and he'll receive the best in academics."

"You've managed to hit on the two things he doesn't need."

The conversation ended abruptly after that, and I placed a call to Baderwood's registrar. In contrast to Rosemary, the registrar reaffirmed my decision.

A charter bus was scheduled to pick up children from the Philadelphia area in two days and my other activities were put on hold while I got Skipper ready. It didn't help that he was reluctant to go, but I assured him it was temporary and would be an adventure he could talk about with his friends when he got back. He handed me his favorite video game and left the room.

With three suitcases packed and lined up in the hallway, I called my brothers. I was sure they wouldn't like the idea of boarding school, but I wasn't prepared for their reaction.

"You don't deserve to be a mother," Val said. "You're sending him away so you can advance your career? Incredible."

I tried to interrupt, to tell him why my actions were necessary, but he shouted over me.

"What's wrong with you? And what about us? Don't we have anything to say about this?"

I held my tongue. Nothing I could say would change his thinking. I hoped Philip might listen but he, too, was upset. I could only hope they'd see the logic once they cooled down.

Skipper was dry eyed when I hugged him at the bus depot, which was more than I could say for myself. I watched him take a seat by the window and then I waved and waved until the driver pulled away. He stared at me but didn't reciprocate.

Skip had been gone barely a week when Sylvia and Jacob Gordon called.

"Nora, we just heard that you're looking for a gallery on Chestnut Street."

Jacob's voice was several decibels higher than normal. I braced myself, expecting him to be upset, but he said the news was an answer to their prayers.

"We've been thinking about retirement, but you know how it is – after thirty years, it's hard to give up. Knowing you're interested makes all the difference."

Relief swept over me. Finally something good had come along. With Skipper gone and my brothers keeping their distance, I felt like I was living in an isolation chamber. We hadn't spoken since we argued, and their silence hurt worse than the hateful words we'd exchanged. Jacob's voice was the lift my spirit needed. The details of the sale were quickly expedited. Even the necessary legalities were handled with smiles and handshakes. Within weeks painters and construction workers were filing in and out while I watched my dreams become reality.

My office was the first area completed and I began using the space despite hammering and sawing in the showroom. Outside the office window the sugar maple leaves glowed yellow, orange and red against a bright blue sky. Others, curled and brown, spun wildly over the Belgian cobblestones and piled up in the corners and basement window wells.

Each morning I parked my car in the rear alley, looked north where I had a clear view of the statue of William Penn atop the City Hall, and imagined him smiling at how his original design for the city had been safeguarded. Not only had the cobblestones been preserved, but also each shop had a pole in front for tying up a horse.

The office was disorganized, something I found hard to accept because it was rare that I allowed office minutia to get in the way of accomplishment. Maybe it was my mind's way of healing because I found myself daydreaming and wandering aimlessly around the gallery after the workers left for the day. There was no reason to rush home. The less time I spent alone, the better. Why not let the gallery absorb me completely? I rationalized that this was the culmination of a long-held dream and I deserved every minute of pleasure. But opening day was creeping closer and the pressure of unopened boxes and file folders was building. I bent to scoop up a scattered pile of customs forms when I heard the squeal of a truck stopping at the delivery door. While the driver climbed the steps, I pushed away from the papers and opened the door.

Once inside, the driver bent his knees slowly and set three heavy boxes on the storage room's freshly painted concrete floor, now a glossy rust color. I signed his clipboard and closed the door behind him, then I slit the tape on a box and pulled out an invitation. The saffron-colored vellum felt creamy and the smell of fresh ink tingled in my nose.

> "You are cordially invited to the opening of
> The Chestnut Street Persian Gallery
> Wednesday, October 16, 2002
> Five to nine o'clock
> Wine and Cheese"

I opened the folder. "Nora Reardon, sixteen years in the field, is pleased to present her unique collection of Oriental antique and revival carpets. The inventory includes a wide range of fabrics and weaving styles from Turkey, Iran, China, India, North Africa, and beyond."

Hans Holbein's portrait of George Gisze resting his arm on a brilliant Turkish kilim was printed in full color on the opposing side. Since my marketing strategy for the invitations included the arts community, I thought this juxtaposition of Oriental rugs and portraiture sent the right message.

My stomach clenched picturing the gallery filled to capacity with people running their hands over the silky nap of the Iranian prayer rugs from Isfahan and Qum. I walked to the alcove where my most valuable antiques were displayed, bathed in a color-enhancing light. From the day the rugs were hung, I could count on their magic for instant refreshment. My sanctuary. My family.

I sagged suddenly and decided to close up the gallery and go home. I wasn't accomplishing anything and the clutter could wait another day. Usually I left by the rear door where my car was parked, but tonight I descended the marble steps to admire my new front door – a honey colored, deeply carved oak with a beveled glass insert and gold lettering: "The Chestnut Street

Persian Gallery, Nora Reardon proprietor." Satisfied, I walked through the narrow side alley.

Once I entered the Schuylkill Expressway and increased speed, I lowered the windows and let the car fill with cold, fresh air. The wind's gentle tug on my hair was cleansing and sensual. I hadn't felt so free, so good, in months. My worries about meeting Abdullah's first payment had been put to rest. My accountant assured me rug sales were excellent, and when I called Abdullah with the good news, he said he'd come to the opening and bring along some friends to meet his newest American entrepreneur. There wasn't a reason in the world why I wouldn't be ready for opening day, despite the disorganization in my new office. The feeling of freedom and contentment overwhelmed me and I decided to spend the next day, Saturday, at home.

Routinely, I called Skip on Saturday mornings and, with fragrant coffee mist filling the kitchen, I took a final bite of marmalade-spread toast and punched in the numbers. This time the phone rang and rang without an answer. I was disappointed he didn't remember it was the time we'd agreed to talk, even though I had to admit our conversations were rarely satisfying. Invariably, I asked questions and he gave one-syllable answers in a tone that sent a clear message: He didn't want to talk to me. I placed the phone in its wall cradle and I told myself he might be busy doing things with the other boys. It would be good to know he was having fun.

14

October 16th was a cool Indian summer day that became a dry, crisp evening. At five o'clock I opened the front door of the gallery and stepped briefly onto the landing. In a few hours the stars would sparkle in an indigo sky outside the city; unfortunately, however, downtown lights would obscure the sight for my guests. Already, the sun cast long shadows across the brick buildings, accentuating the red clay in its glow and catching on the tidy rectangular shapes. The street lamps, with bulbs that shimmered like gas flames, sensed the diminishing light and cast their soft moons along the brick walkways.

At the end of the street a small group was headed toward me. I recognized the gait of old friends Sam and Esther Bezdikian.

"I wanted to be first. Am I?" My dear friend's ascent was slow, and he had trouble with his balance until the man behind him placed a steadying hand on his elbow. I made a mental note to install a handrail as soon as possible - a brass one, brilliantly polished.

"You are and there isn't anyone else I'd rather have to christen my first gallery." Sam's love and good wishes were just what I needed to chase away the winged creatures that had taken residence in my stomach.

Esther was with a man I didn't know. As the caterers dispatched their coats, Sam described him as a rising political figure in New York.

"One day Colin Feeney will occupy Gracie Mansion, you'll see," Sam said with a glance at his smiling friend and a wink for me. "Show him one of your exquisite Orientals for his office, while I look for your brothers. I haven't seen them in ages."

"Oh, they're not here, I mean, they couldn't come. They'll be sorry they missed you."

Sam frowned and studied my face. Fortunately, others arrived and I excused myself. I wasn't going to think about my brothers. Something would break the impasse. Something always did.

As we threaded our way around the bold Yüncü kilims, I saw Sam's friend run his hand over the silk Gördes prayer rugs. "Sam's right about what an Oriental can do for an office. Here, let me show you my special antique collection."

But before Mr. Feeney and I moved toward the alcove at the rear of the gallery, a large cohort of guests arrived, among them Abdullah El Ramil. He'd come with his wife, eight friends, and several magnums of Dom Perignon. Within minutes, he assembled my caterers and put them to work setting out flutes on trays and filling them with champagne. Then in his booming voice he called everyone to toast "a most remarkable woman whose beauty is surpassed only by her knowledge and ability. To your success." He raised his glass and swept his eyes around the room.

Everyone was looking at me. I felt my face flush and prayed it wasn't as red as my dress. The expression on Abdullah's face indicated his satisfaction that everyone in the room now knew who he was.

People milled around, foiling any attempt I made to count how many had come. The crowd was a mix of clients, old friends and promising new contacts. I tried with minimal success to collect business cards from those I didn't know so I could follow up with a phone call or perhaps a personal visit.

I'd begun to notice two very large men who were always near Sam's friend. They showed no interest whatsoever in the rugs – never even glanced at them. They had eyes only for the people. My curiosity peaked and the next time I was within whispering distance of Sam, I asked.

"Those two men arrived with your group," I said, nodding in their direction. "Do you know them?"

Sam frowned and leaned closer to me. "Colin's bodyguards – on him like leeches. And they're not the only ones here."

"What? You're kidding."

"Oh, yeah? Take a look at the man standing directly behind Abdullah and the big one on the right side. Now that you know, you can spot them, huh?"

"I can," I said and shivered.

At about eight-thirty I was speaking to a group about my hopes for the gallery when a movement at the door drew my attention. I blinked several times to be sure I was seeing Muharrem. He hesitated at the doorway and looked awkward and shy in the presence of so many strangers. I quickly waved at him and wrapped up my comments. "I promise a surprise every time you visit my gallery." Then I hurried to welcome him.

"Muharrem! What a wonderful surprise." A broad smile spread across his face and his hunched up shoulders relaxed. I'd sent him an invitation just to let him know what I was doing. I never dreamed he'd actually attend.

"I am in New York for a family sadness. My first time in your country." He moved his eyes from person to person, examining everyone and everything. It was typical behavior for him and possibly the reason he was so good at his job. He saw and heard everything, tucking it away for possible later use.

"I'm very happy to see you. Listen, can you stay for some coffee after the gallery closes?" I glanced at my watch. "In about half an hour? Then we can talk."

"I do not wish to keep your time, Mrs. Reardon."

"Oh, no, really I want to talk to you, if you have the time."

"Yes, of course. I will look at your rugs."

Laughter was building near the kilims where Abdullah stood with his friends. I walked over to join them, noticing that others were gathering around. He was a magnetic figure and he knew it. He gestured with both arms, taking in the entire showroom like an opera singer throwing his voice to the last person on the last row of the highest balcony.

"It is rare for an American to be fond of these variations in shades of the same color. You think they are errors, mistakes in the weaving, yes? We call it *'abrash'* and it is caused by dying yarn in small batches."

Heads nodded and a few murmured thoughtfully as they absorbed this new piece of information. Abdullah began to laugh again. "Do you think of *abrash* as a defect? The work of careless weavers?" There was a slight challenge in his voice, but his eyes sparkled. "Those who know these rugs recognize it as evidence the rug was made in a rural setting by village craftsmen following old traditions. It is there in the small villages where you can see the individuality and artistry of the weaver not found in the factories of the big cities."

I could see the images of his words in their eyes, and by the time the discussion ended, I imagined I could add several hundred dollars to the price tag for romance alone.

Meanwhile, the predicted future occupant of Gracie Mansion crossed the room with a practiced smile aimed at me. His bodyguards, about six feet to his left and right, maneuvered through the crowd in his wake. His black silk shirt and finely tailored slacks obeyed the movement of every joint in his lean body like they'd been sent to military school. He had pale skin and black hair that bore the grooves of the comb that had slicked it straight back and around his large ears.

My hands curled into fists. There was something in the way he walked toward me that raised the hair on my arms and neck.

"Sam's glowing description falls far short of the real thing, Mrs. Reardon." He placed his hand on my shoulder. It was a casual move and his touch was light, but my skin tightened. I swept the room looking for Sam. Under most circumstances, I trusted my first impressions of people, and my intuition was warning me. I managed a tentative smile and moved aside, forcing him to drop his hand.

"You've put together an exceptional gallery. I'm very impressed. I'm also very disappointed you never got around to showing me your antiques, as you promised."

"Oh, sorry. I was distracted by Abdullah's toast. Thank you, for your kind words. Are you interested in Oriental rugs, Mr. Feeney, or did Sam twist your arm to attend the opening?" The answer to either question would tell me more about him and I felt I needed the protection of information.

"A bit of both, in fact," he said. The smile fell from his mouth and his lips receded into a thin line. His hazel eyes, shrouded by thick brows, darkened.

I suddenly needed no confirmation of the discomfort I felt. I began to walk slowly in the direction of my last sighting of Sam and Esther.

He followed. "I'm building a summer home in Cape May, New Jersey. I need a place where I can get away from politics, if you know what I mean. I'll need rugs and I'm thinking you seem to have everything I need," he said, slowing down noticeably to emphasize the last few words.

Muharrem appeared out of nowhere. "Pardon me, Mrs. Reardon, the woman in the blue dress is asking questions about the North Persian Baksheesh rug and wonders if you can give her a moment of your time since she must leave soon."

"I'll call you and we'll make a date to get together, okay?" Feeney said. I gave him a quick nod, excused myself, and walked away with Muharrem.

"Please forgive me. The lady does not require your help, but I have never seen such a look on your face. Have I made a serious mistake?"

"How well you know me, my friend. I am in your debt. Thank you." Feeney and El Ramil weren't the only ones with a bodyguard. The thought made me smile.

I resolved to have a long talk with Sam before I made any contact with Colin Feeney in the future.

When the last guest left, I stood on the landing step and waved. I locked the door and invited Muharrem into my office. I'd been on my feet since early afternoon, but I felt satisfied and energized by the turnout. The only blot on the evening had been the disquieting episode with Feeney. Muharrem followed my lead and sat down. He said he couldn't stay more than a few minutes and I sensed he was concerned for me rather than for his own schedule.

"I'm afraid our coffee lacks the richness of Turkish coffee," I said, handing him a mug from the small service table near my desk. I was glad I had temporarily shoved all the clutter into the closet and tried to forget that it lurked just beyond the door.

"No, not at all. I like American coffee, Mrs. Reardon." He laughed and told me he'd recently tried adding Irish Cream and liked it even better that way.

"I think we have known each other long enough for you to call me Nora."

"Oh, yes, okay." Then he hesitated. "But not in Turkey, if that is acceptable."

"I understand." Turkish business customs required a certain formality, particularly between men and women, and the fact that I was a foreigner probably increased the need for ritual. It would cast doubt on Muharrem's credibility if he did anything that dishonored the expected formalities.

We sat in silence for a few moments while Muharrem took in every detail of the office and the showroom from where he sat.

"You said a sadness has brought you to New York?"

"Yes. I came to the funeral of my cousin. She was thirty-nine years old, four years older than me. Too young to leave the world, yes?"

"Much too young. I'm sorry, Muharrem."

"She was the daughter of my father's favorite brother. He had six brothers and twenty-three nieces and nephews. I came as my father's ambassador."

I remembered that Muharrem's father had not been well and asked about his health since the seizure last year.

"My father is again in the hospital. He is weak."

"I'm so sorry to hear that."

Sadness clouded his eyes, reminding me how upset he'd been in Ankara when he received the call about his father. That day he was torn between his duty to me and his need to be with his family. He quickly regained his composure, his face brightened and he turned back to look at me.

"Now, let me say your gallery is beautiful and the inventory is excellent. I think some is my credit. You will be successful definitely."

He had emptied his mug and I reached to take it from him, asking if he wanted a refill. My hand brushed his and he jumped to his feet.

"No, no. I must go now. Thank you for the very good coffee." He moved awkwardly to the door. It struck me as odd since one of the things I always noticed about Muharrem was his grace despite his size.

At the door he turned back to face me and I had the feeling I was about to hear the real reason for his visit.

15

Chestnut Street was empty except for the two of us standing on the marble landing. Shadows of trees and benches were imprinted along the walkways, dark and sharp-edged beneath the street lamps, pale and indistinct in the distance. As Muharrem stood facing me, the muscles on his cheeks twitched with words he was struggling to release.

"I have spoken to Carlos," he said.

"Yes?"

He took a step to the other side of the landing, a mere three feet from where he'd been. Something about the situation struck me as silly and I laughed. At first Muharrem was startled, but in seconds we were giggling together. Tears streamed down our faces. We laughed at our laughter, unable to stop, not really wanting to.

"I, ha, ha, ha, wanted, I mean I hope I am not rude, ha, ha, but I want to ask-"

"Look, Carlos and I were becoming more than friends." I swiped the tears from my cheeks. "Do you understand?" He nodded and looked relieved. But having gone that far, I wrestled with myself about what I should say. The truth was I felt unsettled about Carlos myself.

He took a breath. "Yes, but why do you no longer work with him?"

"The gallery required a great deal of work. For the present Carlos and I are friends only, and I think it's for the best." I hadn't really answered his question, but it was all I could think of to say.

"Of course. But we, you and I, will continue to work together in my country?"

"Oh, yes. It may be several months yet before I need to add to my warehouse inventory, but, yes, I'm sure we will."

He stepped heavily down the five steps to the walk, stopped, and turned around again. "I am sorry to keep you here in the cold air. Goodnight. Thank you for the coffee. Your gallery – it is excellent."

As I watched him walk toward the parking garage, I decided that his earlier question probably had more to do with my work with him in Turkey than with Carlos. My mind was still spinning from the dance I'd done. I loved Carlos, but my love made me vulnerable to hurt and I'd had enough of that. Muharrem was intuitive. Once he'd had time to think about our conversation he'd understand that I'd told him all I could. So why did I feel so sad? Watching Muharrem walking away, I realized I hated to see him go. When was the last time I'd laughed or really enjoyed being with someone? I wanted to spend more time getting to know him now that we'd made a move from a strictly professional relationship. I called out to him.

My voice startled him and he turned and stood still for several seconds before he walked back.

"When do you return to Turkey?"

"My flight is the day after tomorrow," he said.

"Oh, that's good. May I take you to dinner tomorrow? It'll be my way to thank you for coming to the opening." Again the muscles on his face were working out the words to use.

"Eh, well, yes. I wanted to experience an American restaurant, but my family insisted I stay with them and I could not refuse." His face lit up. "Can we have pizza?"

I laughed again. He was approximately my age, but at that moment he looked like a teenager. "Yes, of course, if that's

what you'd like. There's a pizzeria within walking distance of
here. Can you be here at about six o'clock when I close the
gallery?"

He nodded, turned, and walked at a quicker pace than before.
A shiver of apprehension darted through my body. I'd acted on
impulse, not my usual comportment. And I'd shocked
Muharrem, I was sure. He had the uncanny ability to sense
mood, most likely a natural gift enhanced by witnessing hours
of negotiation.

I locked the doors to the gallery and drove home thinking
about Carlos. Like the lurking clutter in my office closet,
Carlos was tucked away behind activities at the gallery. A
month had passed and I hadn't called him.

In the morning, energized and excited, I began to contact the
new prospects, an activity I especially enjoyed. It meant new
business opportunities would walk through the front door, the
door that told the world Nora Reardon was a proprietor.
Sometimes I felt if the rugs could talk, I'd need nothing else in
the world. They never disappointed me, and they never hurt.

When Muharrem arrived that evening, there were three
customers in the gallery – all neighboring shop owners who
came to welcome me. When they left Muharrem and I walked
east on Chestnut and turned south at Seventeenth Street to
Costanza's Pizzeria. We were seated next to a mural of a
Venetian canal, complete with gondola. The scene was
peaceful but the restaurant vibrated with loud voices, rushing
servers and kitchen clatter. Mandolin music poured from a
speaker over our heads.

A wedding party was celebrating in an adjacent room. I
thought it might be too chaotic for Muharrem, but one glance
at him put my mind at ease. He was mesmerized. He craned to
see the wedding party. Then he stared at the teenagers – the
owner's sons – tossing pizza dough at each other.

"It is a game?" he shouted.

"No. Actually it stretches the pizza dough." The aroma of baking crust and spicy tomato sauce saturated the air. Each table had a candle set in an empty wine bottle with no attempt to stem the flow of candle wax. Over the years the wax had dripped in layers over the bottles, locking them in place and forming a puddle on the tables where lovers carved their initials.

The wedding party spilled noisily into the main dining room and people exploded with applause and shouts of "good luck" and "There's still time to change your mind." Muharrem was beaming.

"Do you have a large family?" I said.

"I believe you will think it is large, but for us it is typical – three younger sisters and three older brothers. I have thirteen nieces and nephews. My wife and I are under much pressure to have children."

Our pizza arrived and for the next few minutes we were busy eating and laughing. It gave me time to puzzle over the fact that Muharrem was married. Had he ever mentioned his wife to me? Possibly he had and I took no notice.

The restaurant was emptying except for several couples and someone had turned down the volume on the music. Muharrem refilled our glasses with the last of the wine and our waitress brought a stack of pizzels to the table. To Muharrem's questioning look, I explained the anise-flavored cookies were an Italian specialty.

"Hmmm, very good," he said. His tongue lashed out around his lips to retrieve some crumbs.

We finished the pizza except for three slices.

"Wanna take this with you?" our waitress said.

"Is that acceptable?" he said looking at me.

"Sure. They'll wrap it for you. Your family can reheat it or someone may eat it cold." Jared had loved leftover pizza for breakfast. The memory didn't pinch, just made me aware that he'd always be with me one way or another.

Muharrem nodded and we left a few minutes later. He carried his foil-wrapped American pizza in both hands like a treasure. When we reached his car in the parking garage, he insisted on driving me to my car in the narrow alley behind the gallery.

"That was fun," he said. "Muharrem's American pizza experience."

After we parted I found myself thinking of my next trip to Turkey.

The following Saturday was clear, cool and minus the howling wind that had banged at the window shutters on the outside deck and stripped the trees of their last few leaves. I pulled on a warm jacket after breakfast and went for a walk.

I'd hired a part-time salesman. Ed Gallo worked many years with the Gordons and, when he learned they were thinking of selling, Ed said he'd retire as well. But when I offered him a job, he jumped at the chance and gave me two weekdays and Saturdays. He was flexible, knowledgeable, and familiar with many clients. His employment freed me up to tend to other matters, although I ended up in the gallery for one reason or another on most weekends. I hoped the necessity would gradually lessen so I could visit Skipper.

At the corner I met the Denbys heading for the park. Marty and Jack ran to the swings and Carolyn and I found an empty bench within sight of the playground.

"How's Skipper doing? We miss him."

"Fine. I miss him too, but I've just opened a gallery on Chestnut Street, and I was so busy I thought it best to enroll him in a boarding school – Baderwood. It's in Vermont and he's doing beautifully." He'd probably be a full grade ahead of Marty when he returned, I thought. I bit my lip and eyed the dandelions at my feet.

"Exciting – the gallery, I mean. I'll stop in the next time I'm in town. I'd really like to see it. In fact Jack and I have been talking about replacing that threadbare monstrosity in our living room. An Oriental would look great."

I chopped my heel against the roots of the dandelion until it lay on its side with clumps of earth dangling from the upended roots.

"Let me know when you're coming."

"Will Skipper be home for Thanksgiving?" she said.

"Yes." Suddenly I remembered I'd forgotten to call Skipper at our appointed time. I stood. "When I get back to the house I'll call him and talk about that." I pictured Skipper and me alone at the table. I still hadn't spoken to my brothers. It was time we broke the ice and I resolved to make that call before the day was over.

"Will you and Jack be going to his folks for the usual family Thanksgiving get together?" I said.

"Not this year."

"Why don't you have Thanksgiving with us? Skipper would love it and it'll be fun," I said.

"We'd really like that." She turned away from me and shouted. "Marty, Jack, come here."

Half an hour later I walked home, excited to tell Skipper about Thanksgiving. But again he wasn't in his room, and I was more disappointed than usual because I wanted to give him some news that might elicit more than his usual one-syllable responses. I decided to call my brothers.

Val answered. He was genuinely glad to hear from me and said they'd been discussing how to "mend our fences." I told him I'd been feeling the same way. He invited me to have an early lunch with them and I agreed.

When I arrived, Val greeted me with tears in his eyes.

"This month has been hell for us. We never want to experience another separation like this again," Val said.

Philip waved me to a chair. "Come, sit down. We want to tell you something," The air in the room felt heavy. I sat on one of their kitchen chairs and they flanked me.

"Do you ever think about how it was when Mama and Papa died?" Val said.

"Why are you bringing that up? I don't want to talk about it."

"I know. You never wanted to talk about it," Philip said. "After it happened, you closed yourself in your room for days at a time. Then he told me Val had had a breakdown and spent weeks in a special clinic being treated for depression.

"Why didn't you ever tell me this?"

"I did tell you - you didn't want to know," Philip said.

"I'm sorry, Val." I looked down at my hands. What else had I buried or denied or forgotten about those frightening days? Did I want to know, even now?

We sat in silence until Philip sighed and started preparing lunch. I watched him, but my memory was traveling back and I couldn't stop it. I saw myself running up the stairs to my room, slamming the door. I flung the window open and let the blast of cold air lift the curtain and plaster it to my face. I didn't push it aside; I confronted it with words, swearing I'd never work for anyone but myself. No one was going to fire me and ruin my life.

The clatter of the dish Philip set in front of me closed the scene. It was several minutes before my anger faded though. I don't remember eating lunch, but I pushed myself back from the table feeling full. We talked about the old neighborhood, school friends, Christmas and Thanksgiving dinners.

"Oh, yes, about Thanksgiving. Skipper will be home for five days and I want it to be very special for him. I've invited the Denbys to join us. I thought Skip would like that, and he'll want his favorite uncles. Can you come?"

"Of course," Philip said. "Let's go in the living room. We saw Skip last week. He looked well."

My face flushed. "It's great that you could get up there to see him. Things are finally slowing down for me and I hope to visit him soon. At least we talk to each other every Saturday."

I reached home at two o'clock and opened the door to the discordant counterpoint of the phone and chimes from the grandfather clock in the entrance hall. The male voice on the phone turned the warm glow of the afternoon to ice. He identified himself as a detective from the Canaan Valley County Police in Vermont. He asked me if Thomas Reardon was my son.

"Yes, what's wrong? Is he all right?"

"He's been reported missing."

16

The kitchen stool behind me screeched on the tile floor as my weight settled against it.

"Missing? How can he be missing?" I pulled the stool closer and sat on it, gripping the phone with one hand and sliding forward on my elbows. A chill spread across my chest.

"I'm so sorry, Mrs. Reardon. Baderwood's principal told me he'd call you. I just needed, ah, wanted to ask you some questions," he said.

I pictured a young man who had stumbled into unfamiliar emotional territory.

"Look, are you sure of your facts? I've been out. I just got home." I glanced at the answering machine and saw the blinking light. "How do you know he's missing? He couldn't leave the school without anyone knowing. This doesn't make sense."

The answering machine was persistent, a red pulse that delivered its own message.

"Mrs. Reardon?"

"Yes, yes, I'm listening." But I wasn't. I was picturing Skipper, seeing his eyes watching me from the bus.

"Mrs. Reardon, my name is Hank Biel. I suggest you call the school. I'll call again later, or perhaps tomorrow," he said.

"Fine, you do that." I slammed the phone against the cradle on the wall and pressed the "Play" button. The sharp, precise voice of Samuel Pritchard, Baderwood's principal, was suddenly in my unwilling ears. He said there was a problem and asked me to call as soon as possible.

I dialed the number. Dr. Pritchard was immediately on the line. He explained that Skipper had had breakfast and then returned to his room to prepare for an overnight camping trip with ten classmates. They were bussed fifteen miles north to Campbell Campground in the Green Mountains, a location the teachers used for biology and ecology projects, as well as for recreation. He disappeared while they were setting up the tents. The police had been alerted, and everything possible was being done to locate him. A search and rescue team would begin canvassing the campground and surrounding areas very soon.

His words gathered like rocks until I felt too heavy to stand.

"Excuse me, Dr. Pritchard. I'm going to the campground. I'll leave soon. It will take me about four hours." He gave me directions and said he'd meet me at the campground administration building where the search team had set up a communication center.

I needed just a moment to get hold of myself and think. I reached into the refrigerator for cold water and saw the pitcher behind several containers. I pulled each out, setting them on the counter without looking. There was a sharp crack and I spun around to see what I'd done. Thick tomato juice spread among shiny, sharp splinters and made trickling sounds at the drain. I stared at the slow-moving liquid spreading over the white porcelain and heard a singsong voice: "little cuts, little cuts, little cuts." I blinked at the sight of blood in the sink until my eyes denied the blood and saw the tomato juice.

Perhaps the dribbling sound imitated a voice or my mind was playing tricks, but the voice was familiar. Suddenly I gagged on the smell of tomato juice and backed out of the kitchen until the sensation passed. I dashed upstairs to my room and dialed my brothers.

Val shouted to Philip to pick up another phone so I could tell them everything I knew. Val immediately said he'd drive me to Vermont. He ran off to prepare, telling me he'd pick me up soon. Philip stayed on the line.

"Skip and I have talked about this very thing." He recounted a conversation they'd had in a crowded mall about what to do if ever he were lost. "I told him 'Just stay put. I'll retrace my steps and find you.' He'll remember that. They'll find him. Try not to worry."

In the background, I heard Val shout and a door slam. He'd be with me in about twenty minutes. I hung up and packed a small overnight bag and prayed I wouldn't need it. Skipper, alone in the mountains. It was unimaginable. I blinked away a scene of him huddled between large boulders, covered with leaves to keep warm, and I ran to the front door to wait for Val. They'd probably already found him. Twenty minutes felt like an hour.

Once in the car, Val handed me a map.

"I've driven these roads hundreds of times. Just help me watch for turnoffs," he said with uncharacteristic calmness. Perhaps this was Val, the engineer. The one I'd never taken time to know.

We drove without conversation, keeping our worries to ourselves. The road spread out in front of us like an endless treadmill. It was better to watch the passing landscape and confirm we were moving forward than deal with what was going on in my head. Skipper alone, lost. And the horrible vision I'd seen in the sink. I shook my head and let the hills, rocks, trees, and the occasional suburban development catch my attention. Children played on backyard jungle gyms, men maneuvered lawn mowers, women bent over flower gardens, a lineman worked at the crossbar atop a telephone pole. For a few seconds I was distracted until I saw a small boy standing alone, apart from his family, and I remembered.

Where was Skipper? How could this happen? Did the chaperones just let the children wander around in the woods? I made up my mind to find out how a child could get lost on a school outing. For now, though, my anger at the school was second to my fear for Skipper. Was he injured and unable to return to the campsite? I suddenly jerked with a new thought. Were there bears or mountain lions in the Green Mountains?

"Are you cold?" Val said, fingers already on the car's heating controls.

"No, I'm fine. Look, there's the first sign for Albany. We need to watch for Route 7 east to Baderwood. From there we'll use the directions to the campground that Dr. Pritchard gave me."

I looked at my watch to confirm what the long shadows already indicated. It was late afternoon. Oh, God, let them find him before dark. It was cold now. What would it be like in a few hours?

"Baderwood came highly recommended. I don't understand how they can lose a child in the woods," I said.

"I've been asking the same question and I want an answer. This should never happen, never. But, I think what we need to do is take one thing at a time, and right now we've got to find Skipper. We can think about the school later."

"Yeah." The old Val would have been all over me about the school, blaming me for insufficient research or something. Was he right? I took someone's recommendation without checking the school out myself. And I never took Skipper to see what his reaction might be. It hurt to acknowledge what I considered efficiency was perhaps recklessness. If I'd discussed my plans with my brothers, would I have done a better job? Well, if Val could change, so could I. Instead of recrimination, what I felt now was companionship. I reached over to take his hand. He responded with a squeeze.

We were on a small two-lane road that needed repaving. The potholes frustrated Val, and for a few moments the old impatience resurfaced. We had to slow down to a crawl or risk breaking an axle. An accident on this road would be disastrous; there wasn't a building in sight.

Finally the sign to the Campbell Campground came in view. We pulled in, turning too sharply, and slid several feet in the gravel. Up ahead, cars, vans and trucks were parked helter-skelter. Uniformed men and women stood in animated groups gesturing and pointing into the woods. My eyes followed a man into the evergreen ocean. In seconds he drowned.

A man in dark blue walked toward us. Val lowered his window.

"Sorry, sir, you can't park here," he said when Val lowered the window.

"I'm the boy's mother," I yelled.

There was a knock on my window and I spun around to face the ruddy cheeks of a young police officer.

"Are you Thomas' mother? I've been watching for Pennsylvania plates. I'm Hank. I spoke to you on the phone. I'm with the police, the Missing Persons Bureau." He opened the car door and offered me a firm, reassuring grip. Val and I followed him to a log cabin larger than all the others along the road. The sign over the porch said: "Campbell Campground Administration, Welcome." A huge stack of cut firewood at one side of the oversized door and a row of well-worn rocking chairs stretching along the other testified to the seasonal extremes of Vermont. I would have traded either for my present season of despair. Hank pulled back a large metal latch and opened the door, exposing a boil of brown park service uniforms and orange-vested search and rescue workers. Voices crackled over radios, filling the air with palpable electricity.

"We have fifteen teams of three officers each fanned out over a three-mile radius from the school's campsite," Hank said, pulling the door closed behind him. "They've been out for more than an hour. Don't worry, we'll find your Thomas, Mrs. Reardon. How far could a seven year old travel?" His smile was weak.

"Skipper, we call him Skipper," I said.

He was immediately alert. "That's information we should have had from the beginning," he said with the first show of authority I'd seen. He moved quickly to the man on the radio.

"Look, I can't just stand here. I want to do something," I said.

"Let the experts handle this, Nora." It was Val's new voice.

"But we could be another two sets of eyes, another two pairs of ears. We could help. I can't stand the waiting."

Hank returned in time to hear the debate. He nudged us into a small, side office and closed the door.

Shut off from the clamor of voices in the outer room, I felt an even deeper separation from Skipper. I needed to run through the woods screaming his name. No mother could sit quietly while her child...

"Mrs. Reardon, if you rush off into the woods – woods I might add you are totally unfamiliar with – we'll soon be looking for you as well as your son." He was looking at me kindly but his tone belied his boyish face and my initial impression of him.

"You might disturb evidence that could give us clues to Skipper's direction." He saw that I was listening and he hammered out his points. A small green twig was stuck under the metal police badge on his chest, and as I stepped back I noticed flecks of earth on his shoulders and ears. So Hank was not one to stand back and allow others to do the work that had to be done. I felt a new surge of confidence in him.

"What's more, if you stay here at the communications center, you'll be aware of everything as it happens. Out there, alone, you'll know nothing except what you can see yourself. Am I getting through to you?"

I smelled the redwood boards that formed the cabin, looked around at the well-worn government-issue furnishings - metal desk, vinyl-upholstered swivel chair, and wall posters of Smokey the Bear's pleading platitudes. Finally, I nodded my agreement. He returned my answer with an encouraging grin and a thumbs-up.

"Good. Let's go get an update," he said.

For several minutes he gathered groups together and barked out new instructions. His arms and hands swiped through the air, mapping the outdoors as if it were present in the room. Val and I took seats against the wall and for the first time I registered the heat and the smell of sweating bodies. Outside, the forest was darkening and I thought I saw flashlights blinking among the trees.

The front door opened and a man and woman dressed in business clothes entered. They swept the room with their eyes and settled on us. They threaded their way across the room carrying several small bags between them.

"Mrs. Reardon? I'm Dr. Pritchard."

He reached for my hand. "And this is Grace Cummings, the school's psychologist. We thought you might not have had time to eat so we brought some food." He set the bags on the floor. "I'm sorry I wasn't here when you arrived. I stopped to pick up Grace because when they find Skipper, she'll be helpful. Is there some place quieter we can go?"

Val reopened the small office and we pulled four chairs up to the desk. They unwrapped sandwiches and lifted the lids on beverages. The cool sweetness of the soft drink was welcome and I thanked them for their thoughtfulness.

I couldn't eat – my stomach was knotted – but between bites of her sandwich Grace Cummings talked about the school's policy of attentiveness to new students.

"Your son – Skipper is it? I overheard someone call him that as we walked through the cabin."

"Yes."

"Odd he didn't correct us. We've called him Thomas from the day of his arrival. You weren't with him as I recall."

I wasn't paying attention. My ears and mind were in the next room. The voices were like a roar on the other side of the wall. I moved to the edge of my chair.

"Skipper is an above average student. I believe his teachers have kept you informed?" Her eyes begged me to sit back and listen. Whether I liked it or not, I was in the hands of another school psychologist. Cummings, Fiori, they knew how to "handle" distraught parents. Mentally, I was ready to bolt through the door, but physically - and this was the decision-maker - my legs felt heavy and lifeless. I placed my hands in my lap and waited for her next comment.

"Tell me, Mrs. Reardon, does Skipper make friends easily?"

"No, he doesn't. He's selective," I said, moving to the edge of the chair again.

"I thought as much," she said. She exchanged a knowing look with Dr. Pritchard.

"Is there a problem? Are you telling me Skipper has a problem? Let me tell you, Skipper is selective because he's been taught to choose his friends carefully."

"Good advice, of course," Dr. Pritchard said.

He was prim and stiff. I wondered how many friends he attracted. I hung my head and took a breath.

"Skipper has many good friends in Philadelphia, some he's had since preschool. It takes time to develop friends." I didn't want to be rude. They were trying to help, to find out information about Skipper, but it was so hard to sit still.

"One of the reasons I recommended that Skipper attend this overnight camp was to help him make friends in a smaller group setting," she said. "He hasn't taken part in any extracurricular activities since he arrived, and I felt he was spending too much time alone."

"Yes, and now look at what's happened." I got up and walked to the door. Why did she have to say that? Why did people make decisions about Skipper, come to conclusions about him without asking me? "Excuse me, but I want to know what's going on."

In the outer office, Hank and two other men were working with a large map that covered the desk and spilled over onto the floor. When Hank saw me, he motioned me to join them. His fingers jabbed at red pins.

"These markings indicate the area already covered. The orange pins are members of the search and rescue team. It's getting hard to see out there and the woods and large boulders in this area make it tough to bring in searchlights."

"What's here?" I said, pointing to a large area without orange pins. "Why aren't there any searchers there?"

"We plan to investigate that area more closely in the morning, that is, if we don't locate Skipper tonight."

I winced and Hank quickly added, "We're not giving up but-"

"Yes, I understand, but what's there?"

"Caves. They've been searched briefly, of course. We know the openings are small and we don't know how far the caves extend, but no kid would crawl into a dark cave. I'm thinking he's hurt, maybe knocked out from a fall or something." He rubbed the fine blond stubble on his chin.

He seemed confident, sure of his assessment, but as I pictured the caves my mind suddenly flooded with Fiori's comments about Jared disciplining Skipper in dark, solitary places. Anger at Jared surged anew and I turned to Hank.

"Hank, please, could you search that area now?" I said. "Skipper is, ah, well, he's used to playing in small tight areas." I tried to keep my voice as level as I could, but I was beginning to tremble. "I know it's an unusual trait, but maybe he was curious. Maybe he wanted a private place to play," I added.

"Mrs. Reardon, children who are lost and frightened don't crawl into caves, especially bright ones like Skipper," said Grace Cummings, who had joined us.

I turned to look at her, tempted to tell her to mind her own business. But if Skipper were lost, it was true he would know better than to crawl into a cave, so if he did, there must have been another reason. Suddenly, the trembling worked its way outward and I wrapped my arms around my waist. Hank noticed. Several different expressions rippled over his face, finally hardening as his eyes narrowed with a new thought.

"Is there any reason for us to think Skipper might not want to be found?" he asked.

"Could Skipper's behavior be considered depression?" Dr. Pritchard said, glancing first at Grace and then at me.

Hank studied my face, then snapped around and shouted: "Doug, Allen, Carol Ann – get out the caving gear. We're going in tonight. And call in for more light. We'll have to use the towers. You know what to do. Quick now." He was spinning around, shouting orders. The room exploded with activity and people poured out the door while another man sent out a message over the radio to pull half of the teams into the cave area and double the search area for the remaining half.

I had moved to the wall, not just to get out of the way, but also to find Val, bury my head in his chest and try to swallow the lump in my throat. But when I closed my eyes I saw thick red blood flowing on white porcelain. I pushed away from Val.

"Take it easy, Nora. They're doing everything they can."

I nodded and turned away to look out a window and saw my own reflection against the blackness – my mouth tight, my eyes shining. The fear I felt for Skipper showed. It was enough for now. I'd deal with the blood later. God, help me to deal. Could Skipper have run away? Did he hate the school so much? He'd always loved school.

Val and I backed up against the wall while everyone seemed to have an assignment, a mission, a place to be. It was like being in the eye of a hurricane. I covered my face and prayed to be swept up and carried out to sea to float on the foam and, if Skipper weren't found, to sink slowly to the bottom. Time was suspended. It hung in the air, heavy and motionless. Or was it my will that time would pass only with good news and until then it had no purpose?

The room emptied except for three men at the radios. In frustration, Val and I walked outside, desperate to be part of whatever was being done. Then Hank beckoned to us from inside a jeep. We headed into the forest following a pale, narrow trail. Ahead, an area of forest glowed like a ghostly bubble erupting from the damp, musty earth. As we got closer we saw twenty-foot towers topped by beacons crisscrossing each other, merging into one single illumination until rocks, trees, and ferns emerged in all their colorful daytime detail.

Search and rescue vehicles arrived and discharged men and women, among them I recognized several who had been in the cabin.

"It won't take long to prepare the gear. Then they'll split up and go in," Hank said. "They'll go in with light and cable ladders – that's just in case there are any vertical drops – and, well, they'll be prepared. That's the main thing you need to know."

He was doing his best to explain. He knew the unspoken possibilities would be harder to hear – so did I.

Could Skipper hear them coming with the ropes scraping the ground, dragging along loose stones that scattered and clicked like mad hard-shelled insects? Or could he see their helmet lamps breaking into the darkness of the cave? I couldn't believe he wouldn't want to be found. Even if he didn't like the other students, even if he didn't want to be at the school, he wouldn't. No, he had wandered away and got curious about the caves. What seven-year-old boy could resist the adventure?

"Oh, I forgot to mention, radios will not operate underground so there may be some time between messages," Hank said. But at that moment a male voice broke in. The crackling made it hard for me to make out the words, but Hank understood. He shouted for Carol Ann who came running. Ropes slapped at her side and metal links of various sizes clanked around her waist. She looked barely a hundred pounds, yet she moved with strong, sure strides.

"Doug says cave three narrows and it looks like there's a drop. He can't get through but he thinks you can. Tell him to rig a cable ladder and have it ready for you to pull through."

She nodded quickly and took off at a run with her gear banging against her body and her booted feet thudding heavily against the ground.

The radio crackled again. This time I understood the voice. Caves one and two had been cleared. No sign of Skipper. Hank began to speak, but I let him know I understood.

"It'll be slow going for Carol Ann if she needs to belly in, but no one is better than that gal. She's experienced and never gives up 'til the job's done."

We waited. I imagined Carol Ann crawling into the cave, pulling the ropes along. Suppose it was too narrow for her, suppose the ropes tangled and trapped her. No one would be able to reach her. I looked at Hank, opened my mouth, and he read my thoughts.

"She's wearing a harness attached to a rope outside the cave. If she gets stuck and can't turn around, she'll signal and the guys at the mouth of the cave will give her the extra power to back up," he said.

I nodded, dumb and numb, just imagining her small, dirt-covered body, compressed by rock on all sides, inching her way forward to what? She didn't know.

"Report," Hank shouted into the radio after what seemed an eternity of silence.

"We're still letting out rope, so she's still moving forward. Wait. She's stopped."

I grabbed Val's arm. "Why doesn't she tell us what she sees?" I said.

"She can't. Phones won't work underground, remember? She could have stopped for any number of reasons," Hank said, launching into several possible scenarios.

I raised my hand. "Okay." My head was pounding from the tension and the alternating images of Carol Ann crawling and Skipper trapped, or hurt, or terrified. It was all I could bear. It was enough to stand upright and feel my heart and head pounding.

An unbearable twenty minutes passed, confirmed by my watch. Reports came in from the other caves searched and found empty. Two caves had ended in vertical drops with water at the bottom. Another unwelcome image. Nothing from Carol Ann.

Their work completed, workers began to group outside the remaining cave. Hank allowed us to go with him to join them but cautioned that depending on what was needed, we might have to move back out of the way. His words made me edgy but I didn't want to know what he meant, and from Val's silence I imagined he felt the same.

Glancing at my watch had become an obsession. I knew it but couldn't stop myself and when half an hour passed, my arms and legs felt like rubber.

"Why is it taking so much longer in this cave than the others? How do you know something hasn't happened to Carol Ann?"

Hank turned and snapped, "We don't. But I know Carol Ann and she's the best we have. I want to give her a bit more time."

"There's the signal. She's coming out," someone shouted.

All eyes were on the small opening while men gathered the rope, the rope that held Carol Ann on its other end. I prayed she was bringing Skipper with her. Slowly the cave's black mouth glowed and Carol Ann emerged. Workers rushed forward to reach her and pull her to her feet. I held my breath, watched her turn around, kneel, and extend her hand inside the cave.

17

Minutes ago there were sounds in the forest. The last few stalwart crickets were chirping in a sluggish chorus from their crevices in the leafy flooring. Overhead, clusters of dried curled oak leaves rattled in the wind and wagged like scolding sprites momentarily distracted from their inevitable plunge. Rescue workers chatted in groups and, occasionally, a voice lifted above the others and barked a command.

Now the sounds of life were ruptured. It amazed me that one could ask the world to stop and it would. I saw Carol Ann reduced and distant, captured in a circle, a vision from the reverse end of a telescope. When finally the cave's mouth expelled Skipper, a barrier shattered and released not only sound but also senses. I shouted to him.

He turned toward me. Did he recognize my voice among the strangers? Was he happy to see me? There was no sign. Perhaps the bright tower lights blinded him temporarily. Carol Ann released his hand and bent to say something to him. But I couldn't wait for him to regain his sight. I ran and wrapped my arms around him. His down-filled jacket was cold to the touch, but when I grabbed his hands they were warm.

"You're not hurt?" I said. I aimed my question at both of them. Skipper didn't say anything and Carol Ann's face reflected my own puzzlement. I wanted to shout with relief that he'd been found uninjured, but instead the fear I felt earlier was creeping back.

"Skipper?" I pulled back to look at him. He turned away from me.

"He started crying when I found him," she said, breaking the silence. "I thought he was hurt, but he seems fine. He didn't want to come out and the more I coaxed, well, he got angry."

Grace Cummings had moved alongside our small cluster at the mouth of the cave. She motioned Carol Ann away from Skipper and I heard her ask: "How'd you get him to come with you?"

"I stopped coaxing him and just started telling him about Ginny, my little girl, and how she was waiting for me to come home. I told him I wasn't going to leave him and before very long my boss would be sending someone in the cave to look for me. He told me he wouldn't go back to school so I just promised him everything would be okay. That's when he finally agreed he'd come with me."

"We should take him home now," Val said, reaching out to put a blanket around Skip's shoulders.

"Sorry, but the medics need to check him out first," Carol Ann said.

I hadn't noticed the four emergency medical technicians standing by with a gurney. When Carol Ann nodded, they lifted Skipper, covered him with a blanket and secured him with straps. He frowned at the straps and looked frightened. I grasped the side of the gurney and looked at my son full in the face. Other than a small red scrape on his forehead and a dusting of brown earth everywhere on his skin and clothing, he appeared unharmed. His lips were tightly pursed. I knew he didn't like to cry but his eyes betrayed him and I sensed the tears just behind his stare. I patted his chest and gave him a smile.

"He seems fine, I mean, a little shook up, but no injuries. They'll probably release him to you right away, don't you think?" Hank's voice barely registered with me. I stumbled along trying to keep up with the receding gurney and its small burden, maintaining the connection to my son in spite of the orange-vested rescue workers who interrupted with their armloads of equipment. Tower lights were coming down and trucks were pulling in closer for loading. The tension-fused atmosphere of less than an hour ago was now a whirlwind of dismantling, packing and coiling.

I looked around, taking in the scene, knowing it would be imprinted forever. What mark would we leave behind? When we were gone, the blades of grass would rise with the sun, the birds would return to sing their songs to each other and order would be restored. One rainfall and even the tire tracks and footprints would disappear. It would take more than sun and songbirds to restore us.

I felt everyone's eyes on me, looks that reflected more than concern. They didn't understand what had happened any more than I did. Another vision played in my head: Skipper emerging from the cave, running to me, crying and clinging to me, happy to be safe in his mother's arms. But that's not what happened. Skipper didn't want to be found and he didn't want me. Did he hate the school so much? Did he hate me for sending him there?

What were the rescue workers thinking? It was my fault? It was the school's job to supervise the children in their care. How could I know Skipper would wander off and crawl into a cave? If they'd waited until morning, he might be... What did they know?

The doors of the ambulance slammed and the siren sounded as they moved forward. Several of the trucks were pulling out. One tower light remained, casting its circular beam onto a rock strewn clearing. Elsewhere the forest had already returned to its hiding place. We reached our car just as headlights swept past us with red lights flashing. I reached for the car door and saw blood in the sink and I heard "little cuts, little cuts, little cuts." Oh, God, that voice. Who? So familiar. And then I knew.

"It was Mama, Val, Mama."

"What? Nora, take it easy. This has been a horrible day, but it's okay now," he said.

"No, Mama cut herself." I turned around and grabbed his arms.

"What are you talking about?"

"Skipper? Where's Skipper?"

"He's in the ambulance, going to the hospital. They want to check him to make sure he's okay. Then we can take him home. Come on, get in the car."

"Are you okay, Mrs. Reardon?" Hank's hand was on my elbow. "They can give you something at the hospital, something to help you get through this."

I nodded and we got into our cars as the ambulance left the circle of artificial light and moved onto the road. The flashing red lights blinked intermittently through the trees.

St. Bernadette of the Shrine Hospital was a sanctuary of quiet efficiency. Just inside the door, a nun sat statue-like in a cubicle and nurses in pale gray jumpers and white shoes moved about their work, taking time to glance and smile at us comfortingly whenever they passed. We sat on rose-colored upholstered chairs that faced a large tropical fish tank in the center of the room.

A stained glass window of Jesus at prayer occupied the wall next to the lobby door. His body was curved over a huge boulder – soft, vulnerable flesh opposed by hard, unyielding stone. In that muted, sunless state, the message was one of anticipation – Jesus waiting for God, the window waiting for the rising sun. I tried to imagine the colors that would splash out on the marble floor during the day and shout that all things were possible.

"Nora, what did you mean when you said Mama cut herself? Did I hear you right?" Val said.

"Yeah. I can't get it out of my mind. Right after Hank called to tell me Skipper was missing, I spilled tomato juice in the sink but thought it was blood and I heard a voice. I didn't know what to make of it then – the blood, the voice – but at the campground it suddenly came to me."

I choked on my words and glanced over to where Hank, Grace and Dr. Pritchard were sitting. I didn't want them to be part of this conversation. They were deep in their own exchange. Grace was gesturing with her hands, sitting on the edge of her seat.

"Look, you don't have to talk about it now. It was probably brought on by fear and worry and doesn't mean anything," he said.

"But that's just it. I do remember. I'd forgotten, but now I remember."

"What? What do you think you remember?" He pulled his seat closer to me.

I ignored the doubt in his question. "After Papa died, I came home from school one day and went looking for Mama. I found her in the bathroom holding a razor. She was singing and watching her blood drip into the sink."

"Nora, for God's sake, why would she do that? Maybe you had a bad dream. We were all a little crazy then."

"Oh, no, oh, no, it's true. Don't try to tell me it didn't happen. Don't you remember the bandages?"

"No."

Why didn't he remember? Maybe he'd blocked out the memory when he was depressed, in the hospital. But I didn't make up this memory. I saw the bandage on her wrist every day and I knew why it was there. I'd seen her do it. Mama, made herself bleed. And I remember feeling afraid. When she died, I blamed her for leaving us, for leaving me alone. But that wasn't all. I should have stopped her. Instead I just let her die.

A doctor walked toward us with a stethoscope dangling from his left hand. He was overweight and swayed from side to side with each step.

"Are you Thomas' family?" he said. Strawberry blond fuzz curled around his pink ears. His eyes were pale blue and huge behind thick lenses. He smiled, exposing unnaturally white, poor-fitting dentures.

"Well, he said, "he's a fine lad and there's not a thing wrong with him. We surely don't need him taking up a bed that we might need for someone who's truly wounded, do we?" He chuckled. Except for the Irish brogue, he'd have made a believable Santa Claus. "Do you have any questions?"

"Did he say anything to you, doctor?" I said.

"Just answered my questions. Does this hurt? How many fingers do you see? That sort of a-thing. He was most cooperative. A fine lad that. Oh, yes, I did ask him what he was doing in a cave."

"And?"

"He said he was running away from school – something I wanted to do several times meself." He broke into a hearty laugh, but checked himself quickly and asked if we had any other questions.

I glanced at Val, but he didn't seem to have anything to say, so we asked when we could take him home.

"A nurse will bring him out in a few minutes." He backed away. "Thank you, then," he said and turned toward the door.

"Sounds like Skipper is all right," Dr. Pritchard said. "I know you'll want to take him home for a few days, but please call when you've decided to bring him back to school."

"Frankly, right now my inclination is to enroll him closer to home, but I want to talk to him first," I said.

"Well, you know best, of course. But he was doing well in his studies, and we can monitor him and contact you weekly, if you like."

I looked away, not wanting him to see my disgust at his suggestion. How could Skipper learn independence with a leash around his neck? I doubted Baderwood was the place for my son.

A door swung open and a smiling Skipper was wheeled into the room. His smile faded as he looked at our group in the waiting room. Hank stepped forward, ruffled his hair and asked for a "high five." The others patted him on the shoulders and told him how glad they were he wasn't hurt. Val knelt beside him and kissed him on one cheek while I kissed the other.

Hank said: "You know, it's late. Why don't you folks spend the night in the area and drive back to Philadelphia tomorrow after you've rested? I can recommend a motel down the road. It's plain but clean. What do you say?"

"I've got a better idea," Grace said. "Please come and spend the night at my home. It's just north of here. We've got lots of room and my mother and daughter love company. Please come. You've been through so much today."

Before I could respond, Val accepted. I looked at Skipper. He could barely keep his eyes open. Grace was looking at me for confirmation and I had to admit the thought of the three of us in a sterile motel room wasn't appealing. I wasn't sure I could sleep, but I knew I was exhausted.

"That's very nice of you," I said. "Thanks."

Val shook Hank's hand and expressed our gratitude for everything he and his workers had done for us. We walked together to the parking lot.

About twenty minutes later we pulled our bags from the car and followed Grace along a winding path, lit on both sides by lanterns. Although I couldn't make out the colors, clusters of chrysanthemums nestled among rocks everywhere, and trees and shrubs hugged the white clapboard house, making it look anchored, safe and warm. I was soothed in a way I hadn't expected and couldn't wait to get inside.

Grace's mother and daughter were waiting for us. Her daughter, wearing a long pink nightgown, appeared to be about the same age as Skipper. She climbed down from her grandmother's lap and ran to her mother. Grace swung her up in the air and her long, brown hair fanned out behind her like a comet's tail.

"Did you miss me?"

"This much," the child said, spreading her arms wide.

Grace set her down and started to introduce her but she had other ideas. She walked over to Skipper, took his hand and asked him if he wanted to see her dogs.

"How many do you have?" he said.

"Midget is the oldest and the smallest. Rusty is the biggest and he has red hair." Her voice drifted as they left the room.

"I told you Penelope loved company," Grace said. "My mother, Elizabeth Bonseur."

"We all love company. Let me make us some tea," her mother said.

She walked with energy out of the large, somewhat cluttered room. Neat piles of magazines and children's books with library jackets were stacked next to a bookcase that wrapped around a corner of the room. Photographs were everywhere on the tables, on the walls and several deep on the mantle. Many were of a man holding Penelope at various ages.

"Thank you, but I really should get Skipper to bed," I said.

"Let Skipper relax with Penelope for a bit. Tea sounds wonderful," Val said. He eased himself into one of the chairs like a frequent visitor. I raised my eyebrows at him and got a big smile in return.

"You don't know how much your hospitality means, Grace," I said.

"Oh, yes I do. When Richard, my husband, died last year, my mother's pots of tea were responsible for my recovery. Of course, her presence was..." She looked away. "Let me show you where you can put your things while we wait for the tea."

A few minutes later we walked into the kitchen and sat in large white wicker chairs with blue and white striped canvas cushions. Hemp rugs in various sizes covered the floor like islands on a hardwood ocean. Mrs. Bonseur poured steaming amber tea into four mugs decorated with nautical designs in red, white and blue.

"Now that's really something," Val said, pointing to a large model of a sailing ship. "It's a Baltimore Clipper, isn't it?"

"You know your ships," Grace said.

"I love sailing."

"Me, too. Richard made that for my thirtieth birthday. Sailing was a family hobby. We used to do a lot of racing at a small yacht club not too far from here. I haven't gotten back into it yet, but I hope to."

Even though Grace didn't seem to mind, I wondered if we were invading sensitive subjects. I searched her face. Her expression was sad but controlled. Her mother's face, on the other hand, shone with pride.

Val placed his empty mug on the polished pine table. "I'll get Skipper ready for bed and call you, okay?"

"And I'll do the same with Penelope. She'd stay up forever if we let her," Mrs. Bonseur said. "The child thinks sleeping is a waste of time."

The room was suddenly very quiet. Grace refilled our mugs while I wondered if she knew I, too, had lost my husband? It was probably in the school records and, of course, here I was with my brother.

"Did you notice Skipper's reaction when he came out of the cave?"

I caught my breath. Had I said that out loud? I'd been thinking about it, contrasting it with Penelope's affectionate greeting when we walked in the door.

She put down her mug. "Yes. Why do you think he acted that way?"

I breathed deeply. "Sometimes people are not meant to be close," I said.

"People like you and Skipper?"

The room was too warm and a rivulet of perspiration ran down the side of my face. I reached up to wipe it away. Grace stretched behind her to a box of tissues on a serving cart, and as she handed it to me with one hand, she took my other hand in hers. I dropped my head to the table and cried.

"Skipper rejected me long ago."

Val called from the other room to ask if I wanted to say goodnight to Skipper.

"Yes, I'm coming."

"You should get some sleep, but I want to know why you think Skipper rejects you."

"I'm not sure I know why."

Skipper was already asleep when I entered the room. Perhaps most children look angelic in sleep. Skipper certainly did. His dark lashes fanned out long and feathery. His hair was long enough to curl at the ends, a sight I hadn't seen since he was three or four years old. Jared took him to the barber regularly to "foster good grooming habits," he'd said. I kissed Skipper's warm cheek.

By the time I left the room, the lights in the living room were off and everyone had gone to bed. Luckily the glow of a nightlight allowed me to find the room Grace had shown me earlier. I tossed my clothes onto a chair and pulled a heavy quilt to my neck. Somewhere in the room a clocked ticked and a train whistle moaned in the distance. The sound reminded me of the last visit I made to clients along the East Coast.

In the past twenty-four hours, I hadn't thought once about the gallery or my clients. Skipper was everything that mattered. Running away, not wanting to be found – these were beyond my understanding. I saw Grace again with Penelope, saw her mother's face shine with pride. I decided to ask Grace to help me.

18

Children's voices and barking dogs filtered through the open bedroom window in the morning. I got up quickly, pulled aside the drapes and saw Skipper and Penelope racing on the grass with three dogs. A brown, black and white basset hound with a grass-skimming belly struggled to keep up with them. I called out but they didn't hear me.

I turned back to the room and surveyed the honey-toned pine furniture and gleaming hardwood floors. The home had appeal well beyond structure and accessories. Grace's family seemed to have all the things I yearned for. My emptiness lay exposed in their presence.

I washed and dressed quickly and walked into the bright kitchen where Grace and my brother sat across from each other, heads bent together in deep conversation.

"Sorry, am I the last one up?"

"Good morning," Grace said. "You are, but today's Sunday so who cares? You haven't missed a thing. Sleep good?"

"Well, not at first but, obviously, once I drifted off..." The aroma of brewed coffee was irresistible and, as though he'd read my mind, Val brought me a mug filled to the brim and gave me a kiss. He'd made himself at home from the very beginning.

"Skipper seems fine this morning," Val said. "He and Penelope are already great buddies. They've been outside since breakfast."

Tears began to roll down my face. I hadn't felt them coming.

"Oh my, I'm sorry. I can't seem to stop." I started to leave the room, but Grace brought me back to the table.

"You're just reacting to yesterday. I'm the same way. I cry when the worst is over."

Val laughed, a throaty, deep rumble that I felt in my chest.

"What are you laughing at? You've been as worried as me and you know it," I said, forcing a smile.

"I'm happy to see you cry," he said. He crossed his legs and leaned back into the chair.

"What?"

"I mean it. You rarely talk about how you feel. Oh, you've got a temper. I've seen that often enough, but that's it," he said.

I didn't want to defend myself in front of Grace. Instead I dabbed at my wet face with a table napkin and shook my head. Grace was grinning at both of us. Her face radiated acceptance and pleasure, erasing any embarrassment I felt.

"I never had a brother or sister to tell me about myself. I guess that can be good and bad, can't it?" she said.

"Let's just say, he's right some of the time. I am worried about Skipper. I thought his behavior was improving, but now this. I don't understand why he won't let me get close to him. You told me to think about why he acts that way and-"

"Hell, I can tell you why." Val pulled himself to the edge of his chair, ready to engage in a favorite subject.

"Hold it," Grace said. "I can see that you love your sister and Skipper, but you're not helping." She paused long enough for Val's posture and expression to change.

"Sorry," he said. "I'm going outside with the kids."

Seconds later his voice rose above the barking dogs and squealing children.

Grace leaned toward me. "Will you let me help you?"

"I really want my boy back," I choked.

"What makes you think you've lost him?"

The room's blues and whites ran together and the Baltimore Clipper was awash. I squeezed my eyes to clear them only to hear Skipper screaming at me, to see the defiance and challenge in his eyes, things Grace knew nothing about.

"Nora?" Grace's voice was a whisper but it jarred me.

"I'm sorry. I know you want to help, but I don't understand any of this so how could you?"

"Because it's what I do. I've been figuring out kids for fourteen years and the longer I do the more I marvel at their complexity and their resilience. You mustn't be afraid to face your problems with Skipper. They can be fixed."

She walked to the window. Her hair blazed in the sun. "Those dogs mean so much to Penelope. She tells them things she won't tell me. It's been almost a year since Richard died and two weeks ago I overheard her telling Rusty, the Irish Setter, not to tell me about the picture of her dad she has hidden in her bed so she can talk to him at night. Of course, I've known about it. I heard her say talking to him makes her brave. She thinks I need her to be brave. Maybe I do.

"How did Skip get along with his dad?" she said. She'd returned to her chair and twisted it so she could face me.

"You know Jared died?"

"I've read the forms you filled out for his enrollment."

I pushed back my chair and stood. I'd been over this territory before with Rosemary. What good had it done? "I know you want to help but I've answered questions about Skipper's relationship with Jared before."

"With a psychologist? Is he still seeing him?"

"Rosemary Fiori. No."

"Why?"

"I went to her because of a specific incident. He never repeated his behavior, and I didn't see the need to dig into anything else."

"How do you feel about that decision now?"

Her words stung.

"My sense is that there's a lot going on in Skipper's head – some of it exposed by his behavior, but perhaps most of his emotions are buried deep below the surface. Does that sound like a possibility?"

I thought about my brother's comment that I didn't deserve to be Skipper's mother. It hurt. I loved my son with all my heart. "I don't know what to do."

"I'm willing to work on it. Will you?"

I nodded.

Skipper's happy mood held all the way home. My spirits were lifted too. Before we left, Grace and I agreed to meet each Wednesday afternoon in New York after a class she was teaching at NYU. I was hopeful. In fact I felt so relaxed it was hard to imagine Saturday had ever happened. Still, I wanted to know why he'd run away.

In the meantime, he was hanging over the car seat, presenting me with a new challenge. He wanted to know if he could have a dog. I countered with the responsibilities involved. He promised he would do everything himself. It was the quintessential parent/child confrontation, and I heard myself make the typical parental response: "I'll think about it."

Skipper dashed for the phone to call Marty as soon as we arrived home, wanting to meet him and play in the park. After the arrangements had been made, I got on the phone with Carolyn. She wanted to know if Skipper was home from Baderwood for the weekend.

"It's a long story. He's probably not going back, but I'll tell you the details later. We just got home and my brother's here. Call me when you get back from the park and I'll come over to get Skipper."

When she mentioned again how much Marty missed Skip, the comment stung. Was she judging me, giving me a subtle jab? My emotional response was the same one I felt when I saw Grace with Penelope together, and after we talked the feeling went away. Maybe opening up to Carolyn and Jack would improve the distance that had grown up between us. I had hope now and that was something I hadn't felt in a very long time.

Openness and vulnerability always seemed like a weakness to me, but meeting Grace called that to question. She was strong. I trusted her too. But what was that based on – a few moments of conversation, an empathetic ear? Carolyn was empathetic and I'd known her for years, yet lately I hadn't wanted to confide anything. I promised myself I'd try at the next opportunity, and that evening at the Denbys, I began slowly to recount Skipper's rescue.

"You must've been scared to death," Jack said, setting a tray of steaming cups on the table. A mist of warm chocolate floated around us. He brandished a can of pressurized whipped cream, smiling devilishly. I waved him off but Carolyn nodded.

"I was. We haven't talked about it yet, but when we get home…"

"I understand," Carolyn said. "You've got to know why he ran away. Maybe they mistreated him or something."

My mind immediately turned to Jared. "It wouldn't be the first time."

Jack took the seat next to Carolyn. "What do you mean?" he said.

"Skipper had a few sessions with Dr. Fiori, the school psychologist, to work out a problem. Everything seemed to be fine and then she told me something I didn't believe could be true, but I'm afraid it is. Jared mistreated Skipper."

A strange expression passed between my friends. After several seconds of what could only be described as a silent debate, Jack spoke.

"Carolyn and I have agonized for a long time over something I saw at your house last year, a few months before Jared was killed. After he died, we decided not to say anything," he said.

"You'd better tell me."

For the next few minutes Jack described an incident beyond my worst imagining. He and Marty had decided to go to the park to play catch and they stopped off to see if Skipper could join them. The front door was ajar when they arrived and they could hear Skipper screaming.

"I told Marty to wait in the hall while I ran in. I found Jared and Skipper in the basement, you know, in the front part where the old coal bin used to be. Jared was standing with the lid of the large floor drain in his hand. When Skip saw me he jumped into my arms and said, 'I'm not scared. I'm not scared.'"

"I asked Jared if it was a rat or something because we've had them from time to time in these old houses, but he didn't say anything. At the time I remember feeling uneasy, but I blew it off and we went to the park."

I pushed away from the table and exploded in sobs. "I have to go."

"Nora, we didn't mean to upset you," Carolyn said.

"It's not you. It's everything – things you don't know. I'll talk to you about it. I want to, but just now I can't."

"Can I walk you home?" Jack said.

I shook my head.

"How about if we keep Skipper here for a bit? Give you some time to yourself. We'll walk him home," Carolyn said.

I nodded and opened the front door, stumbled down the steps and ran home.

An hour later I heard Skipper downstairs and went to the bathroom to wash my face. A quick glance in the mirror reflected swollen, red eyes. I doubted Skipper would notice.

"Did you have a good time?" I said when I found him in the kitchen.

"Marty says he's going to get a dog too." He took a cookie from a jar on the counter. When had he grown tall enough to reach the back of the counter? It seemed like yesterday when I had to reach the jar for him.

"Skip?" I was going to ask him why he ran away, but the words wouldn't come. Now that he was safe, it didn't seem important. I'd talk to Grace first, to see how this latest piece of horror fit. I knew how it fit me – like a vice squeezing so hard I was ready to burst. "Are you glad to be home?"

"Yes, and I don't want to go back to that school."

"Okay. I'm glad you're home too. Go take a bath and call me when you're ready for bed."

An hour later, when he was under his favorite Lion King blanket, I kissed his cheek and left the room with tears gathering in my eyes. I stopped to look out onto the deck when I reached the den. It was dark and it took several minutes to pick out the shadowy outlines of chairs and tables. The large flower urns along the railing stood like stone nannies, useless without their flowery summer charges. A lidded grill flanked the door, unused since Jared's death. I wrapped my arms around my body, trying to remember how it felt to be held by someone who cared for me.

When had I last spoken to Carlos? Was it before the opening of the gallery? I was so busy then – too busy for Carlos, too busy for Skipper. What must Carlos think? What would anyone think after almost two months of silence? What would he say if I called now? It was early morning in Ankara. Perhaps he'd be in his office. I walked quickly to the phone, felt the chill on my wet cheeks, and wondered how long it takes to stop loving someone?

"Carlos?"

"Nora?"

I tried to speak but choked on my words. He sounded so happy to hear from me.

"What's wrong? Are you crying? Please tell me what's wrong."

In the end, I was unable to speak other than to tell him how much the sound of his voice meant to me. He told me to call later. He would wait in his office until then, no matter how long it might take. Thank God he still cared for me. Nothing had changed. He'd really meant it when he told me he understood how busy I'd be preparing the gallery for opening.

But how would he react to what had happened to Skipper? Would he understand why I enrolled Skip in boarding school? Everything I knew about his own loyalty to his family's security, told me he'd understand. I yearned to talk to him about all these things. I wanted him to share my child as he shared my work. It was the key to our future together.

When I redialed his office, he answered immediately. I recounted the call from the police, told him about the search and rescue and, more important, I poured out my heart to him about my fears, not only because of what Skipper had done, but also because of his attitude toward me.

"My mother says she cannot imagine how you can work and care for your son. Now I am sure she is right."

I felt my face flush. "I've made mistakes, but no more than any other parent. Do you think I should give up my business and stay home to take care of Skipper?"

Carlos didn't answer for several seconds and I felt tongue-tied by my emotions – disappointment and anger among them.

"I am not there with you so I am not sure what you must do. I know how much you love our work, but I was brought up believing children are more important than business. Ah, well, for now it is enough to know Skipper is unharmed."

Somehow the conversation moved from Skipper to the gallery, although I don't remember how. Carlos asked question after question. I provided answers, summarizing what I felt had been two successful months.

"Can we talk about a visit? I want to see the results of all your hard work."

We talked for more than an hour. In the silence that followed, I was certain there were mountains of things left to be discussed and I worried that perhaps one of those mountains might be a sleeping volcano, one with enough power to destroy our future.

I walked to the kitchen thinking some hot tea would be calming, but changed my mind, turned at the steps and went to my bedroom where I kicked off my shoes, pulled my sweater over my head and tossed it on a chair. My chest felt so heavy it ached. I pulled the comforter up to my chin and folded my arms across my waist. Help me find the way, Grace, I prayed.

19

After six sessions with Grace, I began to question my judgment. What had begun with optimism had become depressing. Her probing left me feeling exposed and vulnerable, sometimes raw. Other times it was like meeting myself for the first time as I faced old convictions and confronted contradictions. Grace assured me what I felt was normal. She said it meant we were making progress because I was dealing with new ways of seeing. To be honest, I felt unbalanced and disoriented. We differed on another matter too. Grace didn't want to see Skipper. She encouraged me to send him back to Rosemary Fiori.

"I know you don't like her, but I've read her reports of the time she spent with Skipper and they're excellent. Besides, he likes her," she said, "and, professionally speaking, it's best that I don't work with both of you."

"I don't see how you can improve our relationship if we're not together."

"If Rosemary and I do our jobs well, your relationship will automatically improve."

"Automatically?"

"Yep. Believe me."

I wanted to believe her, but it wasn't until our seventh time together that I began to understand.

"I know this will seem like I'm getting off the track, Nora, but I'd like to know about your family," Grace said.

We were sitting close together in the small room the university allowed her to use as a visiting professor. The space, built out from the main building, allowing light to stream in from three walls, held a small desk, a filing cabinet, two reddish-brown leather chairs, and a small square table with pale circles left by sweating glasses. The only item on the table was a box of tissues. Evidently no counselor's office was complete without one.

I described our close Lebanese family, particularly my two older brothers. It was when I talked about losing my parents that I felt my chest tighten.

"How did your life change after their deaths?" Grace said.

"My brothers took an apartment near the university they attended, and I moved in with my aunt and uncle and their kids."

"That must have felt strange, huh?"

She looked at me sympathetically while I thought about Uncle Nitu. Like my father, he was gentle and expressive, a man who sang in the kitchen and the bathroom. I always wondered if running water gave rise to the melodies he carried in his head. His rich bass voice could be heard all over the house. And Aunt Georgina was very much like my mother. She fussed and worried about all of us. They had four children but they absorbed me effortlessly.

"Actually, except for missing my parents, not much changed for me."

"So it was a smooth transition for you."

I glanced away. Smooth? I remembered my inner turmoil at the time and suddenly I saw blood and heard my mother's voice. I jerked my head sideways.

"What are you thinking?" Grace said.

"Nothing related to how we all got along. My aunt and uncle took very good care of me," I said, pinching off the memory.

"You didn't tell me how your parents died. It's unusual to lose both parents in such a short space of time. What was that like?"

"I was fourteen. What do you think it was like? I managed." I glanced down at my hands and unclenched them. The blood throbbed as it flowed back into my fingertips.

"How did your mother cope with losing your father?"

Blood appeared from nowhere, formed a thin line between the floorboards and flowed toward my foot. I jumped out of my chair and walked to the window.

"Nora, don't be frightened to tell me what you're thinking. It might be important," Grace said.

I described the vision I'd been having since Hank called to tell me Skipper was missing at the campground and that I witnessed my mother cutting herself. As I stood looking out the office window, a gust of wind blew the curtain across my face. Suddenly I saw myself in my bedroom at Uncle Nitu's shortly after moving in with them.

"Grace, I remember more," I said, turning around. "When I saw my mother cutting herself, she told me not to be a baby, not to depend on her, to stand on my own two feet. She really scared me. But later, I got sick of being scared. I swore an oath that I'd have my own career so no one could fire me like they fired my father. I wasn't going to let anything stop me from being successful and independent."

We sat quietly for several minutes.

"That's an important memory, my friend. And you did it, didn't you? You developed a successful business and now you support yourself."

"Yes," I whispered, holding myself against the shivers shaking my body.

"Do you believe that's how Skipper needs to be?"

"What do you mean?"

"Standing on his own two feet? Not dependent on anyone?" Grace said.

Suddenly, I was fourteen, looking into Skipper's eyes. In their depths I saw my pain reflected.

The next day I felt numb. Ed said he'd handle the office for me, but being alone with nothing to occupy my mind wasn't helping. I dressed and headed for the office. Once inside, I knew I'd made the right decision – just the smell of the rugs lifted my mood. I tossed my coat and purse across the top of the desk and noticed two messages blinking on the answering machine and a FAX spilling out onto the floor. I ignored them. They could wait while I visited my rugs.

I stepped into the gallery and flipped the light switch. The colors surrounded me like a sunrise - at least that's how I thought of it, and since there was no witness I allowed myself the fantasy. I needed it. Among my rugs, I felt grounded and safe, wrapped in the arms of family. After the stresses of the past few weeks, it felt good.

Back in the office, I separated the paper from the FAX. It was from Sam Bezdikian, asking me what I thought of the attached article in the current issue of Investment Digest.

"While digging in a Scythian burial ground near the Mongolian border, archeologists discovered a fourth century B.C. carpet of sophisticated design well preserved in the permafrost.

"If you're wondering what this discovery has to do with your investment portfolio, listen up. For $20,000 today, a well-chosen nine-by-twelve foot Oriental carpet can sell for well into six figures in a generation or so. In today's waning market, such returns are causing some to consider rugs as an alternative investment. And while you're waiting for your return, the rugs will keep your tootsies and your children's tootsies warm, as well as enrich your life with beauty."

Chuckling to myself, I set the FAX on my desk and jotted a note to call Sam. He'd be waiting. It was a pattern he repeated year after year – a tip, a reminder, an admonishment. Actually a number of my clients were already well aware of the investment value of Orientals. Nevertheless, I scribbled another note to call my advertising agent to suggest such a slant for an ad. It was worth considering.

The FAX also reminded me it was time to assess the inventory. With our weekly therapy sessions, I was reluctant to schedule a buying trip. Something had to be worked out soon and one of the blinking telephone messages held the solution.

Carlos had called in the middle of the night saying he couldn't sleep because he was thinking of me. Intrigued, I dialed his office hoping he'd still be there at four thirty in the afternoon Turkish time. He was.

"I like beginning my day with your voice," I said.

"Well, let's work on that, shall we? Now, here is what I was thinking about instead of sleeping last night: You have not renewed your inventory since last spring, correct?"

Thousands of miles away and yet we were on the same wavelength.

"Yes, you're right."

"And you agree that I may come to visit and see the gallery?"

"Yes, but that's not the only reason I want you here." My face flushed.

"Now it is my turn to agree." He laughed.

"Stop teasing me and tell me what you have in mind."

"Okay, here it is: Why don't you let me gather an inventory for you? Some Persians perhaps?"

"They're hard to find, aren't they?"

"I have a new source. If you agree, I'll put together a shipment and time my arrival so I can be with you to help. Wouldn't it be wonderful to work together?"

"It's asking a lot of you, Carlos. Are you sure?"

"I am very sure."

I was surprised I had no reservations at all. For a few seconds, I allowed this new feeling to sink in. Other than

Abdullah, no one helped me with my business and since the interest on the loan had rewarded him handsomely, he hardly qualified as an altruistic benefactor. My independence was a shield for me, a statement of my strength, a banner I wrapped around myself. But Carlos knew the U.S. market and his contacts were broader than mine. Suddenly, Muharrem crossed my mind.

"Your plan is perfect, but what about Muharrem?" I said.

"Ah, I should have thought of him. How about asking Muharrem to research kilims and other items while I concentrate on the Persians and antiques? Are there particular types you need?"

"I think you've got it covered, partner. Call me when you have a list of purchases and we'll finalize everything. In about two weeks?"

"Partner, eh? I like the way that sounds. Two weeks, yes, that should do it, after all I am highly motivated," he said.

Before we ended our conversation, Carlos told me about a rug broker he'd met in Germany who held an exclusive contract with several weaving villages in Iran. Since the U.S. embargo on Iran, the opportunities had become scarce, and considering the superiority of Persian weavings, the German contact was fortunate, although strong competition was coming from China, India and Pakistan, where increasingly Persian patterns and production techniques were being adopted.

"The silk Tabriz I saw were especially fine," he said. "They have alternating narrow and wide borders of florals with center fields of medallions, blossoms, and starbursts. The colors are marvelous. I saw several with fields that had the look and color of old parchment. I don't know how they do it. He had some rare antique prayer rugs too. Are you interested?"

"Of course. What's rare about them?"

"The size. Some have come from mosques and they are woven to accommodate nine men praying side by side."

Carlos could have continued in his descriptions of the rugs forever, but I needed to open the front door.

"I've got to go. Call me when you and Muharrem complete your work and I'll wire the funds."

After unlocking the front door, I returned to the office to listen to the second message, and immediately wished I hadn't. Colin Feeney, the man I'd met at the opening, was asking me to call him. Well, now that my mood was brighter, he wasn't going to spoil it. He could wait.

At six o'clock I closed the gallery and summoned my courage to call Colin Feeney. His answering service said he'd left for the day.

"But he left instructions to give you his cell phone number," she added.

"Oh, just tell him I returned his call and I'll-"

"Please, Mrs. Reardon, he was very explicit about his instructions. He said to tell you no hour was too late for you to call."

I took the number, rationalizing that it would be better to get it over with. Before I dialed I remembered the promise I'd made to myself to call Sam before any contact with Colin Feeney, but decided I was being silly.

"Nora, did you have a successful day? When you didn't call, I imagined people lined up at your door," he said. This was a man unused to being put off.

"I was alone in the gallery today, and, yes, it was busy and very successful."

"Well, I hope there are still a few good rugs left for me."

"Sure, how many do you want?"

"When I see something I like, I want all of it."

I really disliked this man. At first I wasn't sure but there was no doubt about it now.

"Do you want to buy my gallery, Mr. Feeney?"

"No, no, just some of the best you have."

Was there no way to steer this conversation?

"You're welcome to come to the gallery whenever it's convenient. Or I can send someone to your home – whatever is best for you. Have they finished constructing the house in Cape May?"

"Bravo for your memory. Yes, all done. And what I'd like is for you to come to look at the rooms and then we can discuss my needs. I'm sure you're very good at that."

My temples began to throb. "It's difficult for me to leave the gallery, but I can recommend my manager who has extensive knowledge of Orientals and interior design."

I held my breath. I'd never avoided a customer contact before, but there had to be a way around this.

"Sam Bezdikian said you are successful because of the personal attention you lavish on your clients," Colin said. "I expect nothing less."

His oily voice disgusted me. If I couldn't avoid going to Cape May, I'd take someone with me. One of my muscled warehousemen came to mind. "I'll get to work and call you very soon," I said.

Grace was on the steps of the building chatting with a student when I arrived the following Wednesday. Despite her suggestion to think of my sensations in a positive light, I was full of questions. How could it be wrong to be independent? I'd done it and I was proud. It's what I wanted for Skipper. Isn't it a parent's job to guide a child to independence? How many stories do we hear about adult children moving back with their parents, or, worse, never moving out on their own?

Grace and I walked together to her office and sat on the leather chairs. The furniture was exactly as it had been the week before - even the tissue box, with one tissue jutting up in the same ready position. Though the room had an unused look, the air swarmed with unanswered questions, unspoken thoughts and unuttered accusations. I squared my shoulders.

"What's wrong with teaching a child to be independent?"

"Is that what your mother did for you?"

Why did she keep harping on my mother, on the past? It was the present and the future I wanted to address.

"Yes, she did – ultimately, that is, I mean, yes, I learned."

"How did that feel?"

I heard my mother's words again, those unbelievable words. I watched her blood drip into the sink and felt the fear again. Adrenalin surged through me.

"Do you remember?" Grace leaned toward me and I sought the back of my chair and looked at the ceiling.

"Yes, I remember. I was afraid, totally lost. Later I was angry, and that's when I decided nobody was going to hurt me like they'd hurt my father and mother. I was going to be independent and strong."

"Afraid. Lost. Afraid, but not asking anyone for help. Angry. Independent. Who does that sound like besides you?"

Nothing moved except particles of dust floating sideways though the beams of sunlight coming in the window in front of me - a meaningless ballet, particles drifting without purpose. Grace shifted in her seat and the leather squeaked.

Was there any other answer besides the one forcing its way to my lips? "Skipper." I thought of his eyes – not defiant, not challenging, but wounded. Had I ever seen his eyes that way?

"Yes, I think so too. Do you think he wants to be that strong, independent person you want him to be? *Can* he be at his age? Were you, even at fourteen?"

"No." The word came on an exhaled breath.

"And he can't bring himself to ask you for help. And he's madder than hell at you for your expectations."

I couldn't speak. My breath came in short gasps for several minutes while I considered what she'd said. My boy always seemed sure of himself, even bossy. He was a leader in school. His teachers said so. That's how he seemed, but was he experiencing something else? I didn't know him in that way. He never let me in so how could I know? Did he hide his feelings because he knew I wanted him to?

"Grace, have I boxed Skipper into a position where he can't show me how he feels?"

"If you felt something you knew your mother would disapprove of, would you have expressed it? I want you to think about this, but there's something else I want to know. When we discussed Skipper's relationship with his dad, you left out something, didn't you?" she said.

"No, I don't think so."

"Tell me how things were when you brought your baby home from the hospital."

"He surprised me at every turn. His demanding cries and his temper were frightening to me. I felt so inadequate, while Jared seemed born to be a father. He always knew just what to do, so we worked out a division of labor that worked for us," I said. "We hired a housekeeper, and Jared arranged his work schedule so he could spend major periods of time with Skipper. Jared encouraged me to use my time to get my business started."

"How were things at home between Jared and Skipper?"

My mind raced ahead.

"You've read Rosemary's reports. You know how Jared disciplined Skipper, don't you?" I said.

"Why didn't you mention that when I asked about their relationship?"

"I didn't know what was going on. How could I? From my point of view they seemed happy together. In fact, I remember being jealous because Skipper was so well behaved for Jared and yet he challenged me at every turn. I feel guilty now."

"Why do you think Skipper acted that way; I mean, an angel for Jared and defiant with you?"

"I've thought about that, but it makes no sense to me."

"Forget about your situation for a second. What's a mother's first responsibility to her child?"

I knew where she was going even before she finished her question. "Are you saying Skipper is angry with me because I didn't protect him? Look, Grace, he never seemed afraid of Jared. He was always so perfect around him."

Each statement slammed back at me. I heard my words over and over. Finally, I cried realizing the horror of the cycle I'd set up for my boy. Skipper was acting in the way he thought I wanted. He taught himself to remain emotionally distant from me, and I was the one who showed him how.

Grace sat on the arm of my chair, put her arms around me and assured me that things were going to be better. The last time she said that, things got worse.

20

Butterflies were having a second reunion in my stomach. The first time was in the crowded security area at the airport while I waited for Carlos. Ever since the September eleventh terrorist attack in New York City, only ticket holders were allowed access to the gates, so instead of watching passengers exit one by one from the gateway, I faced a swarm of bodies trudging to the baggage claim and was forced to sweep my eyes from side to side to spot his curly dark hair. When he saw me and separated from the crowd, he pulled me to the side of the corridor and wrapped me in his arms. We let the crowd thin out before walking hand in hand to the baggage claim. More than anything I wanted to accompany him to the Bellevue, but he was obviously tired. We agreed to meet at the office in the morning.

Now, waiting at my office window, I played hostess to the butterflies again. This time it wasn't just his presence. I was eager to show him my gallery and to see the new rugs too. Before coming he'd gone with several of my workers to retrieve the carpets from the cargo container being held at the port. From there they unloaded most of the rugs at the warehouse, setting aside three antiques, a dozen or so Persians and some kilims for the gallery.

The truck entered the delivery alley, stopped just beyond the ramp and crept slowly backwards into position for unloading, its beep-beep-beep keeping time with my heart. When Carlos jumped from the passenger side and saw me at the window, he gave me a perfunctory wave. The next minute he was shouting directions to the men.

Disappointment replaced my excitement. I'd imagined taking his hand at the outside door, leading him through the office into the gallery, and watching his face light up. Instead, he was completely absorbed in organizing and ordering my workmen around. I turned away, walked to the first stack of Chinese wools and yanked at the fringe. When finally the back door opened, I waited, but when I heard no footsteps I turned to see Carlos standing at the doorway studying my face.

"Have you decided where you'd like to place the new items?" I said, looking at the wall.

He slipped his arm around my waist.

"Well, what do you think?" I said.

"I think I've offended you in some way."

"No you haven't. Tell me what you think of the gallery."

"I know that's what you're asking but-"

"Come on, let me show you around." I grasped his hand and led him toward the display window at the front of the gallery.

The rug patterns throbbed around me, repeating over and over – margins and borders, flowers, twisting vines, medallions. They were the Oriental family, related to each other, yet with closer scrutiny revealing their singular uniqueness. A cursory glance was a betrayal, a short changing of the artistry, history and labor. "Look again," they said, "look deeper." The inspired weaving fingers flowed across the loom to pull, twist, knot and cut. If the vision strayed, lost concentration or faltered, the corruption demanded an unraveling until the vision was rediscovered and the weaver could move on. In this way, and only in this way, did the weaver ensure the integrity of his pattern so that the design would deserve repetition by his progeny. They carried on the tradition because they trusted the vision of their fathers, and their reward was unity and stability.

The momentary irritation I felt toward Carlos was a warning pinch. I was learning about my own repeating patterns from Grace, learning to recognize and acknowledge the corruption they had caused in my relationships. She was helping me to see that my drive for success and independence had created a distance between the ones I loved and me. I'd kept them at arm's length while desperately longing for them. Certainly my brothers and Skipper had been affected. Now, I caught myself reacting against Carlos, protecting my territory, when all he wanted was to help me.

Ed Gallo, who'd been working in another area of the gallery, walked toward us.

"Excuse me, Nora. Mrs. Bertold purchased the nine-by-twelve Anatolian kilim," he said. "She's asking for a delivery time and I told her it would be about three days."

"That'll work. Ed, you've heard me speak of Carlos Ghazerian?"

They shook hands and Ed began asking questions about the new inventory. I suggested they bring in the antiques first and Ed grudgingly returned to the customer to complete the sale. Carlos waited for him. I suspected he wanted another audience so he could extol the virtues of Persian rugs one more time. The deep rumble of his voice carried back to me until he and Ed reached the door of the truck.

Ed returned minutes later with a five-by-six foot Tabriz over his shoulder. "What a beauty! A knot count of four hundred per square inch," he said. His thinning gray hair had fallen over his eyes and he brushed it back with a manicured hand. He rolled the rug out next to me and I lost whatever breath was left in my lungs. It was stunning. Two narrow floral borders wrapped around a wider one of medallions in red, pale blue, dark brown and cream on a tan background. The centerfield of light blue was filled with twelve cream-colored medallions and floral bouquets, vines and starbursts.

"See," Carlos said. He ran his index finger along a trailing vine in the center field of the rug. "One immediate clue in distinguishing Turkish from Persian is the difference in color tonalities, but this one has a surprise. The Turkish rugs from Western Anatolia are, on the whole, lighter than the classic Persian, in which a dark blue field is far more common. Just look at this pale blue field. Ah, I love it, don't you?"

I couldn't speak for Ed, but I was enjoying the electricity Carlos generated over the rugs. The voltage was having another effect on me, but it was inappropriate.

"I knew you'd like that one, but prepare yourself for this," Carlos said.

He spread a smaller four-by-five-foot silk Tabriz over the other. This one had the look and color of old parchment he'd told me about on the phone. A tree of life dominated the center. Scrolling vines and animals were scattered sparingly around the tree and a design of small squares and rectangles enclosing floral motifs formed the border and echoed the red, blue, brown, tan and cream elsewhere in the design. It was extraordinarily harmonious and beautifully executed.

"They're even more lovely than I expected, Carlos. Thank you. I know how much work this represents."

"The gallery is the perfect setting for them. You have accomplished something special here."

We worked for two hours hanging the antiques in the alcove and clearing a separate space for the Persians nearby. Customers who wanted to see the best the gallery could offer would need to walk completely through the showroom to get to them.

Several people dropped in while we worked and Ed reluctantly left to help them. Between customers, Carlos described each rug for me, reciting its origin, the weaving family – if he knew it – and all the fine details. Ed was sucking up the information like a kid with his favorite ice cream soda. I told myself again how lucky I was to have him for a manager.

I was called to the phone only once and immediately regretted taking the call when I heard the voice on the end of the line – Colin Feeney.

"I don't mind telling you, I feel neglected, Nora," he said.

"I apologize, but I've been waiting for a new shipment that I know you'll be interested in. We were just unloading the truck when you called. Do you have your calendar handy?"

I hadn't mentioned it to Carlos yet, but I wanted him to accompany me to Colin's beach house. The appointment was made for early the following week, and I promised to put together a collection that would make his summer cottage the envy of Cape May's residents.

"I'll bring a sample of designs, colors and styles. We'll worry about size later, okay?"

"Some of the rooms are quite large, is that a problem?" Colin said.

"No, not at all. Some of my carpets were made for public spaces, even palaces, and they can be custom fit and refinished for a variety of room sizes," I said.

Apparently, my idea of a "cottage" was about to be adjusted. However, I was betting that Colin, the politician, would be using his Cape May residence to impress campaign donors, regardless of what he'd said earlier about wanting a getaway. He wasn't going to be disappointed on either count. Assured of my full attention, his voice became warmed syrup. I told him I had people waiting for me in the gallery and cut him short. In a way I looked forward to the encounter – at the very least it would show him I wasn't interested or available.

By late afternoon, Carlos and I left the gallery in Ed's hands and headed home to have dinner with Skipper – just the three of us, like a family. I doubted Carlos would notice any changes in Skipper, but to me they were dramatic. Instead of feeling guarded with Skipper, I'd begun to look forward to going home to him. Skipper came running to meet us with an Indian war whoop - the latest in his repertoire of expressions. I was partly to blame for his pent up excitement because I'd been talking about Carlos' visit for two weeks.

I hung up our coats and headed for the kitchen. We were having *köfte*, and when Carlos joined me I put him to work making the lamb patties while I made a salad. Without being asked Skipper set the table, managing at the same time to monopolize the conversation by describing a recent history project – a diorama of knights on horseback at an English jousting tournament.

"I'd like to see that, Skip. Sounds complicated," Carlos said.

"I like to do hard things." He'd finished with the table setting. Now he stood facing us like he was about to deliver a speech.

"Really. Why?"

"Because nobody else can do them." Skipper's chin was set and it didn't go unnoticed, judging from Carlos' quick glance in my direction. "And nobody helped me with it either," he added. He paused like he was waiting for comments or questions. Carlos shot me another glance. I wondered what he thought about Skipper's attitude. For my own part, I was questioning the point at which confidence becomes arrogance. I didn't want to raise an elitist.

Over the last few weeks I'd begun a new ritual of sifting through the day's experiences to choose something interesting to tell Skipper. A few hours before Carlos arrived, a University of Pennsylvania student had come into the gallery. By the time she left she'd purchased forty kilim bags for her sorority sisters. I told Carlos and Skipper how it took three of my warehousemen to carry the bags to her van and how funny they all looked carrying them down the street – like a parade. Carlos laughed with me, but the story didn't seem to interest Skipper. He was looking at his plate, pushing his carrots into a straight line with his fork. He did this often with his food, lining up the pieces next to each other until his plate was striped with the individual items. Then he'd eat the pieces one by one by alternating rows.

But I'd misread him. He wasn't disinterested. He had something else on his mind. Out of the blue, Skipper said he was sorry he'd taken my jewelry without asking.

I felt a chill and Carlos looked at me with raised eyebrows.

"What?" Had he stolen something again?

"You know, when I took your jewelry and gave it to my friends at school," he said.

"Oh, that was a long time ago. We don't need to talk about that anymore, Skip. You know it was wrong and you'll never do it again. That's what's important."

"But Dr. Fiori says it's important to say you're sorry, and she says it's very important to ask nicely, and..." He stopped, deep in thought. "When I'm grown up, I'm going to buy presents for my friends just like that girl did because presents make people happy. But I'll buy them with my own money." His smile lit up the room and my heart along with it. Carlos reached for my hand and squeezed and gave Skipper a smile.

"Anyone would be lucky to have you for a friend, Skip," Carlos said, and Skipper's face was a portrait of satisfaction.

I don't remember eating dinner. The conversation flowed from one topic to another. They discussed soccer and Skipper wanted to know if our rules were different from those in Turkey.

"I know the rules for professional players are the same in both countries, but I haven't seen our school children play. My guess is their rules are probably like yours. I'll bet I could teach you some good moves if we could find some time together."

Carlos' life to date may not have included many children, but there wasn't a hint of awkwardness. He was obviously enjoying himself. Next time I faced a problem with my boy, I'd ask him outright for his help instead of prejudging his interest or his capability.

"Sure. That'd be good. Can Marty play too? He's a good soccer player, but not as good as me."

I called the Denbys and made arrangements for Carlos to pick Skipper and Marty up from school the following day and go to the park until dinner. Carolyn and Jack insisted on dinner at their house. Our plans for Thanksgiving hadn't worked out because of what happened at Baderwood, and they were eager to meet Carlos.

Carlos loved the idea. There was an aura of normalcy about everything, like he'd been part of my life forever. I could almost see the grin on Carolyn's face on the other side of the phone. In recent weeks she and I had begun relating to each other like we used to. I had denied myself the pleasure of a close friend for too long.

Carlos brushed past my body more than once as we cleared away the dishes. His hands lingered overly long on mine when he handed me the mugs one by one. We needed to be alone, but when I suggested that Skipper go to his room to do homework he said he didn't have any.

"Good, the later you go to bed, the easier it will be for me to beat you at soccer tomorrow," Carlos said. Skipper took the challenge.

Earlier in the day I'd made sure there was firewood stacked on the deck. We laid the fire, struck a match and sank as one onto the soft pillows of the sofa. The small twigs quickly ignited and wrapped their flames around the logs. Internally, I felt the same ignition with Carlos' arms wrapped around me. There was so much I wanted to say but the sighing fire, crackling sap, and the fragrance of the vaporizing apple and pecan wood were mesmerizing. Then Carlos got up to add another log.

"Since you arrived I've been feeling like you never left," I said.

"I know what you mean, but I can't say it's been the same for me. You've had months of concentrated work. I've been busy too, but not enough to put you out of my mind. For me the months have been very long."

"I thought of you often. I-"

He turned me around gently.

"I think it is important that you hear this." He paused but I sensed it wasn't an invitation for me to speak. "If you had been thinking of me as I was thinking of you, you would have called. For a long time I have felt you were not certain how I fit into your life. In fact, today in the gallery, I felt like an intruder. Am I wrong?"

The fire snapped and yellow and red sparks flew in several directions. Red flames clung close to the wood logs, unwilling to release their hold and become the diminished yellow that flailed wildly in the heated air, finally to be drawn upward by a stronger force.

My face flushed. "You're not entirely wrong. But it isn't because I don't love you or want you with me. Nothing could be further from the truth."

"You are going to have to do better than that because I don't understand. Today I saw resentment, maybe anger, in your face, and it hurt."

I shifted in my seat. "When you arrived at the gallery today, I was thinking only of myself. How I would show you the gallery, where the new items would go. I would do everything because everything depended on me. Instead, you were handling my rugs, supervising my workmen and entering the gallery on your own terms. For a moment I reverted to my old reactions. I'm sorry, Carlos, I guess I haven't yet learned to let go and let others help me. I felt threatened and a little out of control. For such a long time, I believed I had to be completely independent. I didn't know how to trust anyone but myself. So you were right. I resented you and I'm ashamed of myself." My throat tightened. Carlos put his arm around my shoulders. "I've been afraid to let go. My fear of dependence has kept me from accepting you with my whole heart. It kept me detached from my brothers, and, oh, Carlos, it almost ruined my relationship with Skipper. I'd convinced myself that our security was the most important job I had. Now I

know that being his mother should have been my main
focus. I pushed him away and then I couldn't understand
why he hated me. He didn't hate me. He was as frightened
as I was."

I fell forward, choking on my tears. Carlos pulled me back
into his arms where I stayed until the logs crumbled into ash.

"You are lucky, do you know that?" he said, smoothing my
damp forehead.

"Lucky? How can you say I'm lucky after everything I've
just told you?"

Suddenly his lips parted in a wide devilish grin. "Because
you have me."

We burst into laughter and wrestled each other for the
pillow. I felt released, but not freed. He needed to know about
Jared and I silently promised it would be soon. For now I
buried my face in his neck, breathing through my mouth.

"Seriously, I do think you are lucky, lucky to understand
yourself so well. Most people are afraid to face themselves," he
said.

"I had no choice. Look what I was about to lose – Skipper,
my brothers, you."

"In case you don't already know, I'm not the losing kind."

"You don't like to lose or I can't do anything to chase you
away?"

"Ah, it is better to find these things out over time and we
have done enough discovery for one night." He pulled me to
my feet and kissed me. "But I will tell you this: The more I
learn about you, the more I want to be with you."

"Then I am lucky."

Carlos arrived at the office the next morning wearing jeans
and a chamois jacket and looking well rested, which was more
than I could say about myself. I'd tossed and turned thinking of
the day ahead with Colin.

"What needs to be done today, boss?" he said, with a knowing
smile.

"I have something in mind, if you're willing," I said, leading him to my office.

After I closed the door, I explained how I'd met Colin at the gallery opening, that he was a friend of Sam Bezdikian, and that he wanted to look at Orientals for a beach home.

"It'll take about three hours to get to Cape May. Will you go with me?" I said.

"Of course. I have not been to Cape May since I was in school in Washington, D.C."

"Are you sure?"

"It is my pleasure. Oh, and before I forget, I would like to meet Sam. Perhaps I could stop on my way to the airport when I leave next week."

"He'd love that. Actually, I was thinking about going to New York with you."

"I like that even better. We'll talk about it later. Now, let's begin making a tentative list of rugs to take to Cape May." He was out of the office before I could answer.

"Well, I guess I have my answer," I mumbled to myself.

We traveled caravan style along the Garden State Parkway. My warehouse worker, Tony, led the way in the gallery's truck. Tony's helper was BB, who got his nickname from a thick, round scar on his cheekbone where he'd been hit by shot from a BB gun as a kid. Tony was born and raised in Cape May and said he knew exactly where Feeney's summer home had been built.

"Everybody knows his name," Tony said, loading the truck before we left. "Big stink, really big stink." He stopped his work to explain. "They tore down a real old house – historic, you know – to build that place, and people in Cape May don't like that. Nobody could figure out how he got permission, you know. Big mystery."

Beads of perspiration dripped from the ends of Tony's black hair. He was one of my favorite workers – always pleasant and willing to do extra jobs when needed. I'd learned he was attending school to complete his high school education and planned eventually to get an associate degree in business.

When I heard about his ambitions, I funneled as many jobs as I could his way. Today was one of those and, true to form, Tony was eager to offer extra value.

"Where's the property, Tony?" I said.

"At the southern tip of Cape May County. There ain't nothing else there at the end. It's a spot where me and my girl friends – well, you know."

I gave him a wink and he flashed his white teeth and averted his eyes.

"Well, anyway, wait'll you see that view. You got water everywhere – the Atlantic and the Delaware Bay. Bee-u-ti-ful." He rolled his eyes.

The wind picked up considerably as we neared the Cape. There'd been no storm forecast, but the tree branches were leaning hard to the southwest. Still, the sky was deep blue and the sun streaming in the windows was warm enough that we didn't need the car heater.

Carlos probed me for information about Colin. I gave him the basics: approximate age, high-ranking politician with many influential friends, and Colin's comment that the beach house would probably be used for entertaining.

"Is he married? Does he have kids?"

Carlos's questions surprised me, not because of what he'd asked, but because I never thought to ask. My preoccupation with other things – things I never mentioned to Carlos – interfered. I confessed the oversight to Carlos.

"Doesn't matter. We can find out when he shows us the house," Carlos said. "It will figure into the kinds of rugs we suggest to him. Little feet and kilim don't mix well."

When we arrived, Colin was standing at the railing of an upper deck, smiling broadly as we parked in his driveway. I struggled with my hair in the strong wind while I waited for Carlos to join me, and when I next glimpsed Colin his face had changed. It was expressionless.

The house was held aloft by pilings, leaving the street level clear for parking underneath. Newly planted trees, supported by guy wires, and bushes were placed strategically so that in time they would soften the barren look. The building itself was impressive – a combination of gray-blue weathered planks, concrete and glass – lots of glass. One portion of the house cantilevered out over the water. I imagined a magnificent view of the bay and the ocean from the inside. On the other hand, the height of the house wiped out the view for his neighbors. Their objection to this insensitive new neighbor was understandable.

Carlos and I followed a wide flagstone path to a curved metal staircase and climbed to the upper deck where Colin waited for us wearing a reconfigured expression of welcome.

"Your home is an architectural masterpiece," Carlos said, extending his hand. I introduced him as my Turkish connection and Colin, keeping his arm glued to his side, raised his eyebrows in response. Maybe it was the flooring, suspended as it was atop pilings, but I felt we were off to a rocky start.

We followed Colin into the entranceway.

"You meant it when you said the rooms were large, but you said nothing about this breathtaking view of the ocean," I said.

"Every room in the house has an ocean view."

"Was that your idea, or your wife's?" Carlos said.

"Mine and the architect's."

It wasn't a complete answer, but I was sure Colin wasn't married.

"You've made an excellent beginning with the furnishings," I said, glancing ahead into the living room. Colin seemed rooted to the entrance hall. I began thinking of the rugs and which one to unroll first. Watching a client's first impression was always fun for me.

"I like spare surroundings, nothing overdone. Clutter makes me claustrophobic," he said.

"That's important to know, Colin. Your rugs, then, will supply just the right touch of warmth and elegance to your rooms. Am I on the right track?" I said.

Colin nodded, but the movement conveyed no agreement. I decided to move on since it didn't appear he was going to supply any information to help in the selections. I studied the upholstered pieces – two long sofas and three, stocky barrel chairs – all monochromatic.

"Let's begin with a Turkish kilim for this entrance hall," Carlos said. He asked Tony to bring the six-by-eight Anatolian kilim. But Colin didn't react when it was spread on the floor.

"This is a very fine kilim. The slits, which are the result of the weaving technique used in producing a flatweave - or kilim - are barely noticeable here because of unique interlocking wefts," I said to Colin's downcast eyes. "It's an informal look, I think, but very inviting and colorful.

"Tony, bring the four-by-six Kerman Medallion rug." The Kerman was very different and I hoped it might elicit some reaction. "This pile rug is more formal. The colors are subdued and yet it has warmth and luxury. Do you like this look better than the kilim?"

Was I going to have to reach down his throat and grab a word or two? I waited.

"It's hard to say. Let's move to another area. I'd like to see what you'd suggest for the living room," Colin said.

I glanced quickly at Carlos. He raised his eyebrows and I shrugged my shoulders. Colin led the way, walking all the way to the windows where he stood with his legs apart and his arms crossed over his chest. For a moment I thought he was going to make a pronouncement, but he merely stared at us. Behind him the ocean thrashed and I couldn't help wondering whether the undercurrents were stronger in the water or in the room.

"Carlos, what about the merino wool Kashan?" I said into the awkward silence.

"Perfect," he said. He held onto my eyes and gave me an encouraging grin. I needed it.

It took Tony and BB together to lift the twelve-by-fifteen foot, densely-woven wool. They moved aside two chairs, partially unrolled the Kashan, replaced the chairs and repeated the process at the other end of the room. Their easy movements never failed to amaze me.

The Kashan had a medallion within a medallion dominating the center field. The outer one was covered with gold and red stylized flowers and *botehs* – clusters of palm leaves – on a blue field that echoed the ocean. The inner medallion was a striking black and gold design, while the outer edge had a border of soft red and cream rectangles filled with twirling vines. A larger border of gold leaves on a black field repeated the colors in the center of the medallion. The effect was dramatic.

"Feel it, Colin. The silky nap will surprise you," I said.

"Interesting," Colin said without bending.

I took a deep breath and glanced around the room to shake my irritation. Was he covering up the fact that he knew nothing about Oriental rugs? I'd run into that before with clients who tried to impress me with tidbits they'd learned about Orientals. It invariably led to their embarrassment. If they only knew how much dealers like teaching clients about the intricacies of Oriental rugs, they'd relax and enjoy the process of buying so much more.

The dining room was directly to my right and I stole a quick glance. There, in the center of the room, a table was sparkling with crystal, crowned with red roses and set for two. Had that stage been set for me? I tore my eyes away.

"Tony, please bring in the rest of the rugs," I said. "Colin, I suggest you take a look at them and decide if Orientals are a good fit for you." I walked to the window and glanced out at the ocean while Carlos shifted his feet on the wood floor.

Colin, with a sideways glance at Carlos, said that was a good idea. Tony and BB rolled the Kashan, took it to the truck, and brought in the remaining the rugs.

"How many bedrooms?" Carlos asked, while Tony and BB stood waiting with rolled rugs under their arms.

"Four, each with a bathroom. There's also an office and a small reading room up there. My bedroom is on this level on the other side of the building."

At my signal, Tony and BB alternately unfurled the rugs – two African, three Chinese, and a Persian pictorial. I felt we'd done a good job of representing what was available, even if Colin gave no indication of preference for any of them.

Carlos was undaunted. He pointed out the strengths and special features of each rug. While he spoke, I thanked God for his presence and itched to get out of there.

Twenty minutes later the truck was reloaded. I reached for the door and strode down the steps. When my feet hit the gravel, I turned and called back to Colin on the upper deck: "Call if you want to see more."

Once we were in the car and heading out of the drive, Carlos turned to me. "What the hell was going on in there?"

"He's a strange man."

"Strange?"

"He's a politician. You've lived in Washington, you know what they're like."

Carlos turned away and looked out the window. It was a relief not to feel the spotlight of his eyes, but the pause didn't last long.

"I don't understand. We should have made that sale. Once you are invited to the home, the sale is practically guaranteed. I can't believe…"

"Wait a minute." I pulled to the side of the road, got out and walked back to Tony, behind us in the truck. I thanked him and told him to go on ahead. Then I walked back to Carlos debating with myself. How would Carlos react if I told him my suspicions about Colin? And how would I explain why I withheld my feelings…again?

"Nora, what is this?" He waved to Tony as the truck moved ahead.

"He's a man who... I think he didn't like the rugs and didn't want to come right out and say it."

"No, I don't think so. Politicians withhold their thoughts only when it benefits them. That is what I have learned about politicians. What did he have to gain? He is the one who needs rugs."

My head was spinning. *Strength... vulnerability...* Grace's words. But she didn't know Carlos. She couldn't know how much was at risk for me. All she knew was how to bring me closer to my family. *Family...* Carlos said I was already his family.

I turned in my seat to look at him and took a deep breath. "I did keep something from you, but it's because I wasn't really sure. No, that's not true. I was sure, but I didn't know how you'd react because...."

"Wait a minute. You don't believe I'm truly sorry for the way I acted before, when I left you and returned to Turkey. Is that it? You don't trust me. Or, maybe you don't trust me to work with you. It doesn't matter. What matters is that you don't trust me and that's a problem."

"No, that's not it."

The wind began to howl and the car shook. I hung my head and slowly began to tell him everything I was thinking. How I still felt territorial about my business. How I suspected Colin was interested in me. And, yes, I was still unsure of our relationship.

Huge raindrops raged against the car windows. The car filled with their thunder and I had to stop talking. Carlos pulled me close to him and wrapped his arms around me. My body sagged with relief.

"I'm afraid of what I don't know, not of our future together," he said, whispering in my ear.

"The thing is, I've just begun to understand my reactions. And even if I understand, I find it hard to express. But I promise to try."

"Okay, that's good enough for me." He inhaled and placed his hands on his stomach. "I'm starving. Let's find a seafood restaurant and have dinner."

I started up the car and pulled out onto the road. The rain was still pelting the car and the sky was a boil of gray clouds.

"Skip is with my brothers and they'll even take him to school tomorrow, that is, if I'm not home," I said.

"Oh? You don't feel any urgency to rush home?"

"You could say that."

"Well, now, we could take care of two kinds of hunger here in beautiful Cape May. But, hunger aside, there's an important question I want to ask you."

21

A purple fog settled around the car as we looked for a place to eat along the ocean side of the peninsula. When Carlos realized the color was coming from the sunset, he pulled off the road. The sun was a scarlet ruby set in a glowing aura of red and purple clouds, each encased in a silver envelope. Alternating shafts of white and pink fanned out above us, intensifying as the bright globe ebbed under the horizon on its way to foreign stages, where its performance would repeat and costumes would change in the dust and humidity of other climes.

Gradually buildings took on deepening shades of gray, while overhead the clouds rolled against each other like elephants in a wadi. Carlos searched for restaurants along the coast road. Several times he dashed in only to return to the car with a scowl when they couldn't accommodate him. Finally he emerged smiling from The Spotted Auger and waved me in. The restaurant, also an inn, was on the bay, slightly less windy than the ocean side as the storm bore down.

Inside, a fire crackled and hissed in the bar where we were asked to wait. My curiosity was peaked when I saw a conspiratorial smile pass between the maitre d' and Carlos. I looked at him and got a shrug.

We sat in silence with a glass of wine, hypnotized by the flames and warmed by the nectar.

"I wonder..." Carlos said, "aside from what you told me about Mr. Feeney, do you think he was disappointed in the rugs?" He refilled our glasses and reached for a handful of mixed nuts brought by a passing waitress.

"All I can tell you is I know he wants the best. I strongly suspect I'll hear from him when he gets over his childish snit."

The bar area was a showcase for seashells. Shafts of soft lighting from scallop shell sconces climbed the walls to the open-beamed ceiling. The shells' pink veins reminded me of the day my brother held a flashlight under my hand and I stared at my own bones and veins. On the table in front of us, candles floated on turquoise water in the shell of a giant clam.

At last the maitre d' reappeared and beckoned. A private space had been cleared at the end of the room and a screen of dried sea fans shielded a table from most of the other diners. From our window the distant shoreline across the bay sparkled like a string of diamonds and boats bobbed on the rough water.

"This was worth waiting for," I said. I grasped the hand he held out across the dark blue table covering.

"Good, because what I want to ask you is about waiting," he said, returning to the mystery.

Before I could respond, the waiter approached. Carlos turned to me and asked if seafood chowder sounded good. I nodded. "And a salad of cucumber with dill?" He directed the question to the waiter and me. We nodded together like puppets.

The wheels in my head, fueled by curiosity, were spinning out of control. What did he mean about "waiting?" Would his question help us to find answers to our future together? Or did he think too many things stood in our way and waiting was our only choice? Excitement slipped away into anxiety, and by the time the waiter returned with salads, a tureen, and a basket of rolls, my appetite had deserted me.

"Carlos, I don't think I can eat until you talk to me," I said.

His face clouded momentarily. "Ah, I'm sorry. I had this moment planned in my mind." He shrugged and laughed at himself. "I'm such a fool."

"Just tell me. Whatever it is, just tell me now."

He took a deep breath and expelled it slowly. "I want to tell you that I love you, love you to total distraction, and I don't want to waste any more time waiting."

I opened my mouth to assure him I felt the same, but he stopped me.

"Let me get this out, please, before I get tangled in all the complications I know we must deal with. I want you to know everything I have been thinking."

I concentrated on his face and his lips, those lips that gave me so much pleasure. I thought about a time in the future when perhaps we might be separated and I'd want to relive this scene, hear his words, recall his husky voice, and relish the moment again. Patience came at a price and I felt my nails biting into my palms.

"First, I believe you feel as I do. If I'm right, then we must be together. Second, I would be honored to have Skipper as my son."

His words caught me so by surprise that my eyes filled and overflowed. I knew he was fond of Skip, but his words indicated more.

The waiter, hovering nearby, turned and left us.

"Third," Carlos continued, "I am willing to leave Turkey whenever you say. We must discuss this, of course, but I want you to know I am willing to do whatever it takes. I can sell my business altogether, or I can run it from here. We could combine our businesses, or you could continue as you are and I will find something new." He stopped abruptly and took another deep breath. "There, that's everything."

He reached for my hands again with an anxious expression in his eyes, then let go slowly, leaned back in his seat and seemed satisfied to wait. I folded my hands to keep his lingering warmth with me.

A large yacht glided by the window. Inside a brightly lit cabin, three teenaged children, a man and woman, and an elderly man were engaged in a game. Their heads were thrown back in laughter, arms gesturing, fully engaged with each other. In my imagination, I switched their faces to those of my own family. It was what I wanted more than anything else.

When independence became more important to me than my family, everything seemed to fall apart. Grace had forced me to shift my focus and I'd begun to find a new footing. We talked about it as new, but in some ways it felt familiar – like being a child in my dreaming place on the flowered rug under the table where I knew I was important and loved by the people around me. It was an easy security, freely given and received. Slowly I realized there was a gift in the words Carlos didn't say. He never suggested I give up my business. I was free to make my own choice. I swallowed several times before I could speak.

"I can tell you without reservation that I love you. What you've said makes me very happy. But, just for now, can we put aside talking about our businesses? It's just too much to deal with. Work has been my life for so long. I always thought it was the best part of my life, but it's had a destructive side, and I'm trying to find a balance. I just don't know how much I can cut away without losing myself. Do you understand?"

An elderly couple, sitting at the only table within sight, was frowning at me. I supposed my tears had alarmed them so I gave them a reassuring smile and they looked away somewhat embarrassed.

"Yes, but what about you and me and Skipper? Can you tell me how you feel about that?"

"Oh, yes. I want that more than anything. I have absolutely no doubt," I said.

He sighed and poked his fork into the salad that neither of us had tasted. If I thought he was relaxing, I was wrong. He put down his fork and looked at me with such determination that I felt off balance.

"Okay, here's what I propose. I will return to Turkey, talk to my family, although none of this will surprise them because I have talked of nothing else since we were together the last time. I will arrange for someone to manage my business until we can decide what to do. Yes?"

I struggled for composure, managed a nod, and tried to swallow another wave of lumps. Two emotions were colliding in my stomach: joy and fear.

"Can we be married when I return? I'm tired of the Bellevue Stratford."

No words would come, but I smiled and nodded. He got up, pulled me to my feet and kissed me until I could feel everyone's eyes on my back. He placed some bills on the table and we headed for the desk clerk at the inn.

In my daydreaming of our last night together, I'd imagined feelings of sadness and worry over the coming separation. Each time we parted, I feared the changes that might come. Now I understood those feelings were the spawn of indecision. Carlos wasn't leaving; he was preparing for our future together. This was just the beginning.

Sleet pounded the car windshield as we drove to Philadelphia the next morning. We planned to go directly to my brothers' house to tell Skipper. How would he react? I knew he liked Carlos, but I recalled what happened when I suggested Uncle Val's sailboat for his sixth birthday party. Would Skipper resent Carlos too? We were just beginning to relate again to each other. The more I thought about Skipper, the more I worried that he wasn't ready to accept another man in our lives.

I glanced over at Carlos. He was tense, concentrating on the rain-slicked highway. In the quiet I began to think of how to tell Skipper. If I told him alone and he reacted badly, Carlos wouldn't have to know. But even as the thought came, another intruded. I heard Grace's voice telling me how important it was to share. My plan was just the opposite of that. I was taking control, shutting Carlos out.

The windshield wipers lashed back and forth, offering visibility a few seconds at a time. Too bad I didn't have a pair of internal wipers to clear out my old knee-jerk reactions.

"Carlos, I'm worried."

"I know. Me too. This is a big move for both of us, but, as I see it, we can worry together or separately, right?"

I moved closer, took his arm, and lay my head on his shoulder.

"Something else?" he said.

"Maybe. Skip's been through so much. He was close to his father. Things weren't perfect, but he's still adjusting and my preoccupation with the gallery has hurt him. He tries so hard to make everyone think he's good at everything. He's not just showing off – well, of course he is a little – but he wants us to think he's grown up. I'm afraid Jared forced some of that on him when he was very young – perhaps too young. I've been guilty of the same thing." I paused, realizing I was getting into a topic that required time and our total attention. I'd told Carlos about my own interaction with Skipper, but there was Jared...

"What is it?"

"Why don't we stop for some coffee? The roads are bad and I need to talk."

There was a diner at the next circle. It was crowded for midmorning. Either we were not the only ones seeking shelter from the storm or New Jerseyites were late risers. We ordered coffee and shook our heads at the waitress' glowing description of "the largest selection of Danish coffeecakes on the Jersey coast."

"I've been thinking of how to tell Skipper about our plans to be a family. At first I thought it might be best if I told him alone. That's not a good idea, is it?" I said.

"Do you plan to ask Skipper how he feels about having me for a father?"

"Well, not in so many words, but I think I must consider his feelings."

Carlos took several sips of his coffee, never raising his eyes to look at me until he placed the cup back in the saucer. He reached for my hands.

"I admit, I don't have much experience in these matters, but I don't think our decision to marry should have anything to do with Skipper's opinion. If he has problems with me, we'll work them out. Isn't that what parents do? All he needs to know is that we love him and want the best for him.

"One more thing, and then I'll listen to all of your concerns. You say Skipper wants to be a grown up, but we both know he isn't. He's a little boy. What I'd like to do is show him how important he is to both of us. I'd like us to talk to him together, tell him how we feel, tell him our hopes for the future, explain to him that he has a lot to do with how happy we will be as a family."

Grace might have made that speech. I was stunned. I didn't need any more convincing that Carlos would be a full participant in our new life as a family. And when I found the right moment, and the courage, to tell him about Jared, it would be okay too. It was all part of the past. My confidence was building with each moment and I couldn't wait to get home.

Carlos looked puzzled. "Let's deal with your concerns now before we get to your brothers' house."

"No need. I think you've already stumbled onto the best plan."

"Hey, what do you mean 'stumbled'?"

The storm fizzled to strong breezes by the time we arrived at my brother's home. Gray clouds still muscled across the sky, but the sun was bursting through. We found Val, Philip, Skipper and Marty shooting hoops in the driveway. They were so intent on the game we were able to watch for several minutes before Philip noticed us.

"Carlos, come take my place. I'm getting too old for this," my brother said, walking toward us.

They gathered around. I gave Skipper a hug and Carlos scooped him up over his head.

"Actually," Carlos said, "we'd like to talk to Skipper alone for a few minutes. Then we've got some exiting news to tell you."

Val's eyebrows shot up. He looked at Philip and was about to say something when Philip cut him off. "Go ahead, Skip. Call us when you're ready."

Val looked disappointed, but Skipper was overjoyed to be the first to hear exciting news, whatever it might be.

In spite of our carefully designed plans, Carlos and I fumbled with our words. We needn't have worried. Skip let out one of his war whoops and ran from the house.

"Guess what? I'm getting a new dad."

We hadn't said everything we planned, but it didn't matter. Seconds later Skipper came back to give us both a hug.

"Are you going to call him Carlos or Dad?" Marty wanted to know.

The thought obviously hadn't occurred to Skipper and he looked bewildered.

"You know, I have the same problem," Carlos said. "Should I call you Skip or Son?"

Skipper couldn't provide an answer so Carlos announced it would be their first man-to-man talk. Skip grinned.

As usual we all ended up in the kitchen. My brothers bobbed and weaved among the kitchen equipment like boxers in a ring. Within minutes the table filled with nibbles and brewing coffee filled the air. Skipper claimed a spot on Carlos' lap. I wondered if my brothers found the scene as surreal as I did. This wasn't how life worked, was it? At least it had never been my experience. Something or someone would pull aside a curtain at any moment and expose my real life. The true scene would show Skipper's face red and contorted in rage. His voice would pierce the air and everyone would be staring at him. My brothers would be bombarding Carlos with questions to undermine his intentions. Not so - my brothers were listening, Skipper was glowing, and the love of my life was really sitting in my brothers' kitchen talking about our hopes for the future.

Carlos admitted his mother and sister had been encouraging him for months to do whatever was necessary to make me his wife and Skipper his son. In the final analysis, it had been Elena who presented the clearest vision for her son. She told him she'd known for a long time he would find his greatest happiness with a family. When she got to know me, she recognized the perfect partner, he said. She dismissed every problem Carlos presented. She told him stories of the hurdles she and his father had overcome and how each strengthened their marriage. A smooth life is boring, she'd said. We all laughed when Carlos said that after debating with his mother, he was prepared for any objections we might have.

"Your mother sounds exceptional. You're lucky. How will it feel to be thousands of miles away from her? I would give anything to have our mother here." Val's voice thickened.

Carlos looked from Val to me. If he wanted me to say something, he was disappointed. I'd been thinking only of myself. Now, suddenly, I realized there might be other issues we hadn't considered. His eyes lingered on my face and I wondered if he was seeing his mother or me.

Skipper broke the silence. "Carlos, your mother would be my grandmother, right? Marty has two grandmothers. I'd really like to have one."

"Ah, she'd love to hear you say that Skip. How about calling her right now?" He glanced at his watch and Philip handed him the telephone.

"*Merhaba, annecığm.*" Hello, mother. Yes, yes, everything is wonderful. No, no, she's not sending me back." He laughed. "Mother, your new grandson wants to talk to you."

I was so proud of my boy at that moment. He was talking to a complete stranger with confidence. They talked for several minutes. I'd have given anything to know what Elena was saying. It was obvious she was asking him questions and he was agreeing to everything. He said goodbye and handed the

phone to me. I was torn between two voices: Elena in my ear
and Skipper asking Marty to go to his room and help him write
a letter to his *nine*. "That's grandmother in Turkish," he
bragged.

Elena wanted to know if we'd decided on a wedding date. I
admitted we hadn't, but told her I hoped she would visit soon
to meet my family. She agreed immediately.

After the call everyone exploded with questions. Why hadn't
we set a date? Would the wedding take place in Ankara or
Philadelphia? Would Carlos' sister and her fiancé be able to
come? If Carlos moved to Philadelphia, would his mother
move too?

Val wanted to know what Carlos would do about his
business, but before he could respond, I told him we hadn't
made any business decisions yet. Up went the eyebrows again.
They were getting an aerobic workout. Irritation nipped at my
emotional edges, but Philip, as usual, offered the calming
words: "Sounds like there's a lot to do. Let us know how we
can help."

I slipped out of the room and went up to Skipper's bedroom
where the boys were stretched out on the floor with papers. At
the top of a large sheet, Skipper had written "Skipper" in black
and underlined it several times with broad red stripes. It looked
like they were working on words to describe him. Judging
from the handwriting, Skip had just written "smart," and Marty
added "bossy."

I'd have given anything to see the final project, but that
wasn't to be. I tiptoed back down the hall and returned to the
adults. Shortly Skipper presented a sealed envelope to Carlos
with *Nine* carefully printed across the front. His face glowed
with excitement. But later that night, when I tried to kiss him
goodnight in his bed, he pulled the covers over his head.

"How long will Carlos be my dad?"

His head was turned to the wall and I could see the outline of
his knuckles where he bunched the blanket between his fingers.
The shadow of his small body, cast by the pale green nightlight,

spread across the jungle pattern on the wallpaper. The deep yellows and greens – so vivid in the daylight – were varying shades of gray and lacked definition. I stared at the scene, losing myself momentarily among the sheltering leaves I knew to be there, but knowing there was no hiding from his question.

It was awful to live with uncertainty, and Skipper's question resounded deep inside me as well. Jared left us in the morning and never returned. Our adjustment to losing him was bumpy and painful. How could I be sure I wasn't opening the door to more hurt?

"I hope it will be forever." I couldn't think of anything more to say and mumbled something about the fun we were going to have as a family and let it go at that. He never emerged from the blanket and eventually I left the room.

Two days later Carlos and I drove to New York to visit the Bezdikians, enjoy a final evening together and then early the next morning go to the airport. I braced for a bittersweet twenty-four hours.

22

Esther Bezdikian was chatting with the desk clerk in the lobby of her Manhattan apartment building when we arrived. I watched her from the door while Carlos parked the car. She and Sam had lived at the same location since their retirement. They knew everyone in the building, as well as every storeowner within a mile radius – a substantial community of friends. They gathered people like a storyteller drew listeners and Carlos would be no exception.

Although they never said anything, I'd mentioned his name often enough that I believed they already suspected the good news of our plans to marry. They'd be happy for me, and I was eager for this brief but joyous interlude before what I expected would be a long goodbye later in a room overlooking Central Park. My one consolation was that the next time Carlos arrived in Philadelphia it would be to stay. I was counting on that to keep me going.

While I waited, I scanned the area. The high-rise apartment building, many times remodeled, had held onto its 1950s charm. The paint was fresh and the furnishings new, but neither were the latest fashionable choice. The result was a come-and-sit-awhile environment with no pretension – a perfect nest for my old friends.

The years had been kind to Esther's beautiful Mediterranean face. I always thought DaVinci could have used her for his portrait of Mona Lisa. Peace and mystery radiated from her rounded features. Just being in her presence restored order to mind and body. Sam had been blessed with the perfect counterbalance to his ebullience. She was reserved. In fact, I couldn't recall ever hearing her raise her voice, even to laugh. What I do remember was the desire to be close to her from the first moment I met her, and when Carlos finally joined me and I introduced them, I saw the same magnetic force at work on him.

"I'm so sorry Sam isn't here to greet you. We went to pick up a few things at the store, and he told me to go on ahead because he wanted to visit briefly with Mr. D'Angelo, the old grocer. He's probably having a glass of the old man's home brew."

We followed Esther into the dark wood-lined elevator where she tapped the panel and lit the twentieth floor button. In one way I was glad Carlos was meeting Esther alone. Had Sam been there, she would have slipped into the background, relinquishing complete control to her irrepressible husband.

Carlos hadn't taken more than five steps into the apartment when he dropped to his knees.

"Oh, may I?"

"Of course," Esther said, accepting Carlos' behavior as completely normal. She joined him, gingerly, and turned back the edge of the rug so he could examine the knotting. "You haven't seen this one, Nora. It's Egyptian. Do you like it?"

I was shocked. What had become of the nineteenth century Chinese rug I sighed over on my last visit? I stifled the question and closed my eyes remembering the deep blue field covered with white peonies and golden leaves. I sighed again and reminded myself that Esther and Sam were always quick to change. All they needed was some unique feature and out went the old rug and in came the new.

The idea was alien to me. My parents' rugs were an integral part of my home. Replacing the rugs would be like losing my parents again. I'd never thought of it before, but I knew that's how I'd feel and my brothers would agree.

"Don't you like it?" Esther repeated.

"Yes, of course, it's unique. Egyptian, eh? Quite a change from the Chinese."

In the rug's central cream-colored field there was an intricate grillwork of black and gray surrounding a large rust-colored *gul* – a six-sided design of leaves and branches. *Guls* in deeper colors formed the borders. The pattern gave the impression of symmetry until closer inspection revealed subtle differences in the two halves. I began to understand my friends' fascination. This was a rug that could be enjoyed for a variety of reasons.

The front door swung open and Sam's loud bass voice filled the room. Carlos helped Esther to her feet.

"Forgive me. Mr. D'Angelo isn't well and…" He shrugged his shoulders in a gesture of helplessness.

"It's so good to see you, Sam," I said. "This is Carlos and we have something to tell you."

Our announcement brought a predictable gush of exuberance. Esther hugged both of us and Sam bolted to the kitchen for champagne.

"When we were first married," he shouted from the other room, "Esther and I decided our lives were going to be full of celebrations and a bottle of champagne would always be ready. What number is this, Esther?"

Esther sighed. "How should I know? I've lost count because you're forever celebrating something or other." To us she said: "Would you believe he once celebrated a Girl Scout selling cookies in the lobby? He opened a box and shared them with everyone. When we got back to our apartment, he wanted to toast the immeasurable pleasures children give us. And he expects me to keep a record? Ha, not a chance."

"Val and Philip must be very happy about your news." Sam set down a tray of filled champagne flutes. "I remember how they always worried about you. My God, when you told them you were going to Turkey, Val asked me to talk you out of it. 'No way,' I told him. I knew it would be excellent for your career and I was right, wasn't I?"

He handed each of us a pale amber-filled glass with tiny bubbles streaming to the brim. "Health and happiness!" he said.

"Yes, that turned out to be true."

Esther invited us to sit. "Tell me about Skipper," she said. I suspected she wanted to know his reaction to our wedding plans but was reluctant to ask outright because she knew about my difficulties with Skipper since Jared's death.

"He's very excited to have Carlos in our lives and he's overjoyed to have a grandmother."

The rest of the visit was as I'd hoped – joyous, with Carlos promising many future times together.

The view of Central Park and New York City from our hotel room was stunning. We stood at the window taking in the city lights, caressing each other. I wanted to memorize each angle and curve of his body. Later, we sat on a loveseat, plump with pillows, and talked for hours. I confessed I was scared, not only for myself but also for Skipper. Carlos questioned and I answered, stumbling over statements I knew were contradictory. At times I didn't realize the dissonance until I heard the words aloud. Much of the conversation was a rehash of our earlier talk, but I needed to hear his optimism again. He was so sure, so confident we were meant to be together.

"Everything you say is possible, I suppose," he said. "Skipper may resent me. We may have business problems. You may try to control our relationship – maybe the business too. I'll work with you or fight with you – whatever it takes for us to be a family. The only guarantee I can give you is my love."

I nodded. What more could I ask?

"Good, then let's not worry about what we don't know and enjoy what we do," he said. He pulled me to my feet and kissed me. I was overwhelmed by the eagerness of his kiss. Clearly it was time to stop talking.

One earnest embrace was all we dared at the airport. I turned away from him quickly and returned to my car. Saying goodbye was difficult, and I glanced back once more through the rear view mirror. He was disappearing into the dark interior of the airport, followed by two policemen. The scene reminded me of my nightmare at Esenboga. I pressed my foot on the accelerator, shaking my head to dislodge the memory. His promise to be back in a few weeks helped stem the tears just behind my eyes. Once I was out of the airport's tangle of roads and signs, I pulled onto the shoulder to plan my route and refocus my thoughts.

Several hours later I'd called on two clients in Manhattan and another on Long Island. Marketing my wares was probably the only distraction that could have worked for me that morning. Fortunately, I was fond of my clients and their needs were always a challenge in one way or another. Once or twice I struggled to keep my wits about me but it was worth it. All three galleries placed large orders for regular inventory items and, after I discussed the financial rewards of the antiques, there were indications of interest. I'd follow up on that when I got back to the office.

My cell phone rang seconds after I entered the main highway out of New York. I reached over to my purse and groped inside to find the small, familiar rectangle.

"Nora, this is Sam. Where are you?"

"I just got on the expressway. What's wrong?"

"Pull off the road and park someplace."

"For heaven's sake, what is it?"

"Just do it, will you?"

I crossed over two lanes and drove onto the shoulder and stopped.

"Okay, I'm parked. What is it? You're scaring me."

"The police just called me. They found Carlos unconscious in Brooklyn. He's in bad shape, beaten, they think. They found my card in his pocket – that's why they called me. Esther and I are in the car now. He's at New York Metro Hospital. Do you think you can drive? Safely, I mean? We can come and get you. Nora?"

I stared at the cars streaking by. What was going on? How could someone be at the airport and then unconscious in Brooklyn?

"Nora?"

"Yes, yes, I can drive myself. I'll meet you there. How bad is he, do you know?" I choked on the words.

"No, nothing more than I've already said. Please drive carefully."

The road ahead blurred and I blinked to clear my vision. But sitting at the side of the road wasn't going to give me answers. After several deep breaths, I restarted the car and eased it out onto the highway. At the next exit, I turned back to New York City.

Esther and Sam were standing with two police officers when I got out of the fourth floor hospital elevator. They said Carlos had just regained consciousness, but no one was allowed to see him until they finished their questioning.

"It's important the victim isn't distracted," the taller of the two officers said. "Every detail he remembers is valuable to our investigation. We got eyewitnesses at the airport who saw Mr. Ghazerian leave with two policemen."

My last view of him flashed across my memory. I'd never believed in premonitions, until now. "What do the police-" I was cut off by a uniformed man who opened the door to Carlos' room and asked the officers to join him. I strained to see before they closed the door behind them, but the people already in the room blocked my view.

"Did you get to see him?" I said to Esther and Sam.

"When we got here, the nurses were all over him. No, we didn't. His head seemed to be bandaged and they said he was unconscious. As soon as the nurses came out, the police went in. They've been in there at least fifteen minutes."

We sat across from each other in the hallway. The chairs were stiff, molded for convenience rather than comfort. After a few minutes we reluctantly moved to green padded seats in a nearby lounge and poured pale, amber liquid from a coffee machine into Styrofoam cups. I sat facing Carlos' room, ready to pounce if there was any indication that I could see him.

"Nora, tell us how your business is doing?" Sam said.

I told him about the client visits I'd just completed, but after three or four vague comments I couldn't think of anything more to say.

"I want to hear about Carlos' first reaction to your beautiful gallery. I'll bet he was impressed by what you've accomplished," Esther said.

"Oh, yes, he loves it. He brought a new inventory for me from Turkey – some Persian beauties he picked up from a German broker – and we spent several days getting things organized. Last week I took him with me to see your friend, Colin Feeney. I told you he called me, didn't I? He's building a beach house in Cape May and he wants Orientals in all of the rooms. You know, I must tell you, I don't like him very much."

Sam laughed. "That doesn't surprise me. As many people hate him as love him. Strong personalities have that effect on people. He can be ruthless, I hear, when he's looking out for his political interests, but I guess that's normal in his arena. And, just between you and me, he's been accused of being a ladies' man."

"Hmmm, I can confirm that."

"You mean he-"

"Well, I wasn't going to his beach house alone, I can tell you. Call it intuition, but I sensed that about him. It was perfect that Carlos was with me. It gave Mr. Feeney a clear message that I wasn't available."

Sam's expression changed. He stared down the hallway like he remembered something he had to do. I turned to Esther and mumbled about hating to wait.

"Let's walk to the end of the hall," she said. "Sam, come with us, you're as fidgety as a six year old."

"You two go on ahead. I want to make a phone call." He dashed off to the elevator. Esther looked startled and mildly annoyed, but she didn't say anything. We both knew erratic behavior wasn't especially unusual for Sam. As we passed the room, I caught the eye of the nurse at Carlos' bedside and beckoned to her.

"When can I see him? We, I mean, we're going to be married."

"He needs rest. I've told the police they can have one more minute. But- Look, if I let you in, will you promise to stay no more than a minute? It'll probably lift his spirits to see you."

"Oh, yes, absolutely. One minute, I promise."

A parade of badges and buckles passed by, too intent on their notepads and their discussion to notice me slip in behind them. I sucked in my breath and grasped the railing on the bed when I saw Carlos. He was barely recognizable. His dark hair was matted to his head on one side. The other side was thickly wrapped with a bandage large enough to cover his ear. His left arm was taped from shoulder to wrist, and one leg was in a cast and held in traction. What I could see of his face was red and swollen and stitches were visible on his lips in several places. Dried blood clung to the edges of his mouth.

I touched his right hand as gently as I could and whispered his name. He opened his eyes immediately and winced in pain.

"Don't speak. They won't let me stay, but – oh, I love you."

He tapped my hand with his fingers. The effort to comfort me was too much and I broke into sobs just as the nurse came in to ask me to leave. She placed a firm hand in the middle of my back, steered me to the door and leaned her face close to mine.

"I know he looks bad," she whispered," but his vital signs are strong. He's going to be fine. Don't worry. You'll see a big difference in him tomorrow, I'm sure."

I nodded and looked once more at Carlos who seemed already asleep. Then I stumbled into Esther's open arms in the hallway.

Sam returned. He was frowning and uncharacteristically quiet. After several attempts at conversation, and a comment from the nurse that no one would be allowed to see Carlos again for some time, we decided to go to the hospital cafeteria to pass the time. I used it to dial my brothers.

Val was home. I told him as much as I knew.

"Stay as long as you need. You couldn't have better support than Sam and Esther and we'll take care of Skipper. But..."

"What?"

"I was just wondering what we should tell Skipper. Should we tell him Carlos is in the hospital?"

I froze, remembering Skip's fears. But how could I keep something this important from him? Grace's gentle prodding and her encouragement repeated itself.

"Tell him Carlos has been hurt, but that the nurses say he'll be fine in a few days. I haven't told Carlos yet, but I'm going to bring him home with me to heal. Maybe he will be able to call Skip tomorrow. How's that sound?"

Val thought the phone call was a good idea. At least he would know we included him in what we were going through. I hoped he'd understand, as I was beginning to, that life is full bumps but suffering alone hurts everybody. On the surface I believed this with all my heart, but a small part of me wondered if it wouldn't be better to wait until I had good news before saying anything to anyone. Would I then appear to have handled the problem myself, shouldered the worry alone, shielded those I loved from the hurt I felt? The urge was strong but I forced it from my mind. If Skipper was ever to learn how to draw strength from his relationships, I wanted to show him the way. I knew it was important. I just wished it didn't hurt so much.

23

Elena Ghazerian burst into Carlos' hospital room two days later looking like she'd sat on the edge of her seat for the entire flight from Turkey. Her face, puffy from lack of sleep, was sallow and grim. She barely glanced at me as she rushed to Carlos with outstretched arms.

Carlos had placed a call to her immediately after speaking to Skipper to assure both that he was okay. The tactic hadn't worked on Elena. She said she was leaving for the airport as soon as she could pack a bag. I guess I shouldn't have been surprised since my own mother became a warrior when my brothers or I were hurt. This was Elena, the mother, as opposed to Elena, the gracious hostess.

"Elena, why didn't you call? I would have picked you up at the airport," I said.

"I want to speak to the doctor. Where is he?" she said, leaning over Carlos and gently touching his bandages. "I must know the extent of his injuries."

"The doctor is a woman, Elena, and-"

She waved me off. I was inclined to leave the room so they could have a few minutes alone together, but when I saw that her hysteria was upsetting Carlos, I took her hand. "Let's find the doctor," I said, gently guiding her to the door.

Just outside we collided with a policeman who introduced Detective DeFeo and explained he would lead the investigation. Elena pushed forward.

"Why was my son attacked by your police? He did nothing wrong. You make loud noises when other countries abuse human rights, but you are no better. Hypocrites," she said with her arms waving and fingers pointing.

I looked around for help and caught the eye of one of Carlos' nurses. She was already heading our way with a glass of water. She offered Elena a pill.

"No, I don't want your medicine. I want to get out of your country. How soon will my son be well enough to leave and return with me to Turkey? We don't want to be where we are not respected."

She was irrational, contrary to everything I knew about her. Thank God the nurse stopped us both in our tracks.

"You can't do your son any good in your present condition. Please take this. I promise it will help you," she said, offering the small white pill again. "Believe me, under all those bandages is a very strong man. He's going to heal very quickly and be just as he was," she said with a smile.

These were the words Elena needed. She accepted the pill and the three of us walked together to a small waiting area and sat down. Over Elena's head I saw the door to Carlos' room open. Detective DeFeo called the nurse and she left us on the run. Moments later the doctor arrived along with several others while the detective and policeman disappeared in the other direction. Something was happening, but I couldn't move because at that moment Elena leaned toward me, crying softly. I put my arm around her as her body sagged, and I felt a wave of guilt for my ugly thoughts. We waited together. There was nothing more we could do.

When the doctor emerged, she walked toward us and sat next to Elena. I introduced them.

"Carlos is doing very well. He's weak, that's to be expected, and he's had too many visitors today. I've given him a sedative and he's already asleep. The best thing you can do is to get some rest yourselves. Come back tomorrow. I guarantee he will be much improved, you'll see."

I looked at Elena. Her eyes were heavy but she acknowledged the doctor's words. I was grateful, not just because I agreed, but because if Elena hadn't been there, I would have raced after Detective DeFeo against my better judgment. Something was going on. I could feel it. I'd make some calls when I got Elena settled at home.

At the house we sat in silence and drank tea. I fingered the fringe on the table runner, glancing occasionally at Elena. Her thoughts were far from the breakfast room, only a small twitch of her lower lip revealed her distress. Finally, she admitted she was exhausted and I helped her to the guest room bed and closed the door. Once inside my own bedroom, I dialed the detective's cell phone.

"What's going on? Why were you in his room again today? He needs rest." I said when he answered.

"Several people have come forward and we needed to corroborate their information. Things are moving forward. Trust me, as soon as we know more, we'll be in touch," he said, cutting me off before I could ask him about the information.

I was up early the next morning but not before Elena. I found her standing at the window overlooking the deck. Her face was wet with tears.

"Are you all right?" I said, moving next to her and placing my hand on her arm.

"I'm ashamed, ashamed of the things I said to you yesterday. I didn't mean it. I was so frightened. There is so much in the news today about hate and revenge. I could think of nothing else from the time Carlos called until I saw him. He looked..." She began to sob.

I led her to the sofa and sat next to her. "You have every right to feel as you do. I love my country, but what you say is true.

What happened to us on September eleventh has changed the way we feel about Middle Easterners. We're suspicious and afraid. But that's not how we are, I mean, that's not normal for us, and I know it will change back to the way it used to be. The important thing to remember is that Carlos is going to heal. He has no serious injuries, thank God. He'll be home soon," I said.

"Home." She said the word as if she were testing its meaning.

I turned it around in my own mind. Was it a place or a state of mind? Could I be home without Carlos? I knew I couldn't. I also knew I wanted Elena to be part of my family. She'd shown me nothing but kindness and acceptance from the first moment. I looked at her troubled face and remembered my own hysteria when Skipper was lost in the woods.

"Do you know how much I love Carlos?"

"I think so. And I know he wants you and Skipper to be his family, but-"

"I have worries too. Carlos and I have talked about them. Please, tell me your concerns. Believe me when I tell you they are important to me."

She leaned forward, holding her head in both hands. "My concerns are selfish. I know this, but I cannot chase them from my mind."

"It doesn't matter. I want to hear them."

"I'm not sure I can lose him to you." She shook her head and apologized with her eyes.

"Elena, this is hard for me to say because for so many years I've been afraid of the truth, afraid of my needs. It's not just Carlos I want. I need you too. There isn't a day that passes that I don't remember the loss of my parents. Each time they come to mind I feel pain, and for a long time I rebelled against those feelings. I thought it was important for my son to see me as strong and independent, not needing anyone. It was foolish, but I didn't know that until I met Carlos and you. I've found such security in his love for me." I swallowed. Hearing the words seemed to have more impact than when they were merely my thoughts, yet I knew everything I said was true. "I'm ashamed to tell you that I have hurt my son. I even pushed my brothers away. But lately I've come to learn that we need to depend on each other, that there is great strength in closeness. I really need to be close to you. You will never lose your son to me. You will be part of us."

For several moments we stared at each other. I could still hear my words. They formed an almost physical presence in the space between us. Then she hugged me with a fierceness that said everything – not only that she understood, but that she wanted me too.

A week later Carlos was home with me, walking less and less with the cane they sent with him. And he was solidly involved in two daily rituals with Skipper: a physical therapy session and a nightly reading from Arabian Nights. Watching the therapy was difficult, not just because I occasionally saw Carlos wince with pain. He'd been told to expect some discomfort. It hurt me to watch Skipper's unsympathetic, dogged approach. He never made an allowance and insisted each exercise be done properly and for the exact length of time. I said something about it to Carlos.

"It's one of his qualities that I like best," he said. "You call it being bossy, but what I see is how he pays attention to detail. He says he's my coach and he's helping me to get better."

"Well…"

"Believe me, I'm in good hands. We're having fun and I'm learning something new about him every day. He's a great kid."

"But-"

"You worry too much."

The conversation lingered in my mind for several days, fueled by past memories of ugly scenes, defiance, screaming and violent temper. But it'd been months since Skipper displayed any anger toward me. I'd have to replace those bad memories with more recent good ones. One thing I no longer had to wonder about was whether or not Carlos would be a good parent. I was already learning from him, not the least of which was how the wear and tear of living can be positive. He said we were like the antique rugs in many ways: We come out of our family traditions, take on individual color and pattern, and receive our bumps and bruises, which make us more valuable because of what we learn about ourselves and others. I couldn't argue with him.

The other daily ritual of reading tales from Arabian Nights was going on in Skip's bedroom when I got home from work. I tiptoed up the stairs, listening to Carlos' voice. As I turned the corner at the top, I saw him propped up in the bed with his leg resting on a bedside chair. Skipper was in his pajamas, bent at the waist with his legs on the bed and his head resting on the floor, a position I'd seen before and decided was reserved for seven year olds.

"Prince Houssain wandered for hours through the market, searching everywhere for riches. A clever merchant, sensing an opportunity, invited him into his shop. Almost immediately the Prince's eyes fell on a piece of tapestry, a rug, hanging from the merchant's arm. He asked the price. Thirty purses, said the merchant. The Prince balked, telling the merchant the price was exorbitant. But the merchant told him if the price seemed extravagant, he would be all the more amazed when he learned it was worth many times more. Well, said the Prince, this rug must have something very extraordinary that is unknown to me. You have guessed it, the merchant said. Whoever sits on this piece of tapestry may be transported in an instant wherever he desires to be."

Carlos peeked over the edge of the bed to see Skipper frowning.

"That's a silly story. Rugs can't fly," he said, pulling himself up to face Carlos.

"It's a folktale, sort of like wishful thinking with some magic thrown in."

Now Skipper was on his knees, hands on his hips.

"There's no such thing as magic."

Amusement rippled across Carlos' face and I had to put my hand over my mouth. I was curious to know how Carlos would fare with my so-sure-of-himself son.

"What do you think of Santa Claus?" Carlos said.

Jared and I had talked with him about Santa at least two years ago when it was clear that Skipper was puzzling over reindeer flying all over the world and a round, red-suited man slipping down chimneys with bulging bundles of toys.

"I don't believe in Santa Claus."

"But how did you feel about Santa before you learned he was just a folktale?"

"Well…"

"Someday, when you have little children, will you play at being Santa Claus, do you think?"

Skipper hesitated.

"I'll tell you what I think," Carlos said. "I like a little magic in my life."

I joined them in the pause that followed.

"Guess what? Today I sold four magic carpets," I said, wrapping my arms around both of them – another new ritual I hoped would never end.

A few days later Detective DeFeo interrupted our morning coffee to ask Carlos to come to the police station. He said they wanted Carlos to view a lineup to see if he could identify the men who'd picked him up at the airport. When we got to the station we were surprised to find Sam Bezdikian there.

"I took a train this morning so I could be here for the lineup."

"Why?"

"You'll understand in a couple of minutes," he said with a wink.

His wink infuriated me and he knew it, but I couldn't persuade him to tell us more. All he would say was, "First things first," leaving us to guess what that meant. Carlos was called into another room. Sam and I held a conversation that I can't remember.

Carlos came back beaming. "It is amazing. They had the two men who took me from the airport. I wanted to talk to them but they wouldn't let me so I still don't understand why they attacked me. It makes no sense unless they just wanted to beat up on someone who looked like an Arab," he said.

"Not exactly," Sam said, hustling us out the door. "Let's go get something to drink."

We walked across the street slowly to keep pace with Carlos who was using his cane that day. I also sensed that the experience of identifying the men had shaken him somewhat.

"You weren't exactly a stranger to them, Carlos," Sam said.

We found a table at the back of the café. Carlos and I took seats on one side of the table and faced an excited Sam on the other. He pointed his finger at me, but Carlos interrupted.

"I've never seen those men in my life, Sam."

"No, but they were working for someone who knew you. Listen, I became suspicious after you told me how Colin acted when you two went to the beach house. It's not the first time he's been involved in dirty work like this."

"Colin Feeney?" I looked at Carlos but his face was blank.

"Let me finish. I gave the cops a few suggestions, a few names. Billy Ghegan and Joe McGill, the two you picked from the lineup - they've been known to do stuff for Feeney. They're both retired cops. Evidently Colin makes it worth their while to be retired. It's hard to believe he'd stoop to harming you just because you got in his way with Nora but..."

Carlos looked away from me.

"I didn't know he'd react that strongly," I said to Carlos. "I'm so sorry." My face was burning.

Sam continued. "Anyway, Ghegan and McGill have opted for leniency in exchange for Feeney. The police are on their way to pick him up right now. His political career is over. Stupid jerk. He let his ego trash his chances. I liked the guy, but I'm glad he showed his true colors before he got into office," Sam said, shaking his head.

The silence in the car on the way home was palpable. I couldn't bring myself to apologize again because I sensed Carlos was still angry. I wasn't sure if he was angry with Colin or me and it just seemed best to wait and give him time to cool off. He'd been badly hurt and I was partly to blame either way. But what difference would it have made if I'd told him Colin was interested in me? Would he have acted differently? Maybe he would have gone to Cape May alone, ignoring Colin's insistence on my personal attention.

Once inside the house, Carlos said he wanted to make tea and asked me to wait in the den for him. I watched him filling the kettle with water, reaching for the mugs, filling the teapot, dropping in the tea bags one by one. He looked dejected as he waited for the tea to steep. I yearned to put my arms around him but some of my own thoughts kept me in the den. Perhaps he didn't trust me anymore. I'd betrayed him and how could we make a marriage without confidence in each other? This had been the last straw. We'd never be happy together. What other conclusion was there? By the time he came into the den, I had trouble holding back tears.

"Carlos, please believe me, I really thought Colin would be discouraged when he saw us together. I never would have-"

Carlos' face had lost its color. He wasn't angry. He looked determined, like he knew what he needed to say, but didn't want to. He placed his mug on the table and turned around to face me.

"I know that, I-"

"Maybe we should wait until tomorrow. We don't have to talk anymore today," I said. I could already hear the words that were going to break my heart.

Carlos struggled to his feet and walked to the window overlooking the deck. The sun had set hours ago and except for a few rectangles of light in neighboring homes there was nothing visible. I sat rigid, hardly breathing.

"There is something I should have told you." He spoke to the floor.

I sprang to my feet. These were not the words I expected. "Look, I don't even want to know what happened after I left you at the airport. You had a horrible experience. Don't expect to remember everything that happened. All I care about is that you're getting well."

"No, not about that. Something I should have told you a long time ago. Sit down, please. I want to tell you something you don't know about Colin Feeney and me."

"Colin and you?"

"I knew who he was before we went to Cape May. I recognized his name." He picked up his mug and took a deep swallow. I swallowed too.

"Remember when you told me you had borrowed from Abdullah?"

"You weren't happy about it. That's all I remember. You said he was a risk taker. What's that got to do with you or Colin Feeney? I don't understand."

"I'm trying to tell you. This isn't easy for me. I'm not proud of…"

Lights in the windows across from the deck went out, deepening the blackness outside. A darkening was settling over me too.

"When Abdullah started his venture capital business, I was his partner."

"His partner?"

"Yes. I told you we have been friends since childhood. He knew I was restless working in Ankara. He wanted me to work with him for a while to see what would happen. Maybe, if things went well, I could sell the rug business and move to New York."

"You could have told me that. Did your mother disapprove?"

"No. She never knew. I didn't want to upset her. She thought I was content."

"From what I've observed, your mother wants your happiness above all else."

"This was different. The rug business, well, it's all mixed up with family and family traditions. But that's not what I'm trying to tell you. Colin Feeney was one of our clients. He borrowed money from us."

I understood instantly about rugs and family tradition. More than once I surprised myself with the comfort they brought me. But the idea of Colin Feeney in a financial deal with Carlos and Abdullah was having a chilling effect and the hairs on my neck prickled.

"What happened?" I said.

"I never knew why he borrowed or how much. Abdullah took care of all the details. But something went wrong. Feeney couldn't make his payments and things got ugly. There were threats – on both sides. They finally settled in court and Abdullah won the case, but a few days later at his office he received a call from his wife that their son, who had just had his tenth birthday, had not come home from school at the usual time. Later the police found the boy near a shopping mall. All he could tell them was that a lady, who said she was his mother's friend, drove him to the mall to buy sports clothing. Then she disappeared. He was walking home when the police picked him up. Abdullah was certain Feeney was behind it, but they were never able to prove it."

"That's frightening, but you said you'd never met him, so how did Colin know you were working with Abdullah?"

"Abdullah was always impulsive, doing things quickly without thinking. Before I was completely sure about joining him, he printed my name next to his on everything. It was on the paperwork that passed between Abdullah's company and Feeney. Of course Abdullah discussed him with me many times, but since Feeney had never actually met me I never dreamed he would remember my name. Evidently he remembers everything until he gets even."

"He's a beast." My stomach was churning from the anger I felt. "Don't you think it's kind of a miracle that Sam Bezdikian was on hand to make the connection," I said. "Come and sit down. You've been on your feet too long, plus the stress of…well, you know what I mean."

Carlos nodded. I needed to sit myself. Something was playing around the edges of my mind and when I put my thoughts together I smiled.

"I think I know why you didn't tell me about your affiliation with Abdullah," I said.

"Good, because I thought I knew but now I am not sure."

"You wanted me to think you're perfect," I said. My tease worked and his face brightened.

"And you are letting me know I'm not perfect. Is that it?"

"Yes, and I know what I'm talking about. Before I met you, I tried passing myself off as perfect, remember?"

"You were trying to protect your son."

Would I ever tire of his positive outlook? I pulled him close and kissed him. "None of us needs protecting. All we need is each other," I said and gave him a sly smile.

"A very wise man once said that."

24

The pace slowed while Carlos healed. We spent hours talking alone, sometimes with Skipper, other times with my brothers. Elena returned to Turkey for a time, and when she came back she found a family unit with a clear plan for the future – one that included her.

Our wedding was set for the first Saturday after New Year's Day. Carlos would go back to Turkey with his mother in the spring to make arrangements for September through June, which he'd spend in Philadelphia. When Skip finished school in June, we'd spend the summer in Turkey together.

Instead of a honeymoon, we threw a gigantic party that spread people out on every level of the house. I let my eyes drift over the boisterous crowd to locate my family and closest friends. Carolyn and Jack, Philip, Val and Grace were huddled together in the den, and there was something in Val's eyes that told me he and Grace were more than friends. Grace's mother, Elena, Sam and Esther, obviously enjoying each other, made a distinguished square in the entrance hall. I couldn't see the children, but I thought I could hear the sounds of a video coming from Skip's room. I walked to the bottom of the stairs, curious to see them, and glanced into the kitchen. There was Carlos, looking at me. In his eyes I saw us sitting on a magic carpet headed into the future.

About the Author

Fran Marian is a former journalist and public relations director. The Rug Broker, her first novel, was sparked by travel in Turkey, a fascination with Oriental rugs and the fun of throwing problems at a strong woman. Fran lives in Tucson, Arizona. She and her husband John have two sons and five grandchildren.

Discussion Questions for
THE RUG BROKER

1. Would you want Nora for a friend? What do you consider to be her strengths and weaknesses?

2. What does Nora mean when she says the rugs "are more than floor covering"? Is there something in your life which surpasses its monetary value? In what ways?

3. What role did Nora's brothers play in her life? What impact did they have on her? How do you react when someone thwarts your life goals?

4. Nora says she wants financial independence. Do you believe that's what she really wants?

5. Nora goes through several emotional stages with Carlos. Name them.

6. What do you think is the reason for Nora's estrangement from her good friends, the Denbys?

7. Who do you think was more successful, Grace Cummings or Rosemary Fiori? Why?

8. As you consider Nora's relationship with Skipper, are there things you think she should have done differently? Why do you think she didn't?

9. Now that you have read the book, re-read the first sentence. What word might you substitute for "ironic?"